Deemed 'the father  chard
Austin Freeman ha least as
a writer of detective on of a
tailor who went on to train as a pharmacist. After graduating as
a surgeon at the Middlesex Hospital Medical College, Freeman
taught for a while and joined the colonial service, offering his skills
as an assistant surgeon along the Gold Coast of Africa. He became
embroiled in a diplomatic mission when a British expeditionary
party was sent to investigate the activities of the French. Through
his tact and formidable intelligence, a massacre was narrowly
avoided. His future was assured in the colonial service. However,
after becoming ill with blackwater fever, Freeman was sent back to
England to recover and, finding his finances precarious, embarked
on a career as acting physician in Holloway Prison. In desperation,
he turned to writing and went on to dominate the world of
British detective fiction, taking pride in testing different criminal
techniques. So keen were his powers as a writer that part of one of
his best novels was written in a bomb shelter.

21/8/15

£3.95 + £0

BY THE SAME AUTHOR
ALL PUBLISHED BY HOUSE OF STRATUS

A CERTAIN DR THORNDYKE

THE D'ARBLAY MYSTERY

DR THORNDYKE INTERVENES

DR THORNDYKE'S CASEBOOK

THE EYE OF OSIRIS

FELO DE SE

FLIGHTY PHYLLIS

THE GOLDEN POOL: A STORY OF A FORGOTTEN MINE

THE GREAT PORTRAIT MYSTERY

HELEN VARDON'S CONFESSION

JOHN THORNDYKE'S CASES

MR POLTON EXPLAINS

MR POTTERMACK'S OVERSIGHT

THE MYSTERY OF 31 NEW INN

THE MYSTERY OF ANGELINA FROOD

THE PUZZLE LOCK

THE RED THUMB MARK

THE SHADOW OF THE WOLF

A SILENT WITNESS

THE SINGING BONE

The Penrose Mystery

R Austin Freeman

This edition published in 2001 by House of Stratus, an imprint of
Stratus Books Ltd., 21 Beeching Park, Kelly Bray,
Cornwall, PL17 8QS, UK.

www.houseofstratus.com

Typeset, printed and bound by House of Stratus.

A catalogue record for this book is available from the British Library
and the Library of Congress.

ISBN 0-7551-0371-8

Book One

Being the Narrative
of Ernest Lockhart
Barrister at Law

CHAPTER ONE

A Gossipy Chapter in Which Coming Events Cast Their Shadows Before Them

I have been asked to make my contribution to the curious history of the disappearance of Mr Daniel Penrose, and I accordingly do so; but not without reluctance and a feeling that my contribution is but a retailing of the smallest of small beer. For the truth is that of that strange disappearance I knew nothing at the time, and, even now, my knowledge is limited to what I have learned from those who were directly concerned in the investigation. Still, I am assured that the little that I have to tell will elucidate the accounts which the investigators will presently render of the affair, and I shall, therefore, with the above disclaimer, proceed with my somewhat trivial narrative.

Whenever my thoughts turn to that extraordinary case, there rises before me the picture of a certain antique shop in a by-street of Soho. And quite naturally; for it was in that shop that I first set eyes on Daniel Penrose, and it was in connection with that shop, directly or indirectly, that my not very intimate relations with Penrose existed.

It was a queer little shop; an antique shop in both senses. For not only were the goods that it contained one and all survivors from the past, but the shop was an antique in itself. Indeed, it was probably a more genuine museum piece than anything in its varied and venerable stock, with its small-paned window bulging in a double curve – as shop-fitters could make them in the eighteenth century – and glazed with the original crown glass, greenish in tone and faintly streaked, like an oyster-shell, with concentric lines. I dated the shop at the first half of the eighteenth century, basing my estimate on a pedimented stone tablet at the corner of the street; which set forth the name, "Nassau Street in Whetten's Buildings," and the date 1734. It was a pleasant and friendly shop, though dingy; dignified and reticent, too, for the fascia above the window bore only, in dull gilt letters, the name of the proprietor, "D Parrott."

For some time I remained under the belief that this superscription referred to some former incumbent of the premises whose name was retained for the sake of continuity, since the only persons whom I encountered in my early visits were Mrs Pettigrew, who appeared to manage the business, and, more rarely, her daughter, Joan, a strikingly good-looking girl of about twenty; a very modern young lady, frank, friendly and self-possessed, quite well informed on the subject of antiques, though openly contemptuous of the whole genus.

Presently, however, I discovered that Parrott, so far from being a mere disembodied name, was a very real person. He was, in fact, the mainspring of the establishment, for he was not only the buyer – and an uncommonly good buyer – but he had quite a genius for converting mere dismembered carcasses into hale and hearty pieces of furniture. Somewhere in the regions behind the shop he had a workshop where, with the aid of an incredibly aged cabinet-maker named Tims, he carried out the necessary restorations. And they were real restorations, not fakes; honest repairs carried out for structural reasons left open and undisguised. I came to have a great respect for Mr Parrott.

My first visit was undoubtedly due to the ancient shopfront. But when I crossed the narrow street to examine it and discovered in the window a court cupboard and a couple of Jacobean chairs, I decided to avail myself of the courteous invitation, written on a card, to enter and inspect and indulge a mild passion for ancient furniture.

There were three persons in the shop: a comely woman of about fifty, who greeted me with a smile and a little bow, and thereafter took no further notice of me; a stout, jovial, rather foxy-looking gentleman who was inspecting a trayful of old silver; and a small clerical-looking gentleman who appeared to be disembowelling a bloated verge watch and prying into its interior through a watchmaker's eye-glass, which stuck miraculously in his eye, giving him somewhat the appearance of a one-eyed lobster.

"Now," said the stout gentleman, "that's quite an elegant little milk-jug, in my opinion. Don't you agree with me, Mrs Pettigrew?"

I looked at him in some surprise. For the thing was not a milk-jug. It was a coffee-pot. However, Mrs Pettigrew did not contest the description. She merely agreed that the shape was pleasant and graceful.

"I am glad, Mrs Pettigrew," said the stout gentleman, regarding the coffee-pot with his head on one side, "that you regard the lactiferous receptacle with favour. I am encouraged and confirmed. The next question is that of the date of its birthday. I am reluctant to interrupt the erudite Mr Polton in his studies of the internal anatomy of the Carolean warming-pan, but I have no skill in galactophorous genealogies. May I venture?"

He held out the coffee-pot engagingly towards the small gentleman, who thereupon laid the watch down tenderly, removed the eye-glass from his eye and smiled. And I found Mr Polton's smile almost as astonishing as the other gentleman's vocabulary. It was the most amazingly wrinkly smile that I have ever seen, but yet singularly genial and pleasant. And here I may remark that this amiable little gentleman was for some time a profound mystery to me. I could make nothing of him. I could not place him socially or otherwise. By his appearance, he might – in different raiment – have been a dignitary of the Church. His deferential manner suggested some superlative kind of manservant, but his hands and his comprehensive and inexhaustible knowledge of the products of the ancient crafts hinted at the dealer or expert collector. It was only after I had known him some months that the mystery was resolved through the medium of a legal friend, as will be related in due course. To return to the present incident, Mr Polton took the coffee-pot in his curiously prehensile hands, beamed on it approvingly, and, having stuck his eye-glass in his eye, examined the hallmark and the maker's "touch."

"It was made," he reported, "in 1765 by a man named John Hammond, who had a shop in Water Lane, Fleet Street. And an excellent tradesman he must have been."

"There, now!" exclaimed the stout gentleman. "Just listen to that! It's my belief that Mr Polton carries in his head a complete directory of all the artful craftsmen and crafty artists who ever made anything, with the dates of every piece they made. Don't you agree, Mrs Pettigrew?"

"Yes, indeed!" she replied. "His knowledge is perfectly wonderful. Perhaps," she added, addressing Mr Polton, "you can tell us something about that watch. It is said to have belonged to Prince Charlie, and of course, that would add to its value if it were really the fact. What do you think, Mr Polton?"

"Well, ma'am," was the cautious reply, "I see no reason why it should not have belonged to him, if he was not a very punctual gentleman. It was made in Edinburgh in 1735, and there is a crucifix engraved inside the outer case. I don't know what the significance of that may be."

"Neither do I," said the lady. "What do you think, Mr Penrose?"

"I should say," replied the stout gentleman, "that the evidence is conclusive. Charles Edward, being a Scotsman would have a Scottish watch; and being a papistical Romanist, would naturally have a crucifix engraved in it. QED."

Mrs Pettigrew smiled indulgently, and, as Mr Penrose had indicated his adoption of the coffee-pot, she proceeded to swathe it in tissue-paper and make it up into a presentable parcel; and, meanwhile, I browsed round the premises and inspected those specimens of the stock which were more particularly within my province. But it was not a very peaceful inspection, for Mr Penrose persisted in accompanying me and expounding and commenting upon the various pieces in terms which I found rather distracting. For Mr Penrose, as the reader has probably observed, was a wag, and his waggery took the form of calling things by quaintly erroneous names and of using odd and facetious circumlocutions; which was all very well at first and was even mildly amusing, but it very soon became tiresome. A constant effort was necessary to arrive at what he really meant.

However, in the end, I lighted upon a bible-box of dark-brown oak, pleasantly carved and bearing the incised date, 1653, and, as the little chest rather took my fancy and the price marked on the attached ticket seemed less than its value, I closed with Mrs Pettigrew, and, having paid for my purchase and given the address to which it was to be sent, took my departure. And, as I strolled at a leisurely pace in the direction of Wardour Street, I reflected idly on my late experience, and especially on the three rather unusual persons whose acquaintance I had just made. I am not in general a curious man, but I found in each of these three persons matter for speculation. There was Mrs Pettigrew, for instance. Admirably as she played her part in the economy of the shop, she did not completely fit her surroundings. One is accustomed nowadays to finding women of a very superior class serving in shops. But not quite of Mrs Pettigrew's type. She gave me the impression of being very definitely a lady; and I found myself speculating on the turn of the wheel of Fortune that had brought her there.

Then there was the enigmatical Mr Polton with his strangely prehensile hands and his astonishing memory for hallmarks. And there was the facetious Penrose. And at this point, being then about half-way along Gerrard Street, the subject of my reflections overtook me and announced himself characteristically by expressing the hope that I was pleased with my bacon cupboard. I replied that I was quite pleased with my purchase and had thought it decidedly cheap.

"So did I," said he. "But our psittacoid friend has the wisdom to temper the breeze to the shorn collector."

"Our psittacoid friend?" I repeated.

"I refer to the tropic bird who presides over the museum of domestic archaeology," he explained, and, as I still looked at him questioningly, he added, by way of elucidation: "The proprietor of the treasure-house of antiquities in which you discovered the repository of ancestral piety."

"Oh!" I exclaimed. "You mean Mr Parrott."

"Certainly!" he replied. "Did I not say so?"

"Perhaps you did," I admitted, with a slightly sour laugh; at which he smiled his peculiar foxy smile, looking at me out of the corners of his eyes, and evidently pleased at having "stumped" me. It was a pleasure that he must have enjoyed pretty often.

"I take it," he resumed, after a short pause, "that you, like myself, are a devotee of St Margaret Pie?"

I considered this fresh puzzle and decided that the solution was "magpie"; and apparently I was right, as he did not correct me.

"No," I replied, "there is nothing of the magpie about me. I don't accumulate old things for the sake of forming a collection. I buy old furniture and use it. One must have furniture of some kind, old or new, and I prefer the old. It was made by men who knew all about it and who enjoyed making it and took their time. It is much more companionable to live with than new machine-made stuff, turned out by the thousand by people who don't care a straw what it is like. But my object is quite utilitarian. I am no collector."

"Ah!" said he, "that isn't my case. I am a convinced disciple of the great John Daw, a snapper-up of unconsidered trifles, a hoarder of miscellaneous treasure. Nothing comes amiss to me, from a blue diamond to a Staffordshire dog."

"Have you no special fancy?" I asked.

"I have a special fancy for any relic of the past that I can lay hands on," he replied. But perhaps, like the burglars, I have a particular leaning towards precious stones – those and the other kind of stones – the siliceous variety – with which our impolite forefathers used to fracture one another's craniums"

"Your collection must take up a lot of space," I remarked.

"It does," said he. "That's the trouble. John Daw's nest has a tendency to overflow. And still they come. I'm always finding fresh treasures."

"By the way," said I, "where do you find the stuff?"

"Oh, call it not stuff," he protested, regarding me with a foxy smile. "I spoke of treasures. As to where I discover them; well, well, surely there is a mine for silver and a place for gold where they refine it; a place also – many places, mostly cottage parlours, that no bird of prey knoweth, neither hath the travelling dealer's eye seen them, where may be found ancestral Wrotham pots and Staffordshire figures, to say nothing of venerable tickers and crocks from far Cathay. These the wise collector makes a note of – and locks up the note."

I was half amused and half exasperated by his evasive verbiage and his unabashed, and quite unnecessary, caution. A mighty secretive gentleman, this, I reflected; and proceeded to fire a return shot.

"In effect," said I, "you go rooting about in cottage parlours, snapping up rustic heirlooms, probably at a fraction of their value."

"Undoubtedly," he agreed, with a snigger. "That is the essence of the sport. I once, in a labourer's cottage, picked up a genuine 'Vicar and Moses' by Ralph Wood for five shillings. But that was a windfall."

"It wasn't much of a windfall for the owner," I remarked.

"He was quite satisfied," said Penrose, "and so was I. What more would you have? But windfalls are not frequent, and when they fail I fall back on the popinjay."

"The pop— Oh, you mean Mr Parrott?"

"Exactly," said he. "Our friend Monsieur le Perroquet. Actually, I let him do most of the rooting about. He knows all the ropes, and, as we agreed, he doesn't demand payment through the proboscis."

"No," said I, "he doesn't appear to be grasping, to judge by the price of my own purchase; and I gather that you have got most of your stuff – I beg pardon; treasure – from him."

"Oh, I wouldn't say that," he replied. "Mere purchase from a dealer is a dull affair, though necessary. But one wants the sport as well, the pleasure of the chase, not to mention those of the pick and shovel."

"The pick and shovel!" I repeated. "That sounds as if you did a little in the resurrection line. You are not a tomb-robber, I trust?"

I was, of course, only jesting, but he took me up quite seriously.

"But why not? We may grant the impropriety of disturbing the repose of the freeholders in Finchley Cemetery. Besides, they have nothing but their bones, which, at present, are not collectors' pieces. But our rude forefathers had a foolish – but, for us, convenient – habit of taking their goods and chattels to bed with them, so to speak. Now, a man's title of his goods, after his decease, does not extend to an indefinite period. When a deceased gentleman has enjoyed the possession of his chattels for a couple of thousand years or more, I think he ought to be satisfied. His title has lapsed by the effluxion of time; and my title, by right of discovery, has come into being. The expression 'tomb-robber' is not applicable to an archaeological excavator. Don't you agree?"

I admitted that excavation for scientific purposes seemed to be a permissible proceeding, though I had secret doubts as to whether the expression was properly applicable to his activities. He did not impress me as a scientific investigator.

"But," I asked, "what sort of things do you turn up when you go a-digging?"

"All sorts of things," he replied. "Mostly preposterous stone substitutes for cutlery, decayed and fragmentary pots and pans, with an occasional – very occasional – torque or brooch and portions of the deceased proprietor. But I leave those. I don't collect proprietors."

"And I suppose," said I, "that when you find a gold or silver ornament you notify the coroner of the discovery of treasure trove?"

"That," he replied with his queer, foxy smile, "is indispensable. But you seem to be interested in my miscellaneous gleanings. I wonder if you would care to cast a supercilious eye on my little hoard. I don't often display my treasures because your regular collector is usually a man of one idea – indefinitely repeated – and he is disappointed to find that I am not. But you, like myself, are more eclectic in taste and I should have great pleasure in introducing you to Aladdin's Cave, if you would care to inspect its contents."

I was not, really, particularly interested, but yet I was faintly curious as to the nature of his "hoard." It sounded like a very queer collection, and might include some objects of real interest. Besides which, the man himself, despite his exasperating verbosity and obscurities of speech, rather attracted me. Accordingly, I accepted his invitation, and, when we had exchanged visiting-cards and arranged the day and hour of my visit, we separated; he shaping a course in a westerly direction and I bearing east, towards my chambers in Lincoln's Inn.

CHAPTER TWO
Aladdin's Cave

Mr Penrose's residence or John Daw's Nest, as he would have called it, was situated in Queen Square, Bloomsbury, and, what is more, it was one of the few remaining original houses dating back to the time when residents could look out of the windows through the open end of the square, across the meadows to the heights of Highgate. Appropriately to the house of a collector of antiquities, its door was garnished with a pair of link-extinguishers, as well as with a fine brass knocker and an old-fashioned bell-handle.

A flourish on the knocker, reinforced by a hearty tug at the bell-pull, resulted in the opening of the door and the appearance thereat of an elderly man of depressed and nephritic aspect, with puffy eyelids and a complexion like that of a suet pudding. He received the announcement of my identity with resignation, and, having admitted me, took my hat and stick and silently introduced me to a small room, the window of which commanded a view of the leaden statue of her late Majesty, Queen Anne. At this window I had taken up a position from which I could contemplate that rather neglected example of an extinct art when the door opened briskly and Mr Penrose entered.

"Ha!" said he, "I see you are admiring the mimic rendering of our proverbially deceased twenty-shilling Lady."

"I am afraid," said I, as we shook hands, "that your paraphrase fails in precision. You would have to pay thirty shillings today to buy a sovereign, if you could find one."

"There," he retorted, "is exemplified the pedantic accuracy of the legal mind. But I spoke in terms of the past. The sureous reality is now as dead as Madame herself. But what think you of that masterpiece of the plumber's art? I rather like it; and it is the genuine metal. I have tried it with my pocket-knife. To tell you a little secret, I had thought of making an offer for it."

"Do you mean," I exclaimed, "that you want to buy it?"

"If it should come into the market," he replied. "Unfortunately it has not, up to the present."

"But what on earth could you do with a leaden statue?" I protested.

"Put it in my gallery," he replied, "if the floor would stand it."

"You can take it," said I, "that it would not. Why, the thing must weigh tons. Besides, it is much better in the place that it was made to occupy and which it does really adorn in its rather mouldy way."

"In short," said he, "you think me a bit of a vandal" (which was the literal truth). "Well, you needn't be alarmed. It is safe from my acquisitive instincts for the present."

He turned to a nondescript piece of furniture, half sideboard and half armoire, and, opening a door, took out a decanter and two glasses, which he placed on the table.

"Before we venture into Aladdin's Cave," said he, taking out the stopper of the decanter, "shall we fortify ourselves with a morsel of cake?"

He looked at me interrogatively as he picked up the decanter. Of course, there was no cake visible; but my growing skill in interpreting his verbal puzzles enabled me to diagnose the dark-brown wine as Madeira.

Without giving me time to refuse, he filled the two glasses and, having handed me one, proceeded in a very deliberate and workmanlike fashion to empty the other.

"The vintages of the Fortunate Isles," said he, as he refilled his glass, "have always commended themselves to me, rivalled only in my affection by the product of the vines of Xeres" (he pronounced the name in the Spanish manner, "Hereth," as a slight additional precaution against being too readily understood), "preferably the elderly and fuscous variety."

I noted the fact – while he filled his third glass – as explaining the vinous aroma which I had noticed in Parrott's shop as apparently exhaling from his person. It turned out later to be not without significance. Madeira and old brown sherry by no means share the innocuousness of what Penrose would probably have called "the celestial herb."

When I had resolutely declined a refill, he reluctantly returned the decanter to its abiding-place and locked the door thereof.

"And now," said he, "we shall proceed to explore the secret recesses of the cavern."

He conducted me out into the fine, spacious hall, from which a noble staircase gave access to the upper floors. In one swift glance I noted that the appointments were not worthy of the architecture, for the furniture – of which there was a good deal too much – consisted of undeniable "dentist's oak," and there were one or two shabby-looking busts, the obvious plaster of which had been varnished by some optimist in the hope that they might thereby be mistaken for bronze. But I had little opportunity for detailed inspection, for my host threw open, with something of a flourish, an adjacent door and motioned to me to enter; which I did, and found myself in one of a pair of great, lofty communicating rooms, and forthwith began my tour of inspection.

I had expected to find Mr Penrose's collection something of an oddity, but the reality far exceeded my expectations. It was an amazing hoard. Alike, in respect of matter and manner, it was astonishing and bewildering. Of the ordinary collector's fastidious selection, prim tidiness and orderly arrangement there was no trace. The things that jostled one another on the crowded shelves and tables were in every respect incongruous; for, on the one hand, rare and valuable pieces, such as the "Vicar and Moses" and a fine slip-ware tyg, stood cheek by jowl with common, worthless oddments, and, on the other, the objects themselves were devoid of any sort of kinship or relation. The "Vicar," for instance, was accompanied by a broken Roman pot, a few worthless fragments of Samian ware, a dried crab covered with acorn barnacles and half a dozen horse-brasses; while the tyg had as its immediate neighbour a Sheffield coffee-pot, a Tunbridge-ware wafer-box, a pewter candlestick and one or two flint implements.

The confusion and disorder that prevailed were perfectly astounding. These fine old rooms, with such splendid possibilities, suggested nothing more or less than the store of some curio dealer or the premises of an auctioneer on the day preceding a sale of miscellaneous property. I ventured tentatively to comment on the lack of arrangement.

"You have certainly got a very remarkable collection," said I, "but don't you think that its interest would be increased if you adopted some sort of classification? Here, for instance, is a wine-glass, a Jacobite glass, apparently."

"Not apparently," he objected. "Actually. An undoubtedly genuine piece. An appropriate memorial, too. 'Charlie loved good ale and wine.'"

"So he did, as 'his nose doth show' in the portraits. But why put this glass next to that barbaric-looking pot? There is no relation whatever between the two things."

"There is the relation of unlikeness," he replied. "And don't disparage that rare and precious pot. It is extremely ancient. Prehistoric. Neolithic, I believe, is the correct word."

"But why not put all the prehistoric pots together instead of mixing them up with table-glass and Scandinavian carvings?"

"That would seem a dull arrangement," said he. "You would lose the effect of variety, the thrill of unexpectedness. How delightful, for instance, after considering this book of hours and this highly ornate sternutatorium" – he indicated a handsome tortoiseshell snuff-box – "to come upon these siliceous relics of the childhood of the race – also neolithic, I believe – the products of my own fossatory activities."

The "relics" referred to consisted of half a dozen rough flint nodules which looked as if they might have been gathered from a road-mender's heap. They may have been genuine flint implements, but they were certainly not neolithic. No one with the most elementary knowledge of stone implements could have supposed that they were. But my host's easy-going acceptance of them, and his indifference as to the actual facts, brought home to me a state of mind at which I wondered more and more as I examined this amazing collection.

For, in the first place, Mr Penrose displayed the most complete and comprehensive ignorance of "antiques" of every kind. He knew no more of them than their names, and he frequently got those wrong. But not only was he ignorant. He was quite indifferent. He seemed to be totally devoid of interest in the individual things which he had accumulated; and the question that I asked myself was what earthly object he could have had in this enormous and miscellaneous collection. Apparently, he was possessed by an insatiable acquisitiveness, with no other motive behind it. Mere possession seemed to be the object of his desire; and with mere possession he appeared to be satisfied. Not without reason had he likened himself to "The Great John Daw."

My long tour of inspection came at last to an end. I had examined the collection very thoroughly, not only to please my host – though he was evidently gratified and flattered by the interest that I displayed in his 'hoard' – but because it contained, mingled with a good deal of rubbish, many curious and beautiful objects that invited examination. The last piece that I inspected was an ancient gold brooch, richly decorated with gilt filigree work and set with garnets. I lifted it tenderly from the dusty scrap of paper (marked in pencil with the number 963) on which it rested and carried it to the window to look at it in a better light.

"This is a very fine piece of work, Mr Penrose," I remarked.

"Ha!" said he, "the papistical fibula commends itself. I am glad you like it."

"A Roman fibula!" I exclaimed in surprise. "I should have taken it for a Saxon brooch."

"You may be right," he admitted; "in fact, I am inclined to think that you are. At any rate, it is one or the other."

"But," I protested, "surely you keep some sort of record. I see that the pieces are numbered. Haven't you a catalogue?"

"To be sure I have," he replied. "Excellent idea!" We'll get out the Domesday Book and see which of us is right."

He pulled out the drawer of a table and produced therefrom a manuscript book which he opened and began to turn over the leaves. Still holding the brooch, I stepped across to him and looked over his shoulder. And then I got a fresh surprise, though I ought to have been prepared for something unusual. For if the collection was eccentric, the catalogue was positively fantastic. It seemed to be (and probably was) expressly designed to be as completely unintelligible as possible. The brief entries, scribbled illegibly in pencil, were apparently worded in Mr Penrose's peculiar, cryptic dialect, and, for the most part, I could make nothing of them. Running my eye down the pages, I deciphered with difficulty such entries as: "Up +. Mudlarks," "Sammy. Pot sand. Sinbad," "Funereal flower-pot, Julie-Polly," "Carver, Jul. Pop."

I stood gazing in speechless astonishment at this amazing record while Penrose slowly turned the leaves, glancing slyly at me from time to time, apparently to see how I took it. At length – at unnecessary length – Number 963 was found; but it was not very illuminating – to me – for it consisted only of the laconic statement, "Sweeney's resurrection." Apparently however, it conveyed something to him, for he said, "Yes, you are right. I recollect now." But he did not enter into any particulars.

I laid the brooch down on its slip of paper and began to think of departing; and meanwhile he looked at me with a very odd expression; an expression of mingled anxiety and hesitation.

"I have to thank you, Mr Penrose," said I, "for a very pleasant and profitable afternoon. It was very good of you to let me see all your treasures. I *have* seem them all, I suppose?"

He did not reply for a few moments, but continued to look at me in that queer, anxious, irresolute fashion. Suddenly, his hesitation gave way and he burst out in low, impressive tones, in a manner of the deepest secrecy:

"The fact is that you haven't. There is another little hoard, which I don't show to anyone, but just gloat over in secret. I don't even mention its existence. But, somehow I feel tempted to make an exception in your case. What do you say? Would you like to have a peep at the contents of Bluebeard's chamber?"

"This sounds rather alarming," said I. "Were there not certain penalties for undue curiosity?"

"I hold you immune from those," he replied. "Only I stipulate that this private view shall be really a private view, to be spoken of to nobody. I can rely on you to keep my secret?"

I did not much like this. Like most lawyers, I am a cautious man, and cautious men do not care to be made the unprivileged repositories of other people's secrets. But I could hardly refuse; and when I had, rather reluctantly, given the required undertaking, he moved off towards a door in a corner of the room and I followed, wondering anxiously what he was gong to show me and whether it would commit me to any unlawful knowledge.

The room into which he led me – and of which he closed and bolted the door – was a smallish apartment, at one end of which was a massive mahogany cupboard or armoire. When he had unlocked this and thrown open the doors, there was revealed the steel front of a large safe or small strong-room. Apparently the safe-key was not in his bunch, for he returned the latter to his pocket and then, retiring a few paces, stood with his back to me while he dived into some secret recesses of his clothing. In a few moments he turned round, rather red from his exertions, and stepped up to the safe with the key in his hand, while I watched with growing curiosity.

The lock clicked softly, a turn of the handle withdrew the bolts and the ponderous door swung open, disclosing a range of shallow drawers which occupied the whole of the interior. My host, first withdrawing the key and slipping it into his waistcoat pocket, proceeded to pull out the top drawer and carry it to a table under the window. And then I breathed a sigh of relief. There was nothing incriminating, after all. The drawer was simply filled with jewellery, looking, indeed, like a tray from a jeweller's window. My host's secrecy was naturally and reasonably explained by the value of his treasures and their highly portable and negotiable character.

I looked over the contents of the drawer with keen interest, for I am rather fond of gems, though I have no special knowledge of them. My host, too, showed a pleasure and enthusiasm in regard to the things, themselves, which contrasted strikingly with the indifference that he had displayed towards the general collection.

Yet, even here, there was no glimmer of connoisseurship. His manner suggested mere miserly gloating; and his ignorance of these beautiful baubles astonished me. It was suggested by the absence of any classification, by the way in which totally unrelated stones were jumbled together, and the suggestion was confirmed by his comments. For instance, in this first drawer were two cat's-eyes placed side by side; but they belonged to totally different categories. One, a dark yellowish-green stone with a bright band of bluish light, was a cymophane or true cat's-eye – a chrysoberyl. The other, a charming stone of the hue known as "honey yellow," was a quartz cat's-eye and should have been placed with the other quartz gems. I ventured to comment on the fact, referring to the cymophane as a chrysoberyl, but he interrupted me with the protest.

"Chrysoberyl! Violin-bows, my dear sir! Call not the optic of the fair Tabitha a chrysoberyl!"

As he obviously knew – and cared – nothing of the actual characters of precious stones, I did not pursue the question, but continued my inspection of the really interesting and remarkable collection. The admiration that I expressed evidently gave him considerable pleasure and he also made admiring comments from time to time, though without much appearance of taste or discrimination. But his enthusiasm did really wake up when he brought forth the third drawer, which was devoted entirely to opals, and as these beautiful gems are special favourites of mine, we examined them with sympathetic pleasure.

It was a really magnificent collection, and what rather surprised me (considering the collector's comprehensive ignorance) was its genuinely representative character. There were specimens of every variety of the gem. Of the noble, or precious, opal a long range of examples was shown, of all the varied rainbow hues and of various sizes up to nearly an inch in diameter; some in plain mounts but most of them encircled with borders of rose diamonds or brilliants. There were harlequin opals, Mexican fire opals, glowing like blazing coals, black opals, a large series of the common non-prismatic form, of various hues, and one or two examples of the dark, pitchy "root" or matrix streaked and speckled with points of prismatic colour.

But the gem of the collection, in interest if not in beauty, was a cameo, cut in a disc of precious opal embedded in its dark matrix. The oval slab of matrix, carrying the glowing cameo, was worked into a pendant with a broad border of small rose diamonds and coloured stones forming the design of a rose, a thistle and a central star, while, at the bottom, worked in tiny diamonds, was the word "Fiat"; which, with the engraved portrait of a middle-aged gentleman in a wig, gave a clue to the significance of the jewel.

As I pored over this curious memorial, Penrose watched me with a smile of evident gratification.

"My favourite child," he remarked, taking it out of its compartment and handing it to me, together with a magnifying glass. "Just look at the detail of the face."

"I examined it through the lens and was greatly impressed by the perfection of the modelling on so minute a scale.

"Yes," I said, "it is quite a wonderful piece of work. One gets the impression that it might be a really good portrait. "And now I know," I added, as I returned the jewel to him, "why you swore me to secrecy."

He paused with the trinket in his hand, looking at me with a distinctly startled expression.

"What do you mean?" he demanded.

"Well," I replied, "You must admit that it is a rather incriminating object to have in your possession."

He gazed at me uneasily, almost with an appearance of alarm, and rejoined:

"I don't understand you. How, incriminating?"

I chuckled with mischievous satisfaction. For an inveterate joker, he seemed decidedly "slow in the uptake."

"Doesn't it occur to you," I replied, "that a portrait of James Francis Edward, the King over the water, cherished secretly by a presumably loyal subject of his Majesty George the Fifth, tends to suggest highly improper political sentiments? I call it rank sedition."

"Oh, I see what you mean," said he, with an uneasy laugh, apparently relieved – and slightly annoyed – at my schoolboy jest, "but sedition of that kind is a trifle threadbare in these days."

"He returned the jewel to its place in the drawer and carried the latter back to the safe. As he slid it in, he remarked:

"That's the last of the gem collection. The other drawers contain coins. You may as well see them, too."

I went through the coin collection and was rather surprised at its range, for it included ancient coins, Greek, Roman, Gaulish and British and English coins from the Middle Ages down to the late spade guineas. But all that remains in my memory concerning them is that the different periods seemed to be mixed up, with an almost total lack of order, and that there appeared to be an abnormal proportion of gold coins.

When the last of the drawers had been examined and returned and the safe and its enclosing cupboard had been closed and locked, I began once more to think of taking my leave. But my host pressed me to stay and take a cup of tea with him, and, when I had accepted his invitation, he conducted me back through the large gallery to the room into which I had first been shown. Here, the melancholy manservant – who answered to the name of Kickweed – presently brought us tea and drew a couple of arm-chairs up to the table.

"This collection of yours," I remarked, as my host poured out the tea, "must represent a large amount of sunk capital."

"I hardly regard it as sunk," he replied, "seeing that I have the use and enjoyment of my treasures; but the collection is worth a lot of money – at least, I hope it is. It has cost a lot."

"So I should suppose," said I; "and it must cost you something quite substantial in the matter of insurance."

"Ah!" said he, "I am glad you raised that question. For the fact is that the collection is not insured at all. I have intended to go into the matter, but there are certain difficulties that have put me off. Now, I dare say you know a good deal about insurance."

"I know something about the legal aspects," I replied, "and such knowledge as I possess is at your disposal. You certainly ought to be secured against what might be a very heavy loss. What are the difficulties that you refer to?"

"Well," he answered in a low voice, leaning across the table, "I don't want to go about proclaiming myself as the owner of a priceless collection. Might arouse interest in the wrong quarter, you see. And as to the gems, as I told you, they are a secret hoard the existence of which I disclose to nobody excepting yourself. You are the only person to whom I have shown them."

"But," I protested, "somebody must have sold them to you and must be aware that you have them."

"They know that I have – or had – the individual jewels that they sold me, but they don't know that I have a great and valuable collection. And I don't want them to know; but that is the difficulty about the insurance. Before I could insure the collection, I should have to get it valued; and the valuer would have to see the gems; and then the cat would be out of the bag. At least, that is what I suppose. Perhaps I am wrong. Could I effect an insurance for a certain definite sum without calling in a valuer?"

"You mean," I replied, "on a declaration that you had certain property of a certain value? No. I think a company would want evidence that the property insured actually existed and was of the value alleged; and in the event of a fire or a burglary, they certainly would not pay on property alleged to have been lost but which had never been proved to exist. But I think you are raising imaginary difficulties. You could stipulate that the valuation should be a strictly confidential transaction. Remember that the company's interests are the same as your own. If they insure you against burglary, they won't want you to be burgled."

"No, that is true," he admitted. "And you think I could rely on the secrecy of the valuer?"

"I have no doubt of it," I replied, "particularly if you made clear your reasons for insisting on secrecy."

"I am glad you think that," said he, "and I shall act on your advice without delay. I will put the case to the manager of the Society which has insured this house."

"I think you ought to do so at once," I urged. "There must be many thousands of pounds' worth of property in your collection and a fire or a burglary might sweep away the bulk of it in a night."

He repeated, with emphasis, his intention to attend to the matter without delay, and the subject then dropped. After a little more desultory conversation, I rose to take my leave; and the lugubrious Kickweed, having presented me with my hat and stick, let me out at the street door with the air of admitting me to the family vault.

As I wended homewards I found ample matter for reflection in the incidents of my visit; but chiefly my thoughts concerned themselves with my eccentric host. Mr Penrose was certainly a very strange man, and the more I thought about him, the less did I feel able to understand him. He had so many oddities and each of them suggested problems to which I could find no solution. There was the collection, for instance. Including the gems and coins, it must have been of very great value, and its accumulation must have entailed a vast expenditure of time and effort, to say nothing of the prodigious sums of money that must have been spent. But with what object? He had none of the ordinary collector's expertness and enthusiasm. He had no special knowledge of any single class of objects, not even of the gems for which he professed so much affection. The motive force that impelled him to collect seemed to be simple acquisitiveness, the mere *cupiditas habendi*.

But the outstanding feature of his character was secretiveness. He was a secret man of the very deepest dye. His inveterate habit of secrecy coloured every word and action. The ridiculous jargon that he used, his silly circumlocutions and ellipses and paraphrases, were but phases of the tendency, as if he grudged to disclose the whole of his meaning. Even the preposterous catalogue revealed the same trait, for, while it seemed to have been made deliberately unintelligible, it was clear that the absurd entries held some hidden meaning which was intelligible to him.

It was not an endearing trait. None of us likes a secret man. And very naturally. For secrecy implies distrust; and, moreover we are apt – again very naturally – to assume some reason for the secrecy, and to suspect that it is a discreditable reason. Thus it was with me in the present case; and my general dislike of the secret habit of mind was aggravated by the fact that I had become involved in the secrecy. The promise that had been exacted from me in regard to the gems recurred to me with a certain distaste and resentment. I was committed to the concealment of a fact which was no concern of mine and of the bearings of which I knew nothing. The explanations that Penrose had given for keeping secret his precious hoard were not unreasonable. But suppose there were other reasons. The thing was possible. Some collectors are not over-scrupulous; and I recalled, not for the first time, the singular, startled expression with which he had looked at me when I made my foolish joke about the Jacobite jewel.

In short, I was not quite comfortable about that promise. There is something a little disturbing about a secret hoard of valuable gems; and, but for the fact that Penrose was obviously a man of ample means, my professional experiences might have caused me to ask myself whether this very odd collection might not cover some activities of a more questionable kind.

CHAPTER THREE

Exit Mr Penrose

I did not see Penrose again for about a fortnight. Then, having occasion to call at Parrott's shop to inquire after a gate-leg table which I had purchased and which was undergoing some necessary restorations I encountered him, standing opposite to a lantern clock which had been fixed on a temporary bracket and was ticking cheerfully with every sign of robust health. Noting his evident interest in the venerable timepiece, I stopped to discuss it with him.

"You are looking at that clock, Mr Penrose," said I, "as if you contemplated making an investment."

"I don't contemplate," he replied. "I invested in it some time ago. It is a poor thing, but mine own."

"I shouldn't call it a poor thing," said I. "It is quite a good clock and it looks to me as if it were absolutely intact and in its original condition. Which is unusual in the case of lantern clocks. People will tinker with them and spoil them. You were lucky to find an untouched specimen."

"I didn't," said he. "When it came to me – through the usual psittacoid channel – it was a mere wreck. Some misbegotten Daedalus had eviscerated it and wrought havoc with its entrails. Thereupon I sought medicinal advice for the invalid and had it put under treatment."

"You sent it to a clockmaker?" I suggested.

"I did not," he replied. "It had had too much clockmaker already. I consulted the erudite and podophthalmate horologer, and behold! It has renewed its youth like the eagle."

I must confess that this stumped me for the moment, until a flash of supernormal intelligence associated the word "podophthalmate" with Mr Polton's protuberant eye-glass.

"I didn't know that Mr Polton was a practical mechanic," I remarked.

"Oh, don't call him that!" Penrose protested. "He is a magician, a wizard, a worker of miracles. By the way, Mrs Pettigrew, I rather expected to find him here. He promised to see this clock safely established in my gallery."

"He is here," replied Mrs Pettigrew. "He is in the workshop, doing something to Mr Tims' lathe. Would you like to walk across and let him know that you have arrived? You know the way. And perhaps, Mr Lockhart, you would like to go and inspect your table? I think Tims wants you to see it."

I accepted the invitation and, following Penrose, passed out at the back of the shop and crossed a small paved yard to a wide doorway. Passing through this, I entered a roomy workshop, lighted by a skylight and littered with articles of ancient furniture in all stages of decay and dismemberment. There were three persons in the workshop. First there was Mr Tims, a tall, aged man, frail and decrepit of aspect – until he picked up a tool; when he seemed suddenly to develop fresh strength and vitality. Next, there was Mr Polton in shirt-sleeves and an apron (which appeared by its length to have been borrowed from Tims), engaged at the moment in re-fixing the headstock of a wood-turner's lathe. The third person was Mr Parrott, as I learned when Penrose greeted him; and, as this was the first time that I had encountered him in the flesh, I looked at him with some curiosity.

"Monsieur le Perroquet" was a somewhat unusual-looking man and not at all the type of a shopkeeper. Dark, clean-shaved and blue-jowled, he had rather the appearance of an actor; and this suggestion was heightened by a certain precision of speech and clearness of enunciation, and especially by a tendency to the use of studied and appropriate gestures. Obviously, he was not only an educated man but what one would call a gentleman; easy and pleasant in manner, with that combination of deference and dignity that is attainable only by a well-bred man.

When I had introduced myself, Mr Tims produced the dismembered table and exhibited the repairs on the damaged leg.

"You see, sir," he explained, "I've cut out the worm-eaten part and let in a patch of sound oak, Do you think he'll do?"

"Do you propose to stain the patch?" I inquired.

"That's as you please," replied Tims. "I wouldn't. A mend's a mend, but a stained mend looks like a fake."

"I think Tims is right," said Parrott. "Better leave the patch to darken naturally."

To this I assented, and thereupon Mr Tims proceeded to assemble the separated parts while Parrott and I looked on and Penrose divided his attention between the table and Mr Polton's operations on the lathe.

"By the way, Mr Penrose," said I, suddenly remembering our last conversation, "how goes the insurance scheme? Have you solved the difficulty of the valuer?"

Penrose turned to me quickly with a look of annoyance, so that I was sorry I had spoken.

"There is nothing to report at present," he replied with unwonted shortness of manner; and, as if to close the subject, he stepped across to the lathe and manifested a sudden and not very intelligent interest in its mechanism. However, Mr Polton's job was apparently completed, for, when he had replaced the band on the pulley, tested the centres and given the fly-wheel a trial spin, he proceeded to shed the apron and put on his coat, and was forthwith spirited away by Penrose.

I had noticed that when I spoke of the insurance Mr Parrott had seemed to prick up his ears (which, perhaps, explained the annoyance of the secretive Penrose). But he made no remark while the latter was present, though he had evidently heard and noted what had been said, for, when, Penrose had gone, he asked:

"Do I understand that Mr Penrose has actually decided to insure his collection? I have repeatedly urged him to, but he has always agreed with me, and then let the matter slide."

"I am afraid," said I, "that my experience is the same as yours. I advised him to insure without delay, but you heard what he said."

"I heard what he said," Parrott replied, "but it didn't convey much to me, excepting that he is still putting the business off. Which is rather foolish of him. His collection is of no great value, as collections go, but still, it represents a good deal of money, and he would suffer a substantial loss if he had a fire."

"Or a burglary," I suggested.

"There is not much risk of that," said he. "Burglars wouldn't be tempted by a collection of miscellaneous bric-à-brac, most of it identifiable and none of any considerable value. Burglars like more portable goods and things that are intrinsically valuable, such as precious metals and jewellery."

"You have seen his collection, of course?" said I.

"Yes. As a matter of fact, I supplied the greater part of it. And I gather that you have seen it, too?

"Yes. He was good enough to show me his treasures. That was how I came to advise him about the insurance. It seemed to me very unsafe for valuable property like that to be quite unprotected."

"I shouldn't have called it very valuable property," said he. "But perhaps he has some things that I haven't seen. It would be like Mr Penrose to keep his court-cards up his sleeve. Did he show you any really valuable pieces?"

Now, here was the very difficulty that I had foreseen. Obviously, Parrott was unaware of the existence of the hoard of jewels and coins, but he evidently suspected Penrose of possessing something more than he had disclosed. It was very unpleasant, but my promise of secrecy left me no choice. I must either lie or prevaricate.

"It is difficult for me to estimate values," said I, adopting the less objectionable alternative, "but some of the things that I saw must have been worth a good deal of money. There was a Saxon gold ornament, for instance. Wouldn't that be rather valuable?"

"Oh, certainly," he agreed, "but only in a modest way. I don't know what such a thing would fetch, say, at Christie's. But I think you said he was employing a valuer, and having some difficulty with him, apparently?"

"No," I replied. "His difficulty is that a regular valuation would have to be made, which would involve an inspection of his goods and the making of an inventory. He seems to object to having a valuer nosing round his premises."

"He would, naturally," said Parrott. "I have never met such an extraordinarily secretive man. But really, the valuer would not be necessary. I could draw up an estimate that would satisfy the Company – that is, if the property to be insured is only what I have seen. But, as I said, he may have some other things which he has not disclosed to me. Do you think he has?"

Here I must needs prevaricate again; but I kept as near to the truth as I could.

"It is impossible for me to guess what property he has," I said. "You know the man. I know only what he showed me."

Parrott looked dissatisfied with my answer, which was, indeed, pretty obviously evasive, and he seemed disposed to press the matter further; but, at this point, Mr Tims, having completed the assembling of the parts of the table, offered the completed work for my inspection and approval. I looked it over quickly, and, having pronounced it satisfactory, took the opportunity to make my escape before Parrott should have time to propound any more questions.

As I re-entered the shop from the yard, Penrose and Polton were just passing out at the front door, the latter carrying the body of the clock and the former bearing a large parcel, which presumably contained the weights, the pendulum and the bracket. I went to the door and watched them receding down the street until they reached the corner, when Penrose, happening to glance back, observed me and greeted me with a flourish of his free hand. Then they turned the corner and disappeared from my sight; and thus, though I little guessed it at the time, did Mr Penrose pass out of my ken for ever.

For I never saw him again. A few days later, I joined the South-Eastern circuit, and thenceforth, for the next few months, passed most of my time in the county towns in which the assizes were held; and when I came back, Mr Penrose had disappeared.

The fact was communicated to me by Mrs Pettigrew, who, in her kindly and discreet fashion, tried to minimise the abnormal features of the affair.

"Do you mean, Mrs Pettigrew," I exclaimed, "that he has gone away from his home and left no address or indication as to where he is to be found?"

"So I understand," she replied, "but I don't really know any of the particulars."

"But," said I, "it is a very extraordinary affair."

"It would be," said she, "in the case of any ordinary man. But you know what Mr Penrose is. It would be quite like him, if he had occasion, say, to go abroad, to go and keep his own counsel as to where he had gone to. I believe he has done it before, though not for so long a time. I understand that on more than one occasion he has gone out in his car and driven away into the country without saying anything to his servant as to his intentions – just gone out and returned after a few days, saying nothing to anybody as to where he had been."

"Amazing!" said I. "He can't be quite in his right mind. But this affair seems rather different from the other escapades. You say he has been gone for a couple of months. It looks very much as if he had gone for good."

"It does," she agreed; and then, after a pause, she continued: "It has been a great blow to Mr Parrott, for Mr Penrose was by far our best customer. He was really the mainstay of the business; and now that he has gone and that we have lost poor Mr Tims, it is very doubtful if we can carry on."

"Why, what has happened to Tims?" I asked.

"He is dead, poor old thing," she replied. "He got influenza and went out like the snuff of a candle. He was very old and frail, you know. But he was invaluable to Mr Parrott. He was such a wonderful workman."

"Still," I said, "I suppose he can be replaced."

"Mr Parrott thinks not," said she, "and I am afraid he is right. It is very difficult to find a real cabinet-maker in these days. The few that are left are mostly old men, and even they don't understand old furniture as Mr Tims did. But, without a skilled restorer, we can't get on at all. Mr Parrott is an excellent judge, but he is no workman."

In short, what the absent Penrose would have called "the psittacoid emporium" was in a bad way. It had never been a very prosperous concern, I gathered, and indeed I had seldom seen a stranger in the shop; but with the aid of Penrose's numerous purchases (or "investigations," as he would have described them) and the prestige of Tims' skilful restorations, it had just managed to keep afloat.

"I do hope," Mrs Pettigrew said, rather dismally, "that we shall be able to struggle on. It will be an awful disaster for poor Joan and me if the business collapses. Of course, Mr Parrott has not been in a position to pay me much of a salary, but Joan and I have the use of the rooms over the shop, and with her earnings as a secretary we have rubbed along quite comfortably. But it will be very different if I am earning nothing and we have only her little salary to live on, and rent to pay as well. And it will be so unfair to the poor girl, who ought to be considering her own future, to have to carry the burden of a superannuated mother."

I was very sorry for Mrs Pettigrew and I tried to present a more hopeful picture of the financial possibilities. I also reminded her that she had my address and that it was the address of a friend. And so we parted. A little way down the street – but on the opposite side – I met Miss Joan wending homewards and observed her with a new interest. With her short hair and short skirts, her horn-rimmed spectacles and her attaché case, she was the typical Miss Twentieth Century. But as she swung along manfully, she conveyed a pleasant impression of pluck and energy and buoyant spirits, with mighty little of the "poor girl" in her aspect or bearing; and, raising my hat in response to her friendly nod, I hoped that the gathering clouds might pass over her harmlessly.

But when I next visited London the blow had fallen. I made my way to the dingy little street, only to find a gang of painters disfiguring the empty shop with garish adornments. The Tropic Bird had flown. The Popinjay was no more. The vacant window greeted me with a dull, unwelcoming stare. The pleasant little rendezvous had gone out, like poor Mr Tims, with hardly a final flicker; and Mrs Pettigrew and Joan and Penrose, and the mysterious Mr Polton seemed to have faded out of my life like the actors in a play when the curtain has fallen.

BOOK TWO

Narrated by Christopher Jervis, MD

CHAPTER FOUR

The Burglary at Queen Square

My introduction to the strange and puzzling circumstances connected with the disappearance of Mr Daniel Penrose occurred in a rather casual, almost accidental fashion. On a certain evening, at the close of the day's work in the Law Courts, I had walked up with my colleague, Dr John Thorndyke, to New Square, Lincoln's Inn, to restore to our old friend, Mr Brodribb, some documents which it had been necessary to produce in Court. Finding Mr Brodribb in his office, apparently up to his eyes in business, we handed the documents to him, and, when he had checked them, were about to depart when our friend laid down his pen, took off his spectacles and held up his hand to detain us.

"One moment, Thorndyke," said he. "Before you go, there is a little matter that I should like to take your opinion on. I'll just pop on my hat and walk with you to the corner of the Square. It is quite a trifling affair – at least – well, I'll tell you about it as we go."

He rose and, putting on the immaculate top hat which he invariably wore in defiance of modern fashions, stepped through into the outer office.

"I shall be back in a few minutes, Jarrett," said he, addressing his managing clerk, and with that he led the way out.

"The matter," he began, as we emerged on to the broad pavement of the Square, "relates to a burglary, or attempted burglary, at the house of a man whom I may call my client; a man named Daniel Penrose, though, actually, I am being consulted by his executor, a Mr Horridge."

"Penrose, then, I take it, is deceased," said Thorndyke.

"No. Penrose is alive, but he is absent from his home and no one knows where he is at the moment. So Horridge is assuming that his position as executor authorises him to take action in the absence of the testator."

"That doesn't seem a very sound position," Thorndyke remarked. "But what action does he propose to take?"

"I had better explain the circumstances," said Brodribb. "In the first place, the man Penrose, who has a biggish house in Queen Square is the owner of a collection; a very miscellaneous collection, I understand; all sorts of trash from old clocks to china dogs. This stuff is kept in two large rooms on the ground floor, but adjoining the main rooms is a small room which contains nothing but a table, a chair and a large cupboard or armoire. This room is usually kept locked, but, by a fortunate chance, when Penrose went away he left the key in the door, and the butler, a man named Kickweed, finding it there, very properly took possession of it.

"Now, the alleged burglary occurred about ten days ago. It seems that Kickweed, making his morning round of the premises, unlocked the door of the small room to go in and inspect, when, to his astonishment, he found it bolted on the inside. Thereupon he took a pair of library steps round to the side of the house where the window of the small room looks on a narrow uncovered passage. On climbing up the steps he found the window unfastened and was able to slide it up and step over into the room. There he confirmed the fact that the door was bolted on the inside, but that, and the unfastened window, were the only signs of anything out of the ordinary. The cupboard was perfectly intact, with no traces whatever of its having been tampered with; and, although there were some scratches on the table by the window, as if some hard objects had been put on it and moved about, there was nothing to show when those marks had been made."

"The cupboard, I presume, was locked?" said Thorndyke.

"Yes, and with a Chubb lock."

"And what was in the cupboard?"

"Ah!" said Brodribb, "that is the problem. No one knows what it contained or whether it contained anything. But, having regard to the facts that Penrose is a collector, that he always kept this room locked and that the cupboard was fitted with a Chubb lock, the reasonable assumption is that it contained something of value."

"Yes," Thorndyke agreed, "that seems probable. But what does Mr Horridge propose to do?"

"He would like, with my consent – I am co-executor – to have the lock picked and explore the inside of the cupboard."

"That plan seems to present difficulties," said Thorndyke. "To say nothing of the fact that a Chubb lock takes a good deal of picking, there is the objection that, as you don't know what was in the cupboard, you couldn't judge whether anything had been taken. Suppose you find it empty; you don't know that it was not empty previously. Suppose you find valuable property in it; you still don't know that nothing has been taken, and, by having forced the lock, you assume a slightly uncomfortable responsibility for the safety of the contents. Why not just seal the cupboard and let Penrose do the investigating when he returns?"

"Yes," said Brodribb, with a rather dissatisfied air, as he halted at the corner of the Square and looked up at the clock above the library. "But suppose he doesn't return?" He paused for a few moments and then burst out: "The fact is, Thorndyke, that this burglary is only an incident in a most complicated and puzzling affair. There is no time to go into it now, but I should very much like, some time when you have an hour or so to spare, to put the whole case before you and hear what you have to suggest."

"I shall have an hour or so to spare – for you – this evening," said Thorndyke, "if that will suit you."

Brodribb brightened visibly. "It will suit me admirably," said he. "I will get a bit of dinner and then I will trot along to King's Bench Walk."

"You needn't do that," said Thorndyke. "Jervis and I are dining at our chambers this evening. Come along and join us. Then we shall be able to get into our conversational stride with the aid of food and a glass of wine."

Brodribb accepted gleefully, and, when we had settled the time for him to arrive, he turned away towards his office. But suddenly he stopped, searching frantically in a bulging pocket-book.

"Here," said he, holding out a small piece of paper, "is something to occupy your mighty brains until we meet at dinner, when I will ask you to let me have it back."

As Thorndyke took the paper from him, he broke out into a broad smile, and, turning away once more hurried off to relieve the waiting Jarrett. My colleague looked at the paper, considered for a few moments, turned it over to glance at the back, held it up to the light and passed it to me without comment. It was a small scrap of paper – about three inches square – apparently cut off a sheet with a paper-knife, and it bore three words untidily scribbled on it with a hard pencil: "Lobster(*Hortus petasatus*)."

"Well," I exclaimed, gazing at the paper with mild astonishment, "I suppose this has some meaning, but I'm hanged if I can make any sense of it. Can you?"

He shook his head, and, taking the little document from me, put it away carefully in his wallet.

"Do you suppose it is some sort of clue?" I asked.

"I don't suppose anything," he replied. "Let us wait and hear what Brodribb has to say about it. His expression suggested what school-boys call a leg-pull. But I suspect that he has something quite interesting to tell us about the absent Penrose."

Thorndyke's suspicion turned out to be correct, for, when Mr Brodribb arrived at our chambers, dressed immaculately and accompanied by a clerk carrying a brown-paper parcel, he gave us to understand that he had some rather surprising facts to communicate.

"But," he added, "I haven't come here just to eat your dinner and waste your time with idle talk. I want you to regard this as a professional consultation."

"We will consider that question later," said Thorndyke. "Our immediate purpose is to dine, but, meanwhile, I will return your rather cryptic document. I have kept a copy of it in case it may have a bearing on anything, and Jervis has made a minute study of its ostensible meaning."

"I am glad you say 'ostensible'," chuckled Brodribb, as he stowed the document away in his pocket-book. "And what conclusions has the learned Jervis arrived at?"

"My conclusions." said I, "are not very illuminating. Broadly speaking, the inscription is damned nonsense."

"I am with you there," said Brodribb.

"Then, as to the ostensible meaning, I take it that the word 'Lobster' means – well, it means lobster —"

"I'll take my bible oath it doesn't" Brodribb interposed.

"And as to the Latin words, *hortus*, of course, is a garden and *petasatus*, according to the erudite Dr William Smith, means 'having on a travelling-cap', or, alternatively, in more general terms, 'dressed in readiness for a journey.' Which doesn't make any sort of sense. You can't imagine a garden wearing a travelling-cap or being dressed in readiness for a journey."

"Perhaps it was the lobster that wore the cap," Thorndyke suggested, regardless of syntax. "But what is the significance of this document? I presume that it has some connection with the burglary."

"Yes, it has," Brodribb replied; "and if we could only find out what the devil it means, it might be quite an important clue. The paper was found by Kickweed, when he was examining the small room, under the table by the window. He thinks that it came from inside the cupboard; and if he is right, it furnishes evidence that the cupboard had been opened. And if we could only make any sense of the damned thing, it might give us a hint as to what had been taken."

"Yes," Thorndyke agreed, "but this is all very hypothetical. There is no evidence as to when the paper was dropped. It is quite possible that it may have been dropped by Penrose, himself. But as to this cryptic inscription. As Jervis says, it probably has some meaning. Does it convey anything at all to you?"

"As to meaning, most emphatically NO. But," Brodribb continued, grasping his wine-glass fiercely, "it impresses on me what I have always thought; that Daniel Penrose is an exasperating ass!"

At this outburst, Polton (our laboratory assistant and general factotum), who had just removed the covers and was in the act of refilling Brodribb's glass, looked at the speaker with an expression of surprised interest. He even seemed disposed to linger; but as there was no excuse for his doing so, he retired slowly as if reluctant to go.

"Perhaps," Thorndyke suggested when Polton had withdrawn, "that statement might be amplified and its bearings explained. You seem to imply that the cryptic inscription was written by Penrose."

"Undoubtedly it was," Brodribb replied. "It is typical of the man. Let me explain to you what sort of fellow Penrose is; and I want you to bear his peculiarities in mind when I come to tell you my story, because they probably have an important bearing on it. Now, Penrose has two outstanding oddities of character. In the first place, he is an inveterate joker. He seems incapable of speaking seriously; and the form that his facetiousness takes is in calling everything by its wrong name. The tendency seems to have grown on him until it has become a fixed habit and now his conversation is a sort of everlasting crossword puzzle. You have to cudgel your brains when he is speaking, to guess what he really means, and the only certainty that you have is that whatever he says, you know that he means something else."

"It sounds a bit confusing," said I. "But I suppose there is some method in his madness. Could you give us an illustrative example?"

"His method," replied Brodribb, "consists in using allusive phrases, equivalents in sound or sense, or distortions or perversions of words. He would not invest his money; he would investigate it. He would not call our friend John Thorndyke; he would probably describe him as Giovanni Brambleditch."

"I must bear that name in mind," said I, "for use on suitable occasions. But I think I grasp the principle. It is a sort of mixture of puns and metaphors."

"Yes," agreed Brodribb, "that is roughly what it amounts to. And now as to his other eccentricity. Penrose is an extraordinarily secret man. I use the word 'extraordinarily' advisedly. We are all, as lawyers, in the habit of keeping our own counsel. But we don't make secrets of our common and simple doings. If Thorndyke wants to go to the Law Courts, he doesn't sneak out on tip-toe when there is nobody about and leave no information as to where he has gone. But that is what Penrose would do. His habit of secrecy is as inveterate as his habit of facetiousness. He has been known to set forth from his house in his car without giving any notice to his butler or anybody else, to drive away into the country and stay away for several days – probably rooting about for bargains for his collection – and come back without a word of explanation as to where he had been. I assure you that when I had to draft his will I had the greatest difficulty in extracting from him any intelligible particulars of the property that was to be disposed of."

"It is rather remarkable," said Thorndyke, "that he should have made a will at all."

"It is," agreed Brodribb. "Men of that type usually die intestate. And thereby hangs another part of the tale that I have to tell. But I repeat that it is most necessary to bear these oddities of character in mind in connection with what has happened. And now, I will drop Penrose for the present and let you finish your dinners in peace."

I think that Brodribb's resolution to change the subject occasioned some disappointment to Polton; for that cunning artificer developed an unprecedented degree of attentiveness, which caused him to make frequent incursions into the room for the ostensible purpose of filling wine-glasses and performing other unnecessary services. His obvious interest in our rather trivial conversation caused me some slight surprise at the time. But later events explained his curiosity.

When we had finished dinner, and before removing the debris, he drew the three easy chairs up to the fire, placed a small table by that which was assigned to Brodribb and deposited on it the invariable decanter of port and three wine-glasses. Then he proceeded to clear the table by small instalments and by methods strikingly at variance with his usual swift economy of time and labour. But his procrastination was all in vain; for, not until the table was cleared to the last vestige and Polton had made his final and reluctant disappearance, did Brodribb make the slightest allusion to the subject of our consultation.

Then, when the door had closed, the glasses had been filled and Thorndyke and I had produced our pipes, he extracted a slip of paper from his pocket-book and laid it on the table by his side, fortified himself with a sip of wine and opened the proceedings.

CHAPTER FIVE

Mr Brodribb Propounds a Problem

"The circumstances connected with Penrose's disappearance," Mr Brodribb began, "are so complicated that I hardly know in what order I should present them."

"Probably," suggested Thorndyke, "the simplest plan would be to deal with the events in their chronological sequence."

"Yes," Brodribb agreed, "that would probably be the best way. I can refer back to previous occurrences if necessary. Then we will begin with the seventeenth of last October, roughly three months ago. On that day, in the early afternoon, he started out from home in his car and, contrary to his usual practice, he told Kickweed that he did not expect to be back until rather late. He directed that no one should sit up for him, but that a cold supper should be left in the dining-room. As to where he was going or on what business, he naturally gave no hint, but we are justified in assuming that he started forth with the intention of returning that night.

"But he did not return; and so far as we know, he was never seen again by anybody who was acquainted with him."

"Your description," said Thorndyke, "seems to suggest that he is a bachelor."

"Yes," replied Brodribb, "he is a bachelor, and with the exception of an aged father, to whom I shall refer presently, he seems to have no very near relations. Horridge, his executor, is a somewhat distant cousin and a good deal younger man. Well, then,

41

to repeat; on that day that I have mentioned, having given this very vague information to his butler, he went off to his garage, got his car out, closed up the garage and departed. Kickweed saw him drive away past the house; and that was the last that was seen of him by any person who knew him.

"His next appearance was in very remarkable circumstances. At midnight on that same day, or in the early hours of the next, a gentleman, a resident of Gravesend, who was returning home from Chatham in his car, saw a man lying face downwards on a heap of gravel by the roadside. The gentleman pulled up and got out to see what had happened; and as the man seemed to be either dead or unconscious, and there was nobody about excepting a rather squiffy labourer, he carefully lifted the man, with the labourer's assistance, put him into his car and conveyed him to the hospital at Gravesend, which was about a mile and a half from the place where he picked him up. At the hospital it was found that the man was alive though insensible, and on this the gentleman, a Mr Barnaby, went away, leaving the hospital authorities to give information to the police.

"The injured man appeared to be suffering from concussion. He had evidently fallen on the gravel with great violence, for his face was a mass of bruises and both his eyes were completely closed by the swelling due to the contusions. There was a deep, ragged wound across his right eyebrow in which the house surgeon had to put a couple of stitches; and there were various other bruises about his person, suggesting that he had been knocked down by some passing vehicle, but there appeared to be no broken bones or other severe injuries. The visiting surgeon, however, seems to have suspected the existence of a fracture of the base of the skull, and, on this account, directed that the patient should be kept very quiet and not questioned or disturbed in any way.

"The next day he still appeared to be unconscious, or nearly so, though he took the small amount of nourishment that was offered. But he answered no questions, and, by reason of the suspected fracture, no particular attempts were made to rouse him. And so the day passed. On the following day, the nineteenth, he remained in much the same condition; speechless and somnolent, lying nearly motionless, taking no notice of anything that was occurring around him and giving no answers to questions.

"But about eight o'clock at night he roused quite suddenly and very completely, for he seemed at once to be in full possession of his senses. But what is more, he proceeded to get out of bed, and demanded his clothes, declaring that he was quite well and intended to leave the hospital and go about his business. As you may suppose, there was a mighty hubbub. The house surgeon absolutely forbade the patient to leave the hospital and at first refused to let him have his clothes. But the man persisted that he was going, clothes or no clothes. Well, of course, they had no power to detain him, so the end of it was that they produced his clothes, and when he had dressed himself they gave him a light meal and took the particulars of his name and address and what little he could tell them of the circumstances of his accident. But of this he knew practically nothing. All he could tell them was that some vehicle had come on him from behind and knocked him down, and he remembered no more.

"When he had finished his meal and made his statement, such as it was, he asked for his overcoat. But there was no overcoat with his clothes, though the ward sister remembered that he was wearing one when he was brought in. Apparently, a patient who had been discharged earlier in the evening must have taken it by mistake, for there was a spare overcoat of the same kind – the ordinary raincoat, such as you may see by the dozen in any street; and it was suggested that he should take this in exchange for his own. But he would not agree to this, and eventually, as it was a mild night, he was allowed to go as he was.

"Now, he had not been gone more than an hour when the man who had taken the wrong coat brought it back. He had discovered his mistake by finding in the pocket a motorist's driving licence. But the odd thing was that the name and address on the licence did not agree with those that the departed patient had given. And yet there seemed to be no doubt that it was the missing coat, for the night nurse remembered the daubs of mud that she had noticed on it when she had undressed the patient. Moreover, she now recalled that the collar which she had taken off him had borne the initials 'DP,' in roman capitals, apparently written with a marking-ink pencil.

"But there was an evident discrepancy. The patient had given the name of Joseph Blewitt, with an address somewhere in Camden Town; but the name on the licence was Daniel Penrose and the address was his address in Queen Square.

"It was certainly a facer. The coat had to be returned to its owner. But who was its owner? The secretary decided that it was not his business to solve that problem; and, moreover, as there seemed to be something a trifle queer about the affair, he thought it best to communicate with the police. But as it was rather late and there seemed to be no urgency in the matter, he put it off until the following morning; and when the morning came, the police saved him the trouble by calling to make inquiries. And then something still more queer came to light.

"That morning, early, a patrol had discovered an abandoned car backed into the bushes at the bottom of an unfrequented lane leading down to the marshes a mile or so outside Gravesend. On making inquiries, he learned that it had been there all the previous day, for it had been seen by some boys who had gone down to the marshes on their probably unlawful occasions. They had taken no special notice of it, assuming that the owner had gone off on some business into the village in the irresponsible way that motorists have of leaving their cars unattended. But the boys could not say when it had arrived, as they had not been to the marshes on the day before. However, when the patrol pushed his inquiries in the village, he heard of the accident and of the man who had been picked up on the road not very far away. Thereupon, he took possession of the car and brought it into the town, lodging it, for the time being, in the garage belonging to the police station. And then he came on to the hospital to interview the injured man. But the bird had flown and only the coat with the driving licence remained.

"And then, once more, the plot thickened. For the name on the insurance certificate which was found in the car was the same as that on the licence; and if – as seemed nearly certain – the coat belonged to the departed patient, then that patient had given a false name and address. And this turned out to be the fact. No such person as Joseph Blewitt was known at the Camden Town address; and on inquiring at Daniel Penrose's house, it was ascertained that the said Daniel had left home in his car in the early afternoon of the day on which the injured man had been brought into the hospital and had not since been seen or heard of.

"As to what had become of that injured man, all that they could discover was that he – or, at least, a man with two black eyes and generally answering to the description – had taken a first-class ticket to London shortly after the time at which the patient had left the hospital, and that a man, apparently the same, had got out at New Cross. But they could get no farther. From the time when he passed the barrier at New Cross all trace of him was lost."

"Did the police make any efforts to follow him up?" Thorndyke asked.

"At the moment, I don't think they did. Why should they? So far as they then knew, the man had committed no offence. He was no business of theirs. If he chose to vamoose, he was quite entitled to."

"I need not ask if you know of any reason that he may have had for disappearing?"

"Ah!" said Brodribb, "now we come to the inwardness of the affair. I have told the story in the actual order of events, and, at the time when he bolted from the hospital, there seemed no reason for his sneaking off and hiding himself. But, a day or two later, some other facts transpired which threw an entirely new light on his behaviour.

"It appeared that early in the morning of the eighteenth, the day after that on which he left home – and, incidentally, was picked up on the road – the dead body of an old woman was found in a dry ditch at the side of a by-road leading to the main road from Ashford to Maidstone. From the condition of the body as to *rigor mortis* and temperature, the police surgeon inferred that she had been dead about six hours; which, as the body was discovered at about five o'clock in the morning, roughly fixes the time of her death at eleven o'clock on the previous night. Of the cause of death there seemed to be no doubt. She had been knocked down by a motor, the driver of which had either been unaware of what had happened or had cleared off to avoid trouble. The latter seemed the more probable, for, not only must the force of the impact have been terrific to fling the poor old creature right across the grass verge into the ditch, but the tracks of a car, which were plainly visible in the lane, showed it to have been zigzagging wildly and to have actually struck the grass verge at the point where the accident must have occurred.

"At first, it looked as if the motorist had got away without leaving a recognisable trace. But when the police came to make inquiries, they picked up some important information from the attendant at a filling station at Maidstone. He recalled that a little after eleven o'clock on the night of the old woman's death, a car had come to his establishment for a refill of petrol. It was apparently travelling from the direction of Ashford and there were certain circumstances connected with the car and the driver which had attracted his attention. He had noticed, for instance, that the near-side mudguard was badly bent, and there was earth on the wheels, as if the car had been run over a ploughed field. He had also observed that the driver – who was alone in the car – looked rather pale and shaken and seemed to be excited or agitated. Moreover, he smelt strongly of drink; and the man was of opinion that the liquid was not whisky, but smelt more like 'sherry wine.' These facts, taken together, made him suspect that the motorist had been in trouble and he very wisely made a note of the number of the car and had a good look at the driver. His description of the man is not very illuminating, excepting that he noticed the muddy state of the raincoat, which the nurse had mentioned. But the number of the car gave all the necessary information. It was that of Daniel Penrose's car; and, sure enough, in confirmation of the identity, was the fact that the left mudguard of Penrose's car was badly bent and there was a quantity of earth on the wheels. And there is a bit of further evidence, for it appears that Penrose was stopped by a police patrol on the top of Bluebell Hill, on the Maidstone–Rochester Road and asked to show his licence; which explains how the licence came to be in his raincoat pocket. When you consider the devil of a hurry that he was in, you can understand that he would just shove it into the nearest pocket.

"Well, the final phase of the affair – so far – was the inquest on the old woman. Naturally, when they had heard the evidence of the police and the man from the petrol-filling station, the jury found a verdict of manslaughter against some person unknown."

"Unknown!" I repeated. "Then they did not mention Penrose by name?"

"No," replied Brodribb. "The coroner knew his business better than many coroners do. He directed the jury to confine their finding to the facts that had been definitely proved and leave the identification of the offender to the police. But I need not say that the police are keeping a bright look-out for Daniel Penrose.

"So there, you see, we have an explanation of the initial disappearance. Perhaps, not a very reasonable one; but then Penrose is not a very reasonable man. But that explanation does not quite clear up the mystery. He disappeared about three months ago and since then has made no sign. Now, we can understand his bolting off in a panic, but it is less easy to understand his remaining in hiding. On reflection he must have seen that he was really in no great danger, even if he did actually knock the poor old woman down, which is by no means certainly the case. There were no witnesses of the accident. If he chose to deny that he was in any way concerned in it, it would be impossible to prove that he was. He might even have denied that he was ever on that particular road at all."

"You mentioned," said Thorndyke, "that there were distinct tracks of motor tyres. Probably they would be identifiable."

"That would not be conclusive," Brodribb replied. "It would only prove that the tyres were of the same make. But, even if he admitted that he had caused the old woman's death, still, in the absence of witnesses, he could give any account that he pleased of the disaster. Carelessness on the part of the pedestrian is usually quite satisfactory to a coroner or his jury."

"I don't think the matter is as simple as that," Thorndyke objected. "I agree with you that there has been a most amazing indifference to the value of human life since the coming of the motor car. But this was an exceptionally bad case. The man had been drinking; he must have known that he had knocked the woman down, but yet he drove on callously, leaving her to die uncared for, and did not even report the accident. Whatever the coroner's verdict might have been, the police would certainly have prosecuted, and the man would almost inevitably have been committed for trial. But at the assizes he would have had to deal with a judge; and judges as a rule – to which there are, I admit, one or two remarkable exceptions – take a reasonable and legal view of the killing of a human being."

"Well, even so," Brodribb rejoined, "what does it amount to? Supposing he had been convicted of manslaughter? It might have been a matter of six months' hard labour, or even twelve. It could hardly have been more. Killing with a motor car is accepted as something different from any other kind of killing."

"But," said I, "he would not be particularly keen on twelve months' imprisonment with hard labour."

"No," Brodribb agreed, "but what is the alternative? To say nothing of the fact that he is pretty certain to be caught sooner or later, what is his present condition? He – a well-to-do man, accustomed to every luxury, is a wanderer and a fugitive, hiding in obscure places by day and sneaking out in terror by night. It must be a dreadful existence; and how the devil he is living and what he is living on, is beyond my powers to imagine, seeing that, when he went off, he had, presumably nothing more about him than the few pounds that he would ordinarily carry in his pockets."

"I suppose," Thorndyke said, reflectively, "it has not occurred to you to connect that fact with the burglary?"

Brodribb looked at him in evident surprise.

"I don't think," said he, "that I quite understand what you mean. What connection could there be?"

"I am only throwing out the suggestion," replied Thorndyke, "as a bare possibility. But the house seems undoubtedly to have been entered, and entered by a person who appears to have been acquainted with it. The entry was made into the small room; and that room was clearly the objective, as is proved by the fact that the door was bolted on the inside. Then the person who entered apparently knew what was in that room. But, so far as we know, the contents of that room were known only to Penrose. If the cupboard was opened, it was opened with a key; for it is practically impossible to pick a Chubb lock, and a burglar would not have tried. He would have used his jemmy and forced the door."

"By Jove, Thorndyke!" Brodribb exclaimed, slapping the table, at the risk of spilling the wine, "you have solved the mystery! It never occurred to me that the burglar might be Penrose himself. But your suggestion fits the case to a T. Here is poor old Penrose, penniless and perhaps starving. He knows that in that cupboard is portable property of very substantial value. He has the key of the cupboard in his pocket and he knows that he can get into the room easily by just slipping back the catch of the window with a knife. Of course it was Penrose. I was a damned blockhead not to have thought of it before. But you see, Thorndyke, I haven't got your criminal mind."

"But Thorndyke, having made the suggestion, proceeded to sprinkle a little cold water on Brodribb's enthusiasm.

"It isn't a certainty," said he, "and we mustn't treat it as one. It is a reasonable and probable hypothesis, but we may think of others when we consider the matter further. However, the immediate question is what do you want me to do."

"You can guess that," chuckled Brodribb, as I refilled his glass. "What do I always want you to do when I come here taking up your valuable time and drinking your excellent port? I want you to perform miracles and do impossibilities. It seems a pretty large order, I admit, even for you, seeing that the police are unable to locate Penrose, but I am going to ask you to exercise your remarkable powers of resolving insoluble riddles and just tell us where he is."

"But why trouble to hunt him up?" Thorndyke objected. "He probably knows his own business best."

"I am not so sure that he does," Brodribb retorted. "But, in any case, it is not his business that is specially agitating me. There are some other people whose interests are affected and one of them is keeping me very effectively stirred up. However, I suppose I mustn't inflict on you details of the purely civil aspects of the case."

It was easy to gather from the apologetic tone of the concluding sentence and the wistful glance that he cast at Thorndyke, that he wanted very much to inflict those details, and I was not surprised when my colleague replied:

"It wouldn't be an infliction, Brodribb. On the contrary, it would be both interesting and helpful to have a complete picture of the case."

"I suspect," said Brodribb, "that you are only being beastly polite, but I will take you at your word. After all, the civil aspects are part of the problem and they may be more relevant than I realise. So here goes.

"I spoke just now of Daniel Penrose's aged father and I mentioned that there were no other near relations. Now, Penrose Senior, Oliver by name, is a very remarkable old gentleman. He is nearly ninety years of age, but surprisingly well preserved. Up to a week or two ago, he was, mentally and physically, the equal of an ordinary man of sixty. That was his condition at the time of Daniel's disappearance; lively and active, apparently going strong for his hundredth birthday.

"But, within the last fortnight, the old man has been taken ill — a slight touch of influenza it appeared at first, that seemed to offer no particular cause for anxiety. But you know what these hale and robust nonagenarians are. They dodder along peacefully, looking as if they were going to live for ever, until, one fine day, something gives them a shake up and puts them out of their stride; and then they just quietly fade away. Well that is what is happening to old Penrose. He doesn't seem particularly ill. But he shows no signs of recovering. Suddenly the weight of his years seems to have descended on him and he is gradually fading out. It is practically certain that he will die within the next few weeks; and, when he does die, some very curious complications are going to arise.

"Oliver Penrose is what we humble professional people would call a rather rich man. Nothing on the commercial scale of wealth. Nothing of the millionaire order. But there will be an estate, mostly personal, of over a hundred and fifty thousand pounds. And, so far as we know, that estate is not disposed of by will. The old man was rather obstinate about it, though there was some reason in his contention that it was a waste of trouble to make a will leaving the estate to the next of kin, who would inherit without a will. However, that question is of no importance, for, in any case, Penrose Junior would come into the property. If there is a will, he will be the principal beneficiary, and if there is no will, he is the next of kin, and, being the only child, will take the bulk of the estate.

"And now you see the difficulty. Daniel has made a will leaving a considerable proportion of his property to his cousin, Francis Horridge, who is also one of the executors and the residuary legatee. Daniel is not as rich as his father, but they are a well-to-do family and he has some fifty thousand pounds of his own. So Horridge will not do so badly if he should survive Daniel, which he is likely to do, as he is over twenty years younger. But he wants to do better. On the old man's death, the bulk of his property will, as I said, come to Daniel; and, as Daniel's will at present stands, it will fall into the residue of the estate and thus, eventually, come to Horridge.

"But there is a snag. Daniel has disappeared, but the old man is still alive. Now, suppose that Daniel elects to disappear for good. The thing is possible. He may have some resources that are unknown to us. It would be like him to have a secret banking account in a false name; and he may be in such a funk of criminal prosecution that he may never dare to come to the surface again. Well, suppose he remains in hiding. Suppose he has gone abroad or into some entirely new surroundings and has the means to go on living there; just see what a hideous mess will be created. In the first place, there will be an indefinite delay in distributing the old man's estate. Daniel is the next of kin (or else the principal beneficiary, if there should be a will). But his share cannot be allotted until it is proved that he is alive, and it cannot be otherwise disposed of until he is either proved or presumed to be dead. And, similarly, his own will cannot be administered so long as he is presumably alive."

"If he remains absent long enough," Thorndyke remarked, "the interested parties will probably apply for permission to presume his death."

"Well," retorted Brodbribb, "they certainly wouldn't get it at present or for a long time to come. If Daniel remains in hiding, the whole business may be hung up for years. But, even if they do, later, succeed in getting his death presumed, another and still worse complication will have to be dealt with. For, of course, the question of survivorship will be raised. Oliver's next of kin will naturally contend that Daniel died before the old man and that he could, therefore, not have inherited the old man's property; in which case, Horridge stands to lose the best part of a hundred and fifty thousand pounds. And that, I may say, is where I come in. Horridge is in a most frightful twitter for fear Daniel should slip away for good and perhaps die somewhere under a false name. He wants to find Daniel, or at least ascertain whether he is alive; and he is prepared to spend untold gold on the search. He has tried to ginger up the police and induce them to set up a hue and cry, regardless of poor old Daniel's feelings. But the police are not enthusiastic, as they have no conclusive evidence against him, even if they were able to locate him. So he has fallen back on me, and I have fallen back on you. And now the question is, are you prepared to take up the case?"

I had expected that Thorndyke would return a prompt refusal, for there seemed absolutely nothing to go on. To my surprise, he replied with a qualified acceptance, though he was careful to point out the difficulties.

"It is not very clear to me," said he, "that I can give you much help. You must see for yourself that this is really a police case. For the tracing of a missing man, the police have all the facilities as well as the necessary knowledge and experience. I have no facilities at all. Any inquiries that I may wish to make I must make through them."

"Yes, I see that," said Brodribb, "and, of course, I am not really asking you to perform miracles. I don't expect you to go outside and put your nose down on the pavement and forthwith make a bee-line for Daniel's hiding-place. But it occurs to me that you may be able to approach the matter from a different direction and by different methods from those of the police."

"That is possible," Thorndyke admitted, "but even a medico-legal investigator cannot get on without evidence of some kind, and there seems to be practically nothing to lay hold of. Do you know where the car is?"

"In Daniel's garage. It was taken there and locked up as soon as the police had made their examination of it."

"Do you know whether anything was found in it?"

"I have heard of nothing excepting a large empty flask which had, apparently, once contained brown sherry."

"Do you know whether the car has been cleaned since it was returned?"

"I am pretty sure that it has not. Penrose was his own chauffeur and did all the cleaning himself."

"Then you spoke of a raincoat. What has become of that?"

"It is in the parcel that I brought with me and which I put on the table in the lobby. It was delivered at Daniel's house by the police when they had looked it over and Kickweed handed it to Horridge, who at once locked it up, and later, at my request, transferred it to me. I knew you would want to see it."

"Was anything found in the pockets?"

"There was the driving licence, as I told you. Beyond that there was nothing but the stump of a lead pencil, a wooden cigarette-holder and what looked like a fragment of a broken flower-pot. And I may say that these things are still in the pockets. So far as I know, the coat is in exactly the condition in which it was found."

"We will have a look at it presently," said Thorndyke, "though it doesn't seem likely that we shall extract much information from it."

"It certainly does not," I agreed, heartily, "and the little information it may yield can hardly have much bearing on what we want to know. It won't tell us what Penrose's intentions may have been, or where he is now."

"Oh, don't say that!" exclaimed Brodribb. "I had hoped that Thorndyke would practise some of his wizardry on that coat and make it tell us all that we want to know about Daniel. And I hope so still, notwithstanding your pessimism. At any rate," he added, glancing at my colleague, "you are going to give us a run for our money? You agree to that?"

"Yes," Thorndyke replied, "just as a forlorn hope. It is nothing more, and it is unlikely that I shall have more success than the police. Still, I will sort out the facts, such as they are, and see if they offer us any kind of opening for an investigation. I suppose I can see the car?"

"Certainly, you can. I will tell Kickweed to let you have the key of the garage and to give you any help that you may ask for. Is there anything that you will want me to do?"

"I think," replied Thorndyke, "that, as Penrose is quite unknown to me, I had better have a description of his person and it should be as minute and exhaustive as possible; and if a photograph of him is available, I should like to have that, too."

"Very well," said Brodribb, "I will get a description of Daniel from Horridge and Kickweed, separately, and write out another from my own observations. I will let you have the three, so that you can compare them, and I will try to get you a photograph. And that," he concluded, emptying his glass with relish, and rising, "is all, for the present; and I may say that despite Jervis' pessimism, you have taken a load of anxiety off my shoulders. Experience has taught me that when John Thorndyke starts an investigation, the problem is as good as solved."

CHAPTER SIX

Thorndyke Examines the Relics

As we returned from the landing, to which we had escorted Mr Brodribb, I took up the parcel from the lobby table and conveyed it to the sitting-room.

"Well, Thorndyke," I remarked, as I deposited it on the table under the electric light, "you seem to have let yourself in for a proper wild-goose chase."

He paused in the act of digging out his pipe to regard me with an approving smile.

"That is rather happily expressed, Jervis," said he, "having regard to the personal peculiarities of our quarry. But we are not actually committed to chasing him."

"I can't imagine why you undertook the case," I continued. "There is absolutely nothing to go on."

"That is how it strikes me," he agreed placidly, blowing through the pipe preparatory to refilling. "But we couldn't refuse Brodribb."

"The few facts that we have," I went on doggedly, "are all totally irrelevant. Our information stops short exactly at the point where the problem begins. Take this coat, for instance. Here is a fool – and a frightened, artful, secretive fool at that – who does a bolt and leaves his coat behind; and we are offered that coat as a guide to the particular bolt-hole that he has gone down. The thing is ridiculous. If it had been a question of where he had come from,

56

the coat might have told us something. But obviously it can bear no traces of the place that he intended to go to."

"That is perfectly true," Thorndyke admitted, "but it might be worth while to find out whence he had come, if that were possible."

"I don't see why," I objected, adding hurriedly, to anticipate the inevitable reply: "Of course you will say that the significance of a fact cannot be judged until the fact is known; but still, I really cannot see any possible connection between the place whence he came and the place whither he went, especially as the circumstances had changed in the interval."

"Nor can I," said Thorndyke. "But yet it is possible that there may be some connection. It is evident that Penrose started out with a definite objective. He was going to a particular place with some defined purpose; and it seems to me at least conceivable that if we could discover whither he went and on what business, that knowledge might be helpful. Of course, it probably would not; but seeing that we know nothing of the habits and mode of life of this curious, eccentric and secretive man, our only course is to pick up any stray facts concerning him that may come within our reach."

"Yes," I agreed, without much conviction, "and I take it that what is in your mind is that when he bolted he probably made for some place that was known to him and where he believed that he could hide in safety."

"Exactly," Thorndyke agreed. "If we could discover some of his haunts, we might have a clue to a possible hiding-place."

"It may be so," I rejoined, "and if that is your view, I suppose you will begin by seeing what you can glean from this coat"; and with this I proceeded to untie the string and open the parcel.

The coat, when I lifted it out and unrolled it, was seen to be amazingly dirty. It was not merely splashed with mud. On the sleeves and around the bottom of the skirt were great daubs of thick dirt mingled with a number of whitish marks such as might have been produced by contact with wet chalk.

"It is extraordinary," said I, holding the coat up for Thorndyke's inspection. "The fellow seems to have been positively wallowing in the mire."

"Not exactly in the mire," said Thorndyke, looking closely at the great daubs. "This is not road dirt. It is earth; and the earth seems to have been mixed with particles of chalk. Perhaps we had better empty the pockets before we proceed with the examination of the coat."

I thrust my hand into the two pockets and drew out from one the driving licence, crumpled, smeared and marked with the prints of dirty fingers, and from the other a stump of lead pencil, a cigarette-holder and what looked like a fragment of a broken tile. But it was so encrusted with earth that it was difficult to see exactly what it was.

"Brodribb's description," said I, as I handed it to Thorndyke, "doesn't seem to fit. This is certainly not a fragment of a flower-pot. It is too dark in colour. It looks to me more like part of a tile."

Thorndyke took it from me and examined it closely in the bright light of the electric lamp.

"I don't think it is a tile, Jervis," said he, "but we shall see better when we get it clean. The interesting point about it is that the earth in which it is embedded seems to be similar to that on the coat; a mixture of loam and small fragments of chalk – a sort of chalk rubble. We will brush off the earth when we have looked over the other things."

He laid it in a small cardboard tray and put it aside on the mantelshelf. Then he turned his attention to the cigarette-tube which I held in my hand.

"There," said I handing it to him, "is another example of excellent but quite irrelevant clues."

"How irrelevant?" he asked. "And irrelevant to what?"

"To the subject of our inquiry," I replied. "Here is a highly distinctive object, for it was certainly never bought at a shop. As evidence in a case of doubtful identity, it would be quite valuable.

But it is of no use to us. It gives us no hint as to where its owner is at present hiding."

Thorndyke smiled indulgently. "We mustn't expect too much, Jervis," said he; "in fact, we have no reason to expect anything. We are just looking over this jetsam as a matter of routine to note any facts that it may seem to suggest, without regard to their apparent relevancy or irrelevancy to our inquiry. You cannot judge the relevancy of an isolated fact. Experience has taught me, and must have taught you, that the most trivial, commonplace and seemingly irrelevant facts have a way of suddenly assuming a crucial importance by connecting, explaining or filling in the detail of later discoveries.

"Take this cigarette-tube, for instance. It appears to be the property of Daniel Penrose. But how did he come by it? As you say, it was certainly not bought in the ordinary way at a shop. There is no suggestion of mass-production about it. It is an individual thing made by a particular person, and probably there is not another like it in the world. But if we look at it attentively, we can form some idea of the kind of person who made it and can even suggest the probable circumstances in which it was made. Thus, it is composed of a very hard, heavy, black wood, much like ebony in character but with a slight brownish tinge instead of the characteristic dead black. Probably it is African ebony. It is competently turned but with no special display of skill. The mouthpiece has been shaped with a chisel, whereas you or I would have used a file on such a very hard material. The suggestion is that the chisel was a tool to which the maker was accustomed and which he used with facility. Then the rather artless but quite pleasant decoration consists of a pattern of circular white spots, each an eighth of an inch in diameter, made, apparently, by boring holes – probably with a Morse drill – right through the half-finished piece and driving into them little dowels of holly or some other white hardwood, which would be cut off flush when the work was finished in the lathe. Then there is the suggestion that the tube was made from an odd scrap of wood, left over from some larger work."

"How do you arrive at that?" I asked.

"I think," he replied, "it is suggested by this little streak of sapwood. It is a distinct blemish, and one feels that it would have been avoided if a larger piece of wood had been available. So you see that the impression we get is of a workman who was handy with a paring-chisel but also had some skill as a turner; possibly a joiner or cabinet-maker, who had a lathe in his workshop."

"Yes," I agreed, "he may have been, and, on the other hand, he may not. I don't see that it matters. He is not our pigeon. What seems to me of more interest – though mighty little at that – is that there is a good-sized stump of a cigarette still in the tube. It looks as if Penrose had dropped the holder in his pocket with the cigarette still alight; and if he did that – in a motor car, with plenty of petrol vapour about – he must have been either drunk or frightened out of his wits. What is the next proceeding?"

"I think," said he, as he deposited the licence, the cigarette-tube and the stump of pencil provisionally in a cardboard box, "we had better collect as much earth as we can get off the coat to examine at our leisure. We shall want one or two photographic dishes, a clean toothbrush, a glass funnel, a wide-mouthed jar and a few filter-papers. Do you mind getting them while I damp the coat?"

I ran up to the laboratory and collected these articles, and when I returned with them I found Thorndyke with the coat spread out on the table, cautiously damping the larger mud-stains with a sponge; and we at once fell to work on the rather dirty and not very thrilling task of transferring the mud from the coat to one of the dishes, which I had partly filled with water. But the quantity that we collected by scraping with a paper-knife and brushing off into the water was quite surprising; and when, from the state of liquid mud in the dish, it was transformed into wet earth on a filter-paper, it at once took on the character of a definite and recognisable type of soil.

"That," said Thorndyke as he carefully removed the filter-paper from the funnel and set it on a blotting-pad to drain, "we can examine later and, if necessary, with the aid of an expert geological opinion. It appears to be a rather fine reddish loam a little like the Thanet sands, with a few minute white particles, apparently chalk. But we shall see. And now let us take a look at Brodribb's alleged flower-pot."

He brought the tray from the mantelpiece and, taking out the fragment, cautiously wetted its surface. Then, having first carefully washed the toothbrush, he proceeded to brush the earth from the pottery fragment into a small dish until it was completely clean, and, having dried its surface with blotting-paper and his handkerchief, put it aside while he collected the detached earth on a filter-paper.

"You notice, Jervis," said he as he opened out the filter-paper on the blotting-pad, "that it seems to be the same soil as that on the coat. There are more chalk particles and they are larger; but that is what we should expect, as the larger particles would have less tendency to adhere to the coat. And now let us have your considered opinion on this fragment."

I took it from him and examined it with a decent pretence of interest (and an inward conviction that it didn't matter tuppence what it was).

"I still think," said I, "that it looks like a piece of tile. The material is as coarse as brick and it has a slight curvature like that of an old hand-made tile. But I don't quite understand what those marks are. They are evidently not accidental."

"No," he agreed, "and I think they exclude your diagnosis and so does the definite thickening at the edge. But let us proceed systematically. I find it a help to a thorough examination of an object to describe it in detail as if one were preparing an entry in a museum catalogue."

I agreed warmly and invited him to go ahead.

"Very well," said he, "if you feel unequal to the effort, the task devolves upon me. We will take the physical properties in regular order, beginning with the general character.

"This is a fragment of pottery of excessively coarse and crude quality, consisting of a reddish buff matrix in which are embedded numerous angular white particles which have the appearance of burnt flint. The texture is somewhat porous and there is no trace of a glaze on either surface. On taking it in the hand, and allowing for the fact that it is wet, we find it noticeably heavy.

"Size and shape. The fragment forms an irregular oblong, approximately an inch and a half long by three-quarters wide. Of the four sides, three are fractured – recently, you notice – and the fourth – one of the long sides – is thickened into a definite flange or rim, roughly T-shaped in section. The thickness, as shown by the calliper gauge, varies from five thirty-seconds of an inch at the thinnest broken edge to eleven thirty-seconds on the thick unbroken edge.

"On the thick edge are five indented marks such as might have been made with a blunt knife on the soft clay, roughly a quarter of an inch apart; and on the convex surface, next to the long broken edge, are four similar linear indentations, roughly half an inch apart and at right angles to the thickened edge.

"The fragment is curved in both diameters, rather irregularly, but still quite definitely. Let us see, approximately, what those curvatures amount to."

He took a sheet of writing-paper and placed the fragment on it, standing up on its thick edge, and with a sharp pencil carefully traced the outline. The tracing showed the curvature very distinctly; and it became still more obvious when he placed a straight-edge against the concave side and connected the two ends with a ruled line. Then he produced a pair of compasses furnished with a pencil, and, setting the pencil-point on one end of the ruled line, was able, after one or two trials, to strike an arc which passed through both ends of the line and followed the curve of the tracing. On measuring the distance from the centre to the arc, it was found to be three inches and an eighth.

"We see, then," said he, "that the curve has a radius of three inches and an eighth, so that it seems to be part of a circle, six inches and a quarter in diameter. Now, let us try the other curvature.

He stood the fragment up on one of its short ends and made a tracing as before. Measurement of this showed a curve with a radius of two inches and three-quarters.

"We can't take this last measurement very seriously," said he, "as the curve is so very short and irregular. But you see that we now have the material for a fairly reliable reconstruction of the object of which this fragment formed a part. It appears to have been an earthenware vessel of the very coarsest and crudest type, with curved sides – some kind of bowl or pot – approximately six inches across the top, or mouth, and possibly about three inches high. But the height is a matter of mere guess-work. The irregularity in the curvature of the mouth makes it pretty certain that the vessel was built by hand, not thrown on the wheel; and this suggestion is confirmed by the extremely crude and primitive decoration. The thickened rim of the mouth is ornamented by a series of linear markings about a quarter of an inch apart, made, apparently, by indenting with a blunt knife, or perhaps a long thumb-nail, on the soft clay; and there is another series of similar markings, a little wider apart, which encircles the vessel about half an inch below the rim.

"There, Jervis, is a summary of the characteristics which enable us to form a reasonably exact picture of the object which yielded this fragment. Taking them together and in conjunction with the fact that the fragment was found in the pocket of a man who is known to be a collector of antiquities, what conclusion do you arrive at?"

"Concerning the object? Well, I suppose we must conclude that the pot or bowl must have been an extremely ancient vessel, perhaps prehistoric. It would hardly be Roman."

"No," he agreed. "Roman pottery was the product of a developed industry with quite advanced technical methods. This was quite a primitive piece of work; certainly pre-Roman, I should say, and more probably Neolithic than Bronze Age. But that is a question which we can easily settle by inquiries or reference to published work."

"Yes," said I; "and when you have settled it, you will be exactly where you are now, so far as the abiding-place of Daniel Penrose is concerned, and where you were before you carried out this very interesting little investigation. You will have established a fact that can have no possible bearing on the problem that you are asked to solve."

"Who knows?" he retorted. "We have learned that Penrose had in his pocket a fragment of ancient pottery. It is not likely that he picked it up by chance on the road; and if he did not, it is possible that we may have here a clue to the purpose with which he set out on his travels on the day when he disappeared."

"But," I persisted, "even if you knew that, you would be no more forward. He certainly did not set out with the purpose of killing an old woman and becoming a fugitive from the law. You would just have another irrelevant fact."

He smiled as he dropped the fragment into the box, together with the two filter-papers. "It is quite likely that you are right, Jervis," said he. "But we have already agreed that the relevancy of a fact often fails to be perceived until the appearance of some further facts brings its significance into view. It is always much easier to be wise after the event."

With this, he deposited the cardboard box in the drawer of a cabinet, while I hung the wet coat on a peg in the lobby. Then we disposed ourselves in our respective chairs to smoke the final pipe before turning in, and, dismissing the affairs of Daniel Penrose, chatted somewhat discursively on the morning's doings in court. But in the intervals of our talk I found my thoughts drifting back to the cardboard box and to the occupations with which it was associated. And not only then but in the days that followed did that curious little investigation furnish me with matter for reflection.

Of course, Thorndyke was perfectly right in his contention. It is impossible to decide in advance whether a particular item of knowledge may or may not prove at some future time to be of value; and it was a fact that Thorndyke made a rule of acquiring every item of knowledge that was obtainable in connection with a case, without regard to its apparent relevancy. But, still, I had the feeling that, in this present case, he was not merely acting on this rather academic principle. The care and thoroughness and the appearance of interest with which he had made this examination conveyed to me the impression that the facts elicited meant more to him than they did to me.

Yet what could they mean? The disappearance of Penrose had the hospital as its starting-point, or, at the earliest, the accident to the old woman. But the mud and pottery fragment were related to events that had occurred before the accident and which were, therefore, totally unconnected with the disappearance. Then how could they possibly throw any light on the present whereabouts of the missing man, which was the problem that we had to solve?

That was the question that I asked myself again and again. But by no amount of cogitation could I find any answer.

CHAPTER SEVEN

A Visit of Inspection

The dubious and slightly bewildered state of mind to which I have referred induced me to observe Thorndyke's proceedings with a little closer attention than was usual with me. Not that there was really any occasion, for Thorndyke appeared to go out of his way to make me a party to any doings connected with the Penrose case; which tended to increase my suspicion that I had missed some point of evidential importance.

It was some two or three days after Brodribb's visit to us, when we seemed to have a few hours at our disposal, that Thorndyke suggested a call at Queen Square to examine Penrose's car. I had been expecting this suggestion, and, with the hope of getting some new light on the purpose of his investigations, assented cheerfully. Accordingly, when Thorndyke had slipped a good-sized notebook and some other small necessaries into his pocket, we set forth on our quest.

I have always liked Queen Square and have watched, regretfully, its gradual deterioration – or "improvement," as the optimistic modern phrase has it. When I first knew the place, it was nearly intact, with its satellites, Great Ormond Street, the Foundling Hospital and the group of other pleasant old squares adjacent. As we walked towards it we discussed the changes that the years had wrought. Thorndyke, as an old Londoner, sympathised warmly with my regrets.

"Yes," he agreed. "The works of man tell us more about him than we can gather from volumes of history. Every generation leaves, in the products of its activities, a faithful picture of its capabilities, its standard of taste and its outlook on life. The people who conceived and created these delightful, dignified haunts of peace and quiet, had never heard of town-planning and did not talk much about architecture. But they planned towns by instinctive taste and they built charming houses, the dismembered fragments of which we can now study in our museums. There is a beautiful wooden portico at South Kensington which I used to admire when it stood in Great Ormond Street."

"I remember it," said I. "But in the museum they have scraped off the paint and gilding to show the construction; which is all very interesting and instructive, but is not quite what the architect had in view when he designed it. It is rather as if one should offer the anatomical exhibits in the Hunterian Museum as illustrations of the beauty of the human figure. They might have restored the painting and gilding so that visitors could see what a fine London doorway was like in the time of Good Queen Anne."

As I spoke, we turned out of Great Ormond Street and crossed the square, passing the ancient pump with its surmounting lantern and its encircling posts, and directing our steps towards Penrose's house, which had been described as nearly opposite the statue of Queen Anne. As we approached the latter, Thorndyke remarked, continuing our discussion:

"There is another example of what is practically a lost art. It seems to me a pity that leadwork should have been allowed to fall into such a state of decay. Lead may not be an ideal material for statues, but it is imperishable, it is cheap and it is easy to work. In the eighteenth century, the Piccadilly foundries, from which this statue probably came, turned out thousands of works – urns and vases, shepherds and shepherdesses and other rustic figures for use in parks and formal gardens or as architectural ornaments. But they have nearly all gone; melted down, I suppose, to form sheet lead or water pipes. This looks like the house, and a fine old house it is; one of the last survivors of its family."

We ascended to the broad doorstep, enclosed by forged railings bearing a pair of link-extinguishers and the standard for an oil lamp, gave a tug at the old-fashioned bell-pull and executed a flourish on the handsome brass knocker. After a decent interval, the door was opened by a smart-looking maid-servant to whom Thorndyke communicated the purpose of our visit.

"We have called to see Mr Kickweed on certain legal business. I think he is expecting a visit from me. I am Dr Thorndyke."

On this the maid opened the door wide, and, inviting us to enter, conducted us to a small room adjacent to the hall, where she requested us to wait while she informed Mr Kickweed of our arrival. When she had gone, I cast an inquisitive glance round the room, which contained a table, two chairs and a piece of furniture which might have been regarded either as a cupboard or as some kind of sideboard.

"This can hardly be the room in which the burglary took place," said I, "though it fits the description to some extent, but the window seems in the wrong place."

"Very much so," said Thorndyke, "as it looks out on the square and is over the area. And it is the wrong sort of cupboard with the wrong sort of lock. No, this is not the mysterious chamber."

Here the door opened slowly and discreetly to admit a pale-faced, rather unwholesome-looking elderly man who bowed deferentially and introduced himself by name as Mr Kickweed; though the introduction was hardly necessary, for he might have served, in a museum of social anthropology, as a type specimen of the genus, upper manservant.

"Mr Brodribb wrote to me, sir," he continued in a melancholy tone, "to say that you would probably call and instructing me to give you any assistance that I could. In what way can I have the pleasure of carrying out those instructions?"

"My immediate object," replied Thorndyke, "is to inspect Mr Penrose's car. Has anything been done to it since it came back?"

"Nothing whatever, sir," Kickweed replied. "I suppose it ought to be cleaned, but I know nothing about cars. Mr Penrose always attended to it himself excepting when it went out for repairs, and he always kept the garage locked up. In fact, it was locked when they brought the car back."

"Then how did you get the car in?" Thorndyke asked.

"The police officer, sir, who came with the car, fortunately had a few odd keys with him, and one of them happened to fit the lock. He was good enough to leave it with me, so I shall be able to let you in. If you would like to go round there now I will just get my hat and show you the way."

"Thank you," said Thorndyke. "If it is not troubling you —"

"It is no trouble at all, sir," interrupted Kickweed and there-upon he stole out of the room with the light, noiseless tread that seems to be almost characteristic of heavy, bulky men. A few minutes later he reappeared in correct morning dress, including a slightly rusty top hat, and we set forth together. The garage was not far away, being situated in a sort of mews, approached from Guilford Street. As we halted at the door and Kickweed produced the key, I noticed that Thorndyke cast an inquisitive glance at it, and I guessed what was in his mind, because it was also in mine. But we were both wrong. The key was not of the filed or skeleton variety but was just a normal warded key of a simple type. However, it turned in the lock, after a good deal of persuasion, and, the doors being flung open, we entered.

It was a roomy place and fairly well lighted by a wide window above the doors. The car stood in the middle, leaving ample space on either side and still more at the end, where a rough bench had been placed, with a vice and a number of rather rusty tools, together with various oddments in the way of bolts, nuts and miscellaneous scrap.

"I take it," said Thorndyke, glancing at the littered bench, "that Mr Penrose is not a skilled mechanic."

"No sir," Kickweed admitted. "I don't think he is much of a workman. And yet he used to spend a good deal of time here. I don't know what he would have been doing."

"You did not assist him, then?"

"No, sir, I have only been in here once or twice, and then only for a few minutes with Mr Penrose. I never came here by myself, nor, I think, did anybody else. There was only one key, until I got this one, and Mr Penrose kept that himself, and has it still."

"I suppose you don't know of any reason why he should have objected to your coming here alone?"

"No, sir. And I don't think there was any. It was just his way. He has rather a habit of making secrets of nothing."

"So I have understood," said Thorndyke, "and a very bad habit it is, leading to all sorts of unnecessary suspicions and surmises. However, we came here primarily to inspect the car, so perhaps we had better get on with that."

Accordingly, he proceeded to make a systematic and detailed survey of the vehicle, beginning with the bent mudguard, the leading edge of which he examined minutely with the aid of a lens. But, if there had ever been any fibres or other traces of the collision, they had been removed by the police. He then transferred his attention to the wheels, and, after a preliminary glance at them, produced one or two envelopes from his pocket and laid them on the bench.

"The dirt on the face of the tyres," he remarked, "is of no interest to us, as it will have changed from moment to moment. But that on the inside and on the rims of the wheels is more significant. Its presence there suggests that, at one time, the car had been driven over quite soft earth; and the earth was a natural soil, not a road material, a reddish loam similar to that on the coat."

"Yes," I agreed, "it is evident that the wheels sank in pretty deep by the quantity of soil on the rims. And I think," I added, stooping low to look under the car, "that I can see a leaf sticking to the rim of the wheel."

With some difficulty I managed to reach in and pick it off together with the lump of dry loam in which it was embedded.

. "A dead leaf," Thorndyke pronounced when I handed it to him; "I mean a last year's leaf, and it looks like a hornbeam. But we shall see better when we wet it and flatten it out."

He deposited the leaf and earth in an envelope, on which he wrote a brief memorandum of the source of the specimen, and then continued his examination. But there was nothing more to be seen from the outside excepting a general dirtiness, suggestive of a not very fastidious owner. Nor was there anything very significant to be seen when I opened the door. The interior showed no signs of anything unusual. The floor was moderately clean excepting that under the driver's seat, which was thickly plastered with loam. But this was what we should have expected; and the evidence that it furnished that there was almost certainly only one person in the car during that last drive, merely confirmed what we already knew. There were no loose articles in any of the pockets or receptacles other than the insurance certificate and the rather scanty outfit of tools. In fact, the only discovery — and a very modest one at that — was another dead leaf, apparently also hornbeam, trodden flat into the dirt by the driver's seat.

Having finished with the car, Thorndyke once more glanced round the garage and I could see that he was making a mental inventory of the various objects that it contained. But his next question reverted to the car.

"I understand," said he, "that the police found an empty flask in the car."

"Yes, sir," replied Kickweed. "I took that away to wash it and polish it up. It is a silver flask and it seemed a pity to leave it in the dirty state in which it was found. I have cleaned it thoroughly and put it away among the plate. Did you wish to see it?"

"No," replied Thorndyke, "but I should like a few particulars. About how much does it hold?"

"It holds the best part of a bottle. About an imperial pint."

"That is a large flask," Thorndyke remarked, "Did Mr Penrose usually carry it in the car?"

"Do you know, sir, I really can't say. I have only seen it once before. That was about two years ago when I happened to be brushing Mr Penrose's overcoat and found it in the pocket. But I have the impression that he usually carried it with him when he went away from home. He would be likely to because he is rather fastidious about his wine. He drinks nothing but Madeira and old brown sherry; and you can't get good Madeira or brown sherry at roadside inns"

"And as to quantity? It has been stated that when he was last seen he appeared to be under the influence of liquor. Was that at all usual?"

Kickweed shook his head emphatically. "No, sir," he replied. "That must have been a mistake. He may have smelt of sherry. He often does. But sherry has a very strong aroma and a little of it goes a long way in the matter of smell. But in all the years that I have known Mr Penrose, I have never seen him in the slightest degree the worse for drink. He does certainly take a good deal, as I can judge by the wine merchant's deliveries and the empty bottles, but then he takes no beer or spirits or any other kind of wine. They must have been misled by the odour."

"That seems quite likely," said Thorndyke. "By the way, I notice a couple of hazel twigs hanging up there under that hat. Do you happen to know whether Mr Penrose is a dowser?"

"A dowser, sir?" Kickweed repeated with a mystified air.

"A water-finder," Thorndyke explained. "That is what those forked twigs are used for." He took the hat from the peg and laid it on the bench, and, taking down one of the twigs, held it by its two ends and continued: "The specially gifted persons – known as dowsers – who search for underground streams or springs, hold the twig in this way and walk to and fro over the land where they expect to find water; and when they pass over a hidden spring – so it is stated – they become aware of the presence of underground water by a movement of the twig in their hands. It looks as if Mr Penrose had practised the dowser's art.

"Ah!" exclaimed Kickweed, "I remember now that Mr Penrose once showed me one of these things and told me about it. But I thought it was one of his little jokes; for it was not water that he professed to be able to find with it. He said that it was an infallible guide to buried treasure. It would show the treasure-seeker exactly where to dig. But I never supposed that he was speaking seriously. You see, sir, Mr Penrose is rather a jocular gentleman and it is sometimes a little difficult to be quite sure what he really does mean."

"So I understand," said Thorndyke, "and he may have been joking in this case. But the idea of digging seems to have been in his mind. Now, so far as you know, did he ever engage in any sort of digging activities in his search for antiquities?"

"Well, sir," replied Kickweed, "it is rather difficult to say. He is so very facetious. But I have known him to bring home certain articles – lumps of flint and bits of crockery, they looked like to me – which were covered with earth and which I have helped him to scrub clean at the scullery sink. I suppose that he must have dug them up somewhere as he referred to them as 'Treasure Trove' and 'the resurrectionist's loot' and other similar expressions."

"Yes," Thorndyke agreed, "those expressions and the condition of the objects certainly suggest something in the way of excavations. But I don't see any tools suitable for the purpose; and I should suppose that if he had had any he would have kept them here. Do you happen to remember having seen any picks, shovels or similar tools here or elsewhere?"

Mr Kickweed reflected as he ran an inquiring glance round the walls. "As I said, sir," he replied, "I have only been in here once or twice before Mr Penrose went away. But I seem to remember a sort of pick – I think it is called a trenching tool – which I don't see now. And there was a small spade pointed like the ace of hearts, with a leather case for the blade. But I don't see that either. It hung, I think, on one of those pegs. But that was over a year ago."

"It looks," I suggested, remembering the pottery fragment, "as if Mr Penrose may have taken them with him when he left home. They were not in the car when it was found, but it had then been lying unattended for a couple of days. Loose property has rather a way of disappearing from derelict cars."

"It is quite possible," said Thorndyke; and he then appeared to dismiss the subject, for he replaced the hazel twig on its peg and picked up the hat to return that also, but paused, looking with a faint smile into its dusty and decayed interior.

"Mr Penrose," he remarked, "seems to have attached undue value to this relic. But perhaps the marking was done when it was in a more presentable condition."

He exhibited the interior of the hat on the crown of which the name "D Penrose" had been carefully printed with a rubber stamp.

"Yes, sir," said Kickweed, "the name was probably stamped when the hat was new. Not that that would have made any difference, for Mr Penrose stamped his name on everything that he possessed; not only on his underclothing and handkerchiefs and the things that are usually marked, but his hats, shoes, books, paper-knives – everything that was moveable. It always seemed to me a little inconsistent."

"How inconsistent?" I asked.

"I mean," replied Kickweed, "he is in general a very secret gentleman. He makes a secret of the most simple and ordinary things. And yet he prints his full name, not just his initials as most men do, inside his hat and his shoes and his waistcoat lining, and evenon his pocket-knife. Now, if a stranger asked him his name he would probably avoid telling him; but yet, as soon as he takes his hat off, he discloses his identity to all the world."

"I take it," said Thorndyke, "that he usually does the stamping himself?"

"Lord bless you, yes, sir! That rubber stamp has always been kept under lock and key as if it had been the Koh-i-noor, or as if it could have been used for forging his signature. I have never even seen it. But, of course, that signifies nothing. It is just his way.

"Yes," said Thorndyke, "and you are a wise man, to accept his harmless oddities and not let them worry you." He hung the hat on its peg and then, turning to Kickweed, opened a fresh subject.

"Mr Brodribb consulted me about a burglary that occurred in your house a short time ago. There was a question of calling in the police and getting the cupboard opened. How does that suggestion strike you?"

"It strikes me," Kickweed replied severely, "as an improper and a foolish suggestion. It would be improper to tamper with Mr Penrose's property in his absence and without his consent, sir, and it would be foolish because we should be none the wiser when we had opened the cupboard as we don't know what it contained, or whether it contained anything."

Here I interposed rather rashly.

"The suggestion has been made that it is just possible that the person who entered the room may have been Mr Penrose himself."

Kickweed looked, and professed to be, deeply shocked. But I had, nevertheless, a strong suspicion that that was his own opinion.

"But, you know, Mr Kickweed," said I, "there is nothing immoral or even improper in a gentleman's entering his own house to take his own property if he happens to have need of it. Most men, it is true, would prefer to enter by the front door. But Mr Penrose was not like most men; and if he preferred the window, he was entirely within his rights. It was his own window."

I had the feeling that my observations were received with approval and even with some relief. But Mr Kickweed, if he secretly concurred, as I believed that he did, was not committing himself.

"No doubt, sir," said he, "you are perfectly right. But I couldn't imagine Mr Penrose doing anything so undignified, especially as he had the key of the front door in his pocket. And," he added, with a pensive smile, "it was his own front door."

"You were saying just now," said Thorndyke, "that nothing is known as to the contents of that cupboard. Have you no idea at all as to what it contained, or contains?"

"I said knowledge, sir," replied Kickweed. "I know nothing at all as to what is, or has been, in that cupboard."

He spoke with an emphasis that gave us clearly to understand that he was not going beyond his actual knowledge. He was going to hazard no opinions.

"And is it the fact, Mr Kickweed," Thorndyke pursued, "that there is no one in the world who knows, or could form any reasonable judgement as to what that cupboard did, does or might contain?"

Mr Kirkweed reflected, a trifle uneasily, I thought. But Thorndyke's question admitted of no evasion, and he at length replied with some reluctance:

"Well, sir, I wouldn't say that, for there is one person who may possibly know. I have not spoken of him to any one hitherto, because Mr Penrose was very secret about that room, and he is my employer and it is my duty to abide by his wishes, whether expressed or not. But you ask me a definite question and I suppose you are entitled to an answer. I think it possible that Mr Penrose may have confided his secret to a certain friend of his; a gentleman named Lockhart."

"What makes you think that Mr Lockhart may know what is, or was, in the cupboard?" Thorndyke asked.

"The discovery – if it was one – " Kickweed replied, "was quite accidental. Mr Lockhart came to the house by appointment to look over the collection, and Mr Penrose took him into the great gallery. When they had been there some considerable time, I ventured to look in to ask if I should bring them up some tea. But when I entered the big gallery they were not there; but I could hear them talking, and the voices seemed to come from the small room, though the door of that room was shut. But they must have been in there because there was no other room that opened out of the great gallery. Now the small room contained nothing but the cupboard so that if Mr Penrose took Mr Lockhart into that room, it could only have been to show him what was in the cupboard. And I did, in fact, hear sounds of movement in the room as if drawers were being pulled out. But, of course, as soon as I realised what was happening, I went away.

"But there was another circumstance that made me think that Mr Penrose might have let Mr Lockhart into the secret of the small room. When they had finished with the collection they went into the morning-room – the little front room that you went into – and I took them up some tea; and there they were for quite a long time before Mr Lockhart went away. Afterwards I learned from Mr Penrose, himself, that Mr Lockhart had been advising him about insuring the collection, which made it seem likely that Mr Lockhart had been shown all that there was to insure."

"Yes," said Thorndyke, "that seems a reasonable inference. Is Mr Lockhart connected with insurance business?"

"No sir, He is a legal gentleman, a barrister."

"Ah!" said Thorndyke. "Lockhart. Now I wonder if that would be – you don't happen to know what inn he belongs to?"

"Yes, sir. He belongs to Lincoln's Inn, at least, that is his address. I happen to know by having seen a card of his which Mr Penrose left on his dressing-table."

"Is Mr Lockhart an intimate friend of Mr Penrose?"

"No, sir. Quite a recent acquaintance, I believe, though Mr Penrose seemed to take to him more than he usually does to strangers. Still, I was rather surprised at his taking him into the small room. I have never known him to do such a thing before."

Thorndyke made no immediate rejoinder but stood, apparently considering this last statement and letting his glance travel about the place as if searching for some further objects of interest. But it seemed that he had squeezed both the garage and Mr Kickweed dry, for he said, at length;

"Well, I think we have learned all that there is to learn here; and I must thank you, Mr Kickweed, for having been so extremely helpful."

Kickweed smiled a somewhat dreary smile. "I hope I have not been too much so, sir," said he. "I am not a willing helper, though I feel bound to carry out Mr Brodribb's instructions. I understand from him that you are trying to find out where Mr Penrose has gone to; and, if you will pardon me for saying so, I hope you won't succeed."

Thorndyke smiled appreciatively. "Now, why do you say that?" he asked.

"Because, sir," Kickweed replied earnestly, "I feel that this pursuit is not justifiable. Mr Penrose, as I understand, has had a little mishap and thinks it best to keep out of sight for a time. But if he thinks so, it is his own affair, and I don't consider it just or proper that other people, for their own purposes, should hunt him up and perhaps get him into difficulties."

I must confess that I sympathised heartily with Mr Kickweed's sentiments, and so, apparently, did Thorndyke, for he replied:

"That is precisely what I pointed out to Mr Brodribb. But there are legal reasons for ascertaining Mr Penrose's whereabouts, though there are none for disclosing them to others. You may take it from me, Mr Kickweed, that nothing which may come to my knowledge will be used in any way to his disadvantage."

"I am very relieved to hear you say that, sir," Kickweed rejoined with evident sincerity, "because I have felt that there are others who take a different view. Mr Horridge, for instance, has, to my knowledge, been in communication with the police."

"Well," I said, as we retired from the garage and Kickweed locked the door, "I don't suppose he has done any harm if he has no more to tell them than we have been told."

As our way home led through Queen Square, we walked thither with Mr Kickweed, and Thorndyke took the opportunity to ask a few questions concerning Mr Penrose's collection.

"I don't know much about the things," said Kickweed, "excepting that there is a rare lot of them and that they take a terrible amount of dusting. I do most of it with a pair of bellows when Mr Penrose is not about. But if you feel any interest in them, why not step in, as you are here, and have a look at them yourself?"

Now I have no doubt whatever that this was precisely what Thorndyke had intended to do, but, in his queer, secretive way, had preferred that the inspection should seem to occur by chance. At any rate, he accepted the invitation, and we followed Kickweed to the door of the house and were by him admitted to the hall.

CHAPTER EIGHT

Mr Horridge

Mr Kickweed, as has been mentioned, had a light tread, and his movements in general tended to be silent. Thus our entry into the hall of the old house and the subsequent closing of the door were almost noiseless. Nevertheless, our arrival was not unobserved; for, even as Kickweed was pocketing his latch-key, the door of the morning-room opened slowly and quietly and a large, distinctly fat gentleman appeared framed in the doorway.

There was something slightly odd and even ridiculous in the sudden and silent manner in which he became visible, and in the sly, inquisitive glance that he turned on us; as if he had been a plain-clothes officer and we a surprised party of burglars.

"How did you know I was here, Kickweed?" he demanded.

"I didn't, sir," was the reply.

"Oh," rejoined the other, "I thought these gentlemen might have come on some business with me."

"No, sir. They have been inspecting the car. They are Dr Thorndyke and Dr Jervis."

The fat man bowed stiffly. "Ah!" said he, "they have inspected the car. And now?"

"Dr Thorndyke thought he would like to take a look at the collection," Kickweed replied frigidly, evidently resentful of the other man's manner, "so I invited him to step in and look over it."

"Ha!" said the fat gentleman. "You thought it quite in order to do that? "Well, if Dr Thorndyke wants to see the collection there is no reason why he should not. I will show him round the gallery, myself. My name," he added, turning to us, "is Horridge. You have probably heard of me. I am Mr Penrose's executor, and, in his absence, am keeping an eye on his property.

Now, the tone of his remarks filled me with a burning desire to kick Mr Horridge; but that being impracticable, I should certainly, if left to myself, have told him to go to the devil and forthwith walked out of the house. Thorndyke, however, was completely unruffled; and having once more thanked Kickweed, who was slinking away in dudgeon, he accepted the invitation with a suavity bordering on meekness (whereby I judged that he had definite reasons for wishing to see the collection).

"So," said Mr Horridge, as he conducted us along the hall, "you have been examining the car. Now, what did you expect to find out from the car?"

"I did not expect anything," Thorndyke replied.

Horridge giggled. "And did your examination answer your expectations?" he inquired.

"Substantially," replied Thorndyke. "I may say that it did."

Horridge giggled again, and, throwing open a door which opened from the hall, invited us to enter. We accordingly passed in and found ourselves in an immense and lofty room communicating with another of similarly magnificent proportions by an opening from which the original folding doors had been removed.

I looked around me with surprise and extreme distaste, for the noble apartments had been degraded to the status of a mere lumber-room. Of the trim and orderly character of a museum there was not a trace. The walls were occupied by interminable ranges of open shelves and the floor was crowded with plain deal tables, coarsely stained and varnished to disguise their humble material; and shelves and tables were littered with a chaos of miscellaneous objects, all exposed baldly to the air and dust. There was not a single glazed case in the room and the only article of comely furniture was a lantern clock, perched on a bracket, which ticked sedately and actually showed the approximately correct time.

"This is a very singular collection," Thorndyke remarked, casting a puzzled glance over the shelves and tables. "One doesn't quite see what its purpose is; what it is intended to illustrate."

Horridge giggled again in his unpleasant way. "Whatever the intention is," said he, "it illustrates very perfectly poor old Pen's usual state of mind – muddle. But may I ask what is the object of this inspection? Is it just a matter of curiosity or is it connected with the inquiry into Pen's disappearance? Because I don't see how the inspection is going to help you."

"It is not very obvious, certainly," Thorndyke admitted. "But one never knows what light chance-facts may throw on the problem. I think it will be worth while for me to see what things Mr Penrose has collected and where he obtained them."

Horridge grinned – and the explanation of the grin was presently forthcoming. Meanwhile he rejoined: "Well, cast your eye over the oddments and see what takes your fancy. Then you can go into the question of where they came from. What would you like to start with?"

Thorndyke glanced once more along the shelves and then announced his choice.

"I see there is a good deal of ancient pottery, mixed up with other exhibits. Perhaps it would be well to sort that out and see where the pieces were found. Now, here is a little dish of Gaulish red ware. The slip of paper that it rests on bears the number, 201. That, I presume refers to a catalogue."

"It does," replied Horridge, giggling delightedly. "I will get you the catalogue and then you will be able to find out all about the specimen."

He went to a table near the end of the room and pulled out a drawer from which he extracted a stout quarto volume. This he brought to Thorndyke and, having handed it to him with something of a flourish, stood looking at him and giggling like a fool. But the reason for his merriment became apparent when Thorndyke opened the book and turned to the number. Observing the slow smile which spread over my colleague's face I looked over his shoulder and read the entry, scrawled, not very legibly, in pencil:

201.   Sammy.   Pot Sand.   Sinbad.

"This is not very illuminating," Thorndyke remarked; on which Horridge burst into a roar of laughter.

"Oh, don't say that!" he gurgled. "I understand from old Brodribb that you could see through a brick wall. Well, here's your chance. The whole catalogue is written in the same damn' silly sort of jargon. Of course, Pen knows what it means, but he doesn't intend that anyone else shall. Perhaps you would like to note down a few samples to think over at your leisure."

Thorndyke instantly grasped the opportunity.

"Thank you," said he. "A most excellent suggestion. If you will be so very kind as to show Dr Jervis the collection, I will make a few notes on the pottery and extract the entries from the catalogue. If we could identify some of the localities, we might get quite a useful hint."

This suggestion did not at all meet the views of Mr Horridge, who was evidently as curious as to Thorndyke's proceedings as I was, myself. But he could not very well refuse; for Thorndyke, seeing a chance of carrying out his investigations – whatever they might be – uninterrupted by Horridge's chatter and free from his inquisitive observation, was quietly persistent and, of course, had his way, as he usually did.

"Very well," Horridge at length agreed, with a rather bad grace, "then I'll just take Dr Jervis round the shelves and show him the curios. But I don't know much about them, and I don't suppose he cares much."

Accordingly, we set forth on a voyage of exploration round the crowded, disorderly shelves; and, realising that my function was to keep Horridge's attention distracted from Thorndyke's activities, I plied him with questions about the exhibits and commented on their interest and beauty with the utmost prolixity and tediousness at my command. But it was a wretched make-believe on both sides; for, while Horridge was answering my questions (usually quite ignorantly and all wrong, as even I knew), he kept one eye cocked in Thorndyke's direction, and my attention was similarly occupied.

But Thorndyke gave us but a poor entertainment. Drawing a chair up to a table near the window, he seated himself with his back to us and the catalogue before him. This he pored over for some time, making occasional entries in his note-book. Then he rose, and, having taken a survey of the shelves, began to select pieces of pottery, each of which he took in turn to the table where he examined it critically, compared it with the entry in the catalogue and copied the latter into his note-book. He began with the Roman pottery, but, from long acquaintance with his habits and methods, I suspected that this was only a tactical move to conceal from Horridge his actual purpose. For I knew that it was his invariable habit, when he had to work in the presence of inquisitive observers, to confuse the issues in their minds by actions which had no bearing on the matter in hand.

As to his real purpose, I had no doubt that it was in some way connected with the fragment which we had examined; and as Horridge conducted me round the loaded shelves, I kept a sharp look-out for pottery exhibits which might correspond to the hypothetical vessel which Thorndyke had sketched in his reconstruction. There were two pieces (in different places and among totally unrelated objects) which, so far as I could see without close inspection, answered the description; one, a largish, rather shallow bowl of which a large part was missing, and the other a deeper pot which had been broken and rather unskilfully mended and which was complete save for a small part of the rim.

This pot corresponded very closely both in shape and size with Thorndyke's reconstruction, and it seemed to me, even, that the piece which was missing from the rim was about the size of our fragment. Accordingly, I gave that pot my special attention.

One after another Thorndyke gravely examined specimens of Roman, Saxon and Iron Age pottery in which I felt sure he could have no interest whatever. At last, after circling around, so to speak, he arrived at this pot, picked it up, and with a glance at the number on its paper, bore it over to the table. As he set it down and seated himself, I saw him take something from his pocket, but as his back was towards us I could not see what it was, or what he did with it. I assumed, however, that it was some measuring instrument and that he was ascertaining the dimensions of the piece that was missing. At any rate, his examination was quite brief, and, when he had copied the entry in the catalogue, he carried the pot back to its place and proceeded to look about for further objects for study.

By this time, however, Horridge had begun to be rather bored and was disposed to make no secret of the fact.

"I should think," said he, with an undisguised yawn, "that you've got enough material to occupy you for a month or two; and I'll wager that you don't make any sense of it then."

Thorndyke looked thoughtfully at his open note-book.

"Perhaps you are right," he agreed. "These entries will take a good deal of deciphering and probably will yield no information, after all. I don't think we need trespass on your patience any longer."

"Oh, that's all right," said Horridge, "but, before you go – if you've seen all that you want to see – perhaps you might as well have a look at the small room – the one that was broken into, you know. You heard about that burglary, I think? Old Brodribb said he was going to consult you about it."

"Mr Brodribb did consult me," Thorndyke replied, "on the question of opening the cupboard by force or otherwise. I advised him that, in the absence of Mr Penrose, it would not be proper to force the cupboard and that, as the contents of the cupboard were unknown, the proceedings would be useless as well as improper."

"But what about calling in the police?" Horridge suggested.

"I don't think the police would force a cupboard, without the owner's knowledge or consent, if it were locked and showed no signs of having been tampered with."

"Well," Horridge grumbled, "it's very unsatisfactory. Someone may have got away with a whole lot of valuable property and be able to dispose of it at their leisure. However – if you have finished with the catalogue, do you mind putting it back in its drawer?"

As Thorndyke complied with this rather odd request, our host walked quickly up the long room to a door in the corner, and I had the impression that he inserted a key and turned it. But, as he stood half turned towards us and in front of the handle and keyhole, I could not see distinctly, nor did I give the matter any particular attention.

"It is odd," he remarked, still standing before the door, grasping the handle, "that Pen should have left the key in this door when he went away. He was always so deadly secret about Bluebeard's chamber, as he called it in his silly way. He never let me see into it. I always thought he had something very precious in it; and I'm inclined to think so still."

With this, he opened the door and we all entered the mysterious chamber; a smallish room and very bare of furniture, for it contained only a single chair, a mahogany table, placed under the window, and a massive cupboard, also of mahogany, with a pair of doors like a wardrobe.

"So this is the famous cupboard," said Thorndyke, standing before it and looking it over critically; "the repository of hidden treasure, as you believe. Well, looking at it, one would say that whatever precious things were once in it, are in it still. But one might be wrong."

Having made this rather ambiguous pronouncement, he proceeded to a more particular inspection. The escutcheon of the Chubb lock was examined with the aid of a lens, and the interior of the keyhole with the tiny electric lamp that he always carried. From the lock he transferred his attention to the cupboard itself, closely examining the sides, standing on the chair to inspect the top, and, finally, setting his shoulder to one corner and his foot against the skirting of the wall, tried to test its weight by tilting it. But beyond eliciting a complaining creak, he could make no impression on it.

"I've tried that," said Horridge. "It's like shoving against the Eddystone lighthouse. The thing is a most ungodly weight, unless it is screwed to the floor. It can hardly be the stuff inside."

"Unless," I suggested, "Mr Penrose indulged in the hobby of collecting gold ingots. But even a collection of plate can be pretty heavy if there is enough of it."

"At any rate," said Thorndyke, "one thing is clear. That cupboard has not been opened unless it was opened with its own key."

"Don't think the lock could have been picked?" said Horridge.

Thorndyke shook his head. "Burglars don't try to pick Chubb locks," said he. "They use the jemmy, or else cut the lock with centre-bits."

Horridge grunted and then amplified the grunt with the remark:

"Looks a bit as if our friend Kick had raised a false alarm."

"That can hardly be," Thorndyke objected. "I understand that he found the door bolted on the inside and had to enter through the window."

"Yes, that was what he said," Horridge admitted grudgingly in a tone that seemed to imply some scepticism as to the statement.

"It is conceivable," Thorndyke suggested, "that the visitor may have been disturbed, or that he gave up the attempt when he found it impossible to pick the lock. You see, there is no evidence that he was a skilled burglar. No difficulties were overcome. He simply opened the window and stepped in. The really astonishing thing is that Penrose should have left the place so insecure – that is, assuming that there actually was some valuable property here. The window, as you can see, has no shutters, or even screws or stops, and it looks on to an alley which I understand is invisible from the street. Let us see what that alley is like."

He moved the table away from the window, glancing at a number of parallel scratches on its polished surface, slid up the window and looked out.

"It is quite remarkable," said he. "The window is only a few feet from the ground and the alley is closed by a small wooden gate which has no bolt or latch and seems to be secured only by a lock; which is probably a simple builder's lock which could easily be opened with a skeleton key or a common pick-lock. There is no security whatever. That stout bolt on the room door is, of course, useless as it is on the inside; and the lock is probably a simple affair."

As he spoke, he opened the door and plucked out the key which he held out for our inspection.

"You see," he said. "Just a plain warded lock which a skilled operator could turn with a bit of stiff wire. Penrose seems to have pinned his faith to the Chubb lock; and perhaps events have justified him."

He slipped the key back into the lock; and this seemed to bring the proceedings to an end. After a few perfunctory expressions of hope that our visit had satisfied us and that we had seen all that we wished to see, our host escorted us through the great gallery and the hall and finally launched us into the street.

CHAPTER NINE
Thorndyke Tests a Theory

As we took our way homeward I tried to arrange in my mind the rather confusing experiences of the last hour or two. Those hours, it seemed to me, had been virtually wasted, for we had learned nothing new that bore directly on our problem. This view I ventured to propound to Thorndyke, beginning, naturally with Mr Horridge, who had made a deep and disagreeable impression on me.

"Yes," Thorndyke agreed, "he is not a prepossessing person. A bad-mannered man and distinctly sly and suspicious. You probably noted his mental attitude towards Kickweed."

"Yes, distinctly hostile; and I gathered that he is inclined to suspect him of having faked that burglary for his own ends. I suppose, by the way, that it is not possible that he may be right?"

"It is not actually impossible," Thorndyke replied, "but there is nothing to support such a suspicion. Kickweed impressed me very favourably, especially by his loyalty to Penrose. If he is not a liar, the position with regard to the small room is this: someone entered that room: that someone either knew or thought he knew what it contained. He either failed to open that cupboard or he opened it with its own key. The only evidence that he did open it is the piece of paper that was found, which you notice, was similar to the slips of paper under the specimens in the gallery, excepting that it bore no catalogue number. That paper strongly suggests that the

89

cupboard had been opened, but is not conclusive, since it might have been dropped by Penrose on some other occasion. But, as I said, its presence is strongly suggestive of a hurried opening of the cupboard at night. There were one or two other points that probably did not escape you."

"You mean the extraordinary weight of the cupboard? That certainly impressed me as significant though I am not quite clear as to what it signifies. It might be due to some ponderous contents, but it seemed to me to suggest an iron safe inside."

"Yes," said Thorndyke, "that is undoubtedly the explanation. The cupboard is a mere wooden case enclosing a large iron safe. That was quite clear from the construction, which is very much like that of an organ case. The sides and top are fixed in position by large screws instead of being keyed in with proper cabinet-maker's joints. The wooden case was built on after the safe had been placed in position."

"Then," said I, "the Chubb lock is a mere hollow pretence."

"Exactly. The wooden case could have been taken off with a common screw-driver. You noticed the scratches on the table?"

"Yes. But, of course, there is no evidence as to when they were made."

"No," he agreed. "Probably they were made at various times. But they are of interest in relation to the arrangement of the cupboard. You must have noticed that they were in two groups, roughly two feet six inches apart and all approximately parallel. They looked like the scratches that would be made by the runners of drawers of that width; and comparing them with the cupboard, one saw that, allowing for the space taken up by the wooden case, there would just be room for a range of drawers of that width. The reasonable inference is that the iron safe houses a range of largish drawers and that these have been taken out from time to time and placed on the table so that their contents could be looked at by the light from the window."

I agreed that this appeared to be the case, but I could not see that it mattered very much whether it was so or not.

"It seems to me," I added, "that we are acquiring a lot of oddments of information none of which has the slightest bearing on the one question that we are asked to answer: Where is Penrose hiding at the present moment?"

"It would be safer," said he, "to say, 'seems to have'. I am picking up all the information that I can in the hope that some of it may turn out to have a bearing on our problem."

"By the way," said I, "why were you so keen on seeing the collection? You were, you know, or you would not have put up with Horridge's insolence. You had some definite point to clear up respecting that pottery fragment. What was it?"

"The point," he replied, "was this. To an archaeologist, that fragment alone would have been an object of interest, since, as you saw, it was possible to make from it a rough, but quite reliable reconstruction. But Penrose is not an archaeologist. He is, as we understood, a mere collector of curios. To such a man, a tiny fragment would be of no interest by itself.

"On the other hand, to an archaeologist, a broken pot is, practically, of the same scientific value as a complete pot. But to the mere collector, or curio-monger, the completeness of a specimen is a matter of cardinal importance. If he has an incomplete specimen, he will spare no trouble or expense to make it complete. He is not concerned with its scientific interest but with its value as a curio.

"Knowing, then, what we did of Penrose it occurred to me as a bare possibility that this apparently worthless fragment that we found in his pocket might be the product of a definite search *ad hoc*. That he might have revisited some place from which he had obtained an incomplete specimen with the express purpose of searching for the fragment which would make it complete. The edges of the fragment were freshly fractured. It had been broken off the pot in the course of digging it out. Therefore, the missing piece of the pot was still in the place where the digging had taken place and was certainly recoverable. It was just a speculative possibility, but it was worth testing as we are so short of data, so I decided to look over the collection when I got a chance."

"And I gather," said I, "that you obtained confirmation of your very ingenious theory?"

"I am hoping that I did," he replied; "but we shall see when we get home. If I have, we shall have some sort of a clue to the place from which that disastrous homeward journey started."

I forbore to remark that it did not seem to me to matter two straws where it started from, since it was evident that he thought the information worth acquiring. So I merely asked what the clue amounted to.

"Unfortunately," he replied, "it amounts to very little. This is the entry in the catalogue corresponding to the pot which I examined."

He indicated the entry in his note-book, and I read: "Moulin à vent. Julie (Polly)."

"What a perfect and complete ass the fellow must be," I exclaimed, returning the note-book in disgust, "to write meaningless twaddle like that in what purports to be a museum catalogue!"

"I agree with you most warmly," he replied. "But the man's oddities are an element in our problem. And, of course, these preposterous entries in the catalogue are not meaningless. They have a meaning which is deliberately concealed and which we have got to extract."

"In the case of this one," I asked, "can you make any sense of it? Can you, for instance, discover any connection between an earthen pot and a windmill?"

"Yes," he replied, "I think that is fairly clear, though it doesn't help us much. There is a place in Wiltshire, near Avebury, known as Windmill Hill, where a certain distinctive kind of Neolithic pottery has been found and which has been named the Windmill Hill type. Probably, this pot is an example of that type, but that is a question that we can easily settle, though it doesn't seem to be an important one. The information that we want is probably contained in the other two words; and, at present, I can make nothing of them.

"No," I agreed, "they are pretty obscure. Who is Julie? What is she? And likewise: Who is Polly? Good God! What damned nonsense it is!"

He smiled at my exasperation. "You are quite right, Jervis," said he. "It is monstrous that two learned medical jurists should have to expend their time and intellect in solving a set of silly puzzles. But it is part of our present job."

"Do you find any method in this fellow's madness?" I asked. "I noticed you copying out a lot of this balderdash."

"There is a little method," he replied. "Not much. But this entry, relating to that little embossed red ware dish that you saw, will illustrate Penrose's method. You see, it reads: 'Sammy. Pot Sand. Sinbad.' Now, this Gaulish red ware is usually described as Samian ware, so we may take it that 'Sammy' means 'Samian.' The interpretation of 'Pot Sand' is also fairly obvious. There is a shoal in the Thames Estuary off Whitstable on which it is believed that a Roman ship, laden with pottery, went aground and broke up. From time immemorial, oyster dredgers working over that shoal have brought up quantities of Roman pottery, including Samian ware, whence the shoal has been named The Pan Sand, and is so marked on the Admiralty charts. Penrose's 'Pot Sand' is, therefore, presumably the Pan Sand; and as to Sinbad, we may assume him to have been a sailor, probably an oyster dredger or a whelk fisher."

"I have no doubt that you are right," said I, "but it is difficult to consider such childish twaddle with patience. I should like to kick the fellow."

"I should be delighted if you could," said he, "for, since you would have to catch him before you could kick him, that would mean that our problem would be solved. By the way, we shall have to contrive, somehow, to make the acquaintance of Mr Lockhart. I wonder if Brodribb knows him."

"You think he could tell us what was in that small room. But I doubt if he would. Penrose would probably have sworn him to secrecy, and, in any case, it would be a matter of professional confidence. But it seems to me that the burglary is a side issue, though I know you will say that we can't judge which issues are side issues."

"At any rate," he retorted, "the burglary is not one. It is very material. For, if Penrose was the burglar, he must be in possession of property which he intends to dispose of, by which, if we knew what it was, we might be able to trace him. And if the burglar was not Penrose, we should very much like to know who he was."

I did not quite see why; but, as our discussion had now brought us to our doorstep, there was no opportunity to pursue the question; for, as I had expected, Thorndyke made straight for the laboratory, and I followed, with mild curiosity as to the test that I assumed to be in view. As we entered, the sound of Polton's lathe in the adjacent workshop informed us that he had some job on hand there, but his quick ear had noted our arrival and he came in at once to see if his services were required.

"I need not disturb you, Polton," said Thorndyke. "It is only a matter of a small plaster mould."

"You are not disturbing me, sir," replied Polton. "I am just turning up a few spare tool handles to pass the time. You would like the quick-setting plaster, I suppose?"

"If you please," Thorndyke replied; and as Polton retired to fetch the material, he produced from his pocket a small tin box from which he tenderly shook out into his hand a slab of moulding wax. Looking, at it as it lay on his palm, I saw that it was a "squeeze" of the edge of the pot, the gap in the broken rim being represented by a wart-like swelling of the shape of the missing piece. Noting the exact correspondence, I remarked:

"You hardly want the plaster. The shape of the squeeze is exact enough for comparison."

"Yes," he agreed, "but an actual measurement is always better than a judgement of resemblance."

Here, Polton returned with a jar of the special plaster, a rubber bowl, a jug of water and the other necessaries for the operation.

Unobtrusively, but firmly taking possession of the squeeze, he laid it in one of the little paper trays that he used for making small moulds or casts, brushed it over lightly with a camel-hair brush containing a trace of oil, and then proceeded to mix the plaster. This had to be done quickly, since the special plaster set solid in about five minutes; and I could not but admire the calm, unhurried way in which Polton carried the process through its various stages. At exactly the right moment, the plaster was dropped on to the squeeze, blown with the breath into all the interstices, and then the remainder poured on until the little tray was full to the brim, and even as the last drops were being persuaded out of the bowl with a spoon, the change began which transformed the creamy liquid into a white solid like the "icing" on a wedding cake.

At this point Thorndyke retired to fetch the fragment, and Polton and I took the opportunity to clean the bowl and spoon and spread on the bench a sheet of newspaper to receive the inevitable crumbs and scrapings; a most necessary precaution, for plaster, in spite of its delicate whiteness, is one of the dirtiest of materials. The particles which detach themselves from a cast seem to spread themselves over a whole room, with a special predilection for the soles of shoes, whence they distribute impressions on stairs and passages in the most surprising and unexpected fashion. But a sheet of paper collects the particles and enables them to be removed tidily before they have the opportunity to develop their diabolical tendencies.

When Thorndyke returned our labours were completed and the little tray reposed on the paper with the plaster tools beside it.

"Is it hard enough to open?" Thorndyke asked.

Polton tested with his finger-nail the smooth, white mass that bulged up from the tray, and, having reported that it was "set as hard as stone," proceeded carefully to shell it out of the paper container. Then he scraped away the projecting edges until the wax was free all round. A little cautious persuading with the thumb induced the squeeze to separate from the plaster, when Polton laid them down side by side and looked expectantly at Thorndyke. The

95

cast was now clearly recognisable as the replica of a portion of the outside of the pot, including the rim and the gap where a piece of the rim had been broken away.

Thorndyke now produced the fragment of pottery, and, holding it delicately between his finger and thumb – for the plaster was still moist and tender – very carefully inserted it into the gap; and as it dropped in, exactly filling the space, with a perfect fit at every point, he remarked:

"I think that settles the question of identity. This fragment is the piece that is missing from the museum pot."

"Yes," I agreed, "The proof is absolutely conclusive. What is not quite obvious to me is the importance of the fact which is proved. I see that it strongly supports your theory that the fragment was the product of a definite search, but it is not clear to me that even the confirmation of your theory has any particular value."

"It has now very little value," he replied. "The importance of the fact which this experiment has established is that it carries us out of the region of the unknown into that of the known. If this fragment was part of the museum pot, then the place from which that pot came is the place from which this fragment came."

"Yes," said I, "that is clear enough. And it is fair to assume that the place whence this fragment came is the place from which Penrose started on his homeward journey. But as we don't know where the pot came from, I can't see that we have got so very far from the unknown. We have simply connected one unknown with another unknown."

Thorndyke smiled indulgently. "You are a proper pessimist, Jervis," said he. "But you will, at least, admit that we have narrowed the unknown down to a very small area. We have got to find out where that pot came from; and I don't think we shall have very much difficulty. Probably the catalogue entry embodies some clue."

"But," I persisted, "even if you discover that, I don't see that you will be any further advanced. You will know where Penrose came from, but that knowledge will not help you to discover where he has gone to. At least, that is how it appears to me. But perhaps there is some point that I have overlooked."

"My impression is," Thorndyke replied, "that you have not given any serious consideration to this curious and puzzling case. If you would turn it over in your mind carefully and try to see the connections between the various facts that are known to us, you would realise that we have got to begin by retracing this last journey to its starting-point."

With this, he picked up the cast with the embedded fragment of pottery to put them into the box with the other "exhibits"; and, as he retired, Polton (who had been listening with a curious intentness to our conversation) gathered up the newspaper and the plaster appliances and went back to his lathe.

CHAPTER TEN

Introduces Mr Crabbe

Thorndyke's rather cryptic observation gave me considerable food for thought. But it was not very nourishing food, for no conclusion emerged. He was quite right in believing that I had given little serious consideration to the case of Daniel Penrose. It had not greatly interested me, and I had seen no practical method by which the problem could be approached. Nor did I now; and the only result of my cogitations was to confirm my previous opinion that I had missed some crucial point in the evidence and to make me suspect that there was in this case something more than met the eye.

This latter suspicion deepened when I reflected on Thorndyke's concluding statement: "You would realise that we have got to begin by retracing that last journey to its starting point." But I did not realise anything of the sort. The problem, as I understood it, was to discover the present whereabouts of Daniel Penrose; and to this problem, the starting-point of his last known journey seemed completely irrelevant. But in that I knew that I must be wrong; a conviction which merely brought me back to the unsatisfactory conclusion that I had failed to take account of some vital element in the case.

But it was not only in respect of that disastrous return journey that I was puzzled by Thorndyke's proceedings. There was his unaccountable interest in the burglary at Queen Square.

Apparently, he believed the burglar to have been Penrose himself; and in this I was disposed to concur. But suppose that we were able to establish the fact with certainty; what help would it give us in tracing Penrose to his hiding-place? So far as I could see, it would not help us at all; and Thorndyke's keenness in regard to the burglary only increased my bewilderment.

Naturally, then, I was all agog when, a few days later, Thorndyke announced that Mr Lockhart was coming in to smoke a pipe with us on the following evening; for here seemed to be a chance of getting some fresh light on the subject. Lockhart was being lured to our chambers to be pumped, little as he probably suspected it, and if I listened attentively, I might catch some of the drippings.

"You haven't forgotten," said I, "that Miller is likely to call tomorrow evening?"

"No," he replied, "but we have no appointment so he may choose some other time. At any rate, we must take our chance; and it won't matter so very much if he does drop in."

It seemed to me that the superintendent would be very much in the way and I sincerely hoped that he would choose some other evening for his visit. But Thorndyke presumably knew his own business.

"How did you get hold of Lockhart?" I asked. "Did Brodribb know him?"

"I didn't ask him," Thorndyke replied. "I saw Lockhart's name in the list of cases at the Central Criminal Court so I dropped in there and introduced myself. When I told him that I was looking into Penrose's affairs, he was very ready to come in and hear all about the case."

I laughed aloud. "So," said I, "this poor deluded gentleman is coming with the belief that he is going to be the recipient of information. It is a rank imposition."

"Not at all," he protested. "We shall tell him what we know of the case, and no doubt we shall learn something from him in exchange. At least, I hope we shall."

"Then," said I, "you are an optimist. If he knows anything that you don't you can be pretty certain that he learned it under the seal of the confessional."

Thorndyke agreed that I was probably right. "But," he added hopefully, "we shall see. It is sometimes possible to learn something from what a man refuses to disclose."

I made a mental note of this observation and kept it in mind when our visitor arrived on the following evening, for it suggested to me that Thorndyke's questions might be more illuminating than the answers that they might evoke, particularly if our friend should turn out to be uncommunicative. But this did not, at first, appear to be the case, for, after a little general conversation, he led up to the subject of Daniel Penrose of his own accord.

"I did not quite gather what it was," said he, "that your clients expected you to do. If it is a permissible question, what sort of inquiry are you engaged in?"

"It is a perfectly permissible question," replied Thorndyke. "I can tell you all about the case without any breach of professional confidence as the main facts are already in the public domain. What I am expected to do is to discover the place in which Mr Penrose is at present hiding, or at least to locate him sufficiently to make it possible to produce him, if necessary."

"And apparently he doesn't want to be produced? But why not? Why has he gone into hiding? My very discreet informant told me that he had gone away from home and left no address but she didn't mention any reasons for his disappearing. Are there any substantial reasons?"

"He thinks that there are," replied Thorndyke. "But, if you are interested, I will give you a sketch of the circumstances of his disappearance, so far as they are known to me."

"I am very much interested," said Lockhart. "Penrose is a queer fellow – the sort of fellow who might do queer things and I don't know that I am so violently fond of him. But he always interested me as a human oddity, and I should like to hear what has happened to him."

Thereupon, Thorndyke embarked on a concise but detailed account of the strange circumstances which surrounded Penrose's disappearance from human ken; and I listened with almost as much attention as Lockhart himself. For Thorndyke's clear summary of the events in their due order was a useful refresher to my own memory. But, what specially amused and delighted me was the masterly tactical approach to the cross-examination which I felt pretty sure was to follow. Thorndyke's perfectly open and unreserved narrative, treating the whole affair as one generally known, in respect of which there was not the slightest occasion for secrecy, was an admirable preparation for a few discreet questions. It would be difficult for Lockhart to adopt a reticent attitude after being treated with such complete confidence.

"Well," said Lockhart, when the story was told, "it is a queer affair, but, as I remarked, Penrose is a queer fellow. Still, there are some points that rather surprise me."

"For instance?" Thorndyke suggested.

"It is a small matter," replied Lockhart, "and I may be mistaken in the man, but I shouldn't have expected him to be the worse for liquor. You seemed to imply that he was definitely squiffy."

"It is only hearsay," Thorndyke reminded him, "and an inexpert opinion at that. The report may have been exaggerated. But, in your experience of him, should you say that he is a strictly temperate man?"

"I wouldn't go so far as that," said Lockhart. "He is most uncommonly fond of what he calls 'the vintages of the Fortunate Isles' and the 'elderly and fuscous wine of Jerez,' and I should think that he gets through a fair amount of them. But he impressed me as a man who would take a glass, or two or three glasses of sherry or Madeira pretty often, but not a great quantity at once. Your regular nipper, especially of wine doesn't often get drunk."

"No," Thorndyke agreed, "though sherry and Madeira are strong wines. What were the other points?"

"Well," replied Lockhart, "doesn't it strike you that the actions of Penrose are rather disproportionate to the cause. He seems to have been abnormally funky. After all, it was only a motor accident, and there isn't any clear evidence that it was his car. He could have denied that he was there. And, in any case, it doesn't seem worth his while to bolt off and abandon his home and all his worldly possessions. If he had committed a murder or arson or something really serious, it would have been different."

"It was manslaughter," I remarked; "and a rather bad case. And the vintages of the Fortunate Isles didn't make it any less culpable. He might have got a longish term of hard labour, even if he escaped penal servitude."

"I don't think it was as bad as that," said Lockhart. "At any rate if I had been in his place, I would have stayed and faced the music; and I would have left it to the prosecution to prove that I was on that road."

"That," said Thorndyke, "is a matter of temperament. From your knowledge of Penrose, should you have taken him for a nervous, panicky man?"

Lockhart reflected for a few moments. "You speak," said he, "of my knowledge of Penrose. But, really I hardly know him at all. I made his acquaintance quite recently, and I have not met him half a dozen times."

"You don't know his people then?"

"No. I know nothing about his family affairs. Our acquaintance arose out of a chance meeting at a curio shop in Soho. We walked away from the shop together, discussing collecting and antiques, and he then invited me to go and inspect his treasures. Which I did; and that is the only occasion on which I was ever in his house. But I must say that it was a memorable experience."

"In what way?" Thorndyke asked.

"Well," replied Lockhart, "there was the man, himself; one of the oddest fishes that I have ever encountered. But I dare say you have heard about his peculiarities."

"I understand that he is a most inconveniently secretive gentleman, and also that he has an inveterate habit of calling things by their wrong names."

"Yes," said Lockhart, "that is what I mean. He speaks not in parables, but in a sort of crossword puzzles, leaving you to make out his meaning by the exercise of your wits. You can imagine what it was like to be shown round a collection by a man who called all the specimens by utterly and ridiculously inappropriate names."

"Yes," said Thorndyke; "rather confusing, I should suppose. But you did see the collection; and perhaps he showed you the catalogue too?"

"He did. In fact, he made a point of letting me see it in order, I think, to enjoy my astonishment. What an amazing document it is! If ever he should have to plead insanity, I should think that the production of that catalogue would make medical testimony unnecessary. I take it that you have seen it and the collection, too?"

"Yes," said Thorndyke, "I examined the catalogue and made a few extracts with notes of the pieces to which they referred. And I was shown round the collection by Mr Horridge, Penrose's executor. But I have an idea that he did not show us the whole collection. We saw only the collection in the great gallery; but probably you were more favoured, as you were shown round by the proprietor?"

The question was very adroitly thrown out; but, at this point Mr Lockhart, as I had expected, developed a sudden evasiveness.

"It is impossible for me to say," he replied; "as I don't know what the whole collection consisted of. I assumed that he had shown me all that there was to see."

"Probably you were right," said Thorndyke; and then, coming boldly to the real issue, he asked: "Did he show you the contents of the small room?"

For some moments Lockhart did not reply, but sat looking profoundly uncomfortable. At length, he answered in an apologetic tone: "It's a ridiculous situation, but you know what sort of man Penrose is. The fact is that when he showed me his collection, he made it a condition that I should regard the transaction as a strictly confidential one and that I should not discuss his possessions or communicate their nature or amount to any person whatsoever. It is an absurd condition, but I accepted it and consequently I am not in a position to tell you what he did actually show me. But I don't suppose that it is of any consequence. I take it that you have no special interest in his collection."

"On the contrary," said Thorndyke, "we have a very special interest in the collection, and particularly that part of it which was kept in the small room. Since Penrose went away, there has been a burglary – or a suspected burglary – at his house. The small room was undoubtedly entered one night, and there is a suspicion that the big cupboard was opened. But, if it was it was opened with a key, as there was no trace of any injury to the doors. On the other hand, it is possible that the burglar failed to pick the lock and was disturbed. But Penrose has the only key of the cupboard, so there are no means of ascertaining, without picking the lock or forcing the door, whether there has or has not been a robbery; and we have decided that it would not be admissible to do either in Penrose's absence. Nevertheless, it is important for us to know what was in that cupboard."

"I don't see why," said Lockhart. "If it is not admissible to force the door – and I entirely agree with you that it is not – I don't see that it would help you to know what was in the cupboard – or whether it contained anything at all. Supposing that it had certain contents, you cannot ascertain, without opening it, whether those contents are still there or whether they have been stolen. But if you say that the lock has not been picked nor the door forced, and Penrose has the only key, doesn't that prove pretty conclusively that no burglary has taken place?"

At this moment a familiar sound came to justify my fears of an interruption. I had taken the precaution to shut the outer oak door when Lockhart had entered. But the light from our windows must have been visible from without. At any rate, the well-known six taps with a walking-stick – in three pairs, like the strokes of a ship's bell – spelled out the name of the visitor who stood on our threshold. Accordingly, I rose and threw open the doors, closing them again as the superintendent walked in.

"Now, don't let me disturb anyone," exclaimed Miller, observing that, at his entrance, Lockhart had risen with the air of taking his departure. "I am only a bird of passage. I have just dropped in to collect those documents and hear if the doctor has any remarks to make on them."

Thorndyke walked over to a cabinet, and, unlocking it, took out a small bundle of papers which he handed to the superintendent.

"I can't give a very decided opinion on them," said he. "It is really a case for a handwriting expert. All that I can say is that there are none of the regular signs of forgery; no indications of tracing or of very deliberate writing. The separate words seem to have been written quickly and freely. But I got the impression – it is only an impression – that there is a lack of continuity, as if each word had been executed as a separate act."

"I don't quite follow that," said Miller.

"I mean," Thorndyke explained, "that – assuming it, for the moment, to be a forgery – the forger's method might have been, instead of copying words continuously from an original, to take one word, copy it two or three times so as to get to know it thoroughly, then write it quickly on the document and go on to the next word. Written in that way, the words would not form such completely continuous lines as if the whole were written at a single operation. But you had better get the opinion of a first-class expert."

"Very well," said Miller, "I will; and I will tell him what you have suggested. And now, I had better take myself off and leave you to your conference."

"You need not run away, Miller," Thorndyke protested, very much to my surprise. "There is no conference. Fill up a glass of grog and light a cigar like a Christian."

He indicated the whisky decanter and siphon and the box of cigars, which had been offered to, and declined by, Lockhart, and drew up a chair.

"Well," said Miller, seating himself and selecting a cigar, "if you are sure that I am not breaking in on a consultation, I shall be delighted to spend half an hour or so in your intellectual society." He thoughtfully mixed himself a temperate whisky and soda, and then, with a quizzical glance at Thorndyke, inquired: "Was there any little item of information that you were requiring?"

"Really, Miller," Thorndyke protested, "you underestimate your personal charms. When I ask for the pleasure of your society, need you look for an ulterior motive?"

Miller regarded me with a crafty smile and solemnly closed one eye.

"I'm not looking for one," he replied. "I merely asked a question."

"And I am glad you did," said Thorndyke, "because you have reminded me that there *was* a little matter that I wanted to ask you about."

Miller grinned at me again. "Ah," he chuckled. "Now we are coming to it. What was the question?"

"It was concerned with a man named Crabbe. Jonathan Crabbe of Hatton Garden. Do you know him?"

"He is a personal friend," Miller replied. "And he is not Mr Crabbe of Hatton Garden just at present. He is Mr Crabbe of Maidstone Jail. What did you want to know about him?"

"Anything that you can tell me. And you needn't mind Mr Lockhart. He is one of the Devil's own, like the rest of us."

"I know Mr Lockhart very well by sight and by reputation," said the superintendent. "Now, with regard to this man Crabbe. He had a place, as you say, in Hatton Garden where he professed to carry on the business of a diamond broker and dealer in precious stones. I don't know anything about the diamond brokery, but he was a dealer in precious stones all right. That's why he is at Maidstone. He got two years for receiving."

"Do you remember when he was convicted?"

"I can't give you the exact date offhand," replied Miller.

"It wasn't my case. I was only an interested onlooker. But it was somewhere about the end of last September. Is that near enough?"

"Quite near enough for my purpose," Thorndyke replied. "Do you know anything more about him? Is he an old hand?"

"There," replied Miller, "you are asking me a question that I can't answer with certainty. There were no previous convictions against him, but it was clear that he had been carrying on as a fence for a considerable time. There was definite evidence of that. But there was another little affair which never got beyond suspicion. I looked into that myself; and I may say that I was half inclined then to collar the worthy Jonathan. But when we came to talk the case over, we came to the conclusion that there was not enough evidence and no chance of getting any more. So we put our notes of the case into cold storage in the hope that something fresh might turn up some day. And I still hope that it may, for it was an important case and we got considerable discredit for not being able to spot the chappies who did the job."

"Is there any reason why you should not tell us about the case?" Thorndyke asked.

"Well, you know," Miller replied, "it was only a case of suspicion, though in my own mind, I feel pretty cocksure that our suspicions were justified. Still, I don't think there would be any harm in my just giving you an outline of the case, on the understanding that this is in strict confidence."

"I think you can take that for granted," said Thorndyke. We are all lawyers and used to keeping our own counsel."

"Then," said Miller, "I will give you a sketch of the case; what we know and what I think. It's just possible that you may remember the case as it made a good deal of stir at the time. The papers referred to it as 'The Billington Jewel Robbery.' "

"I have just a faint recollection of the affair," Thorndyke replied; "but I can't recall any of the details."

"It was a remarkable case in some respects," Miller proceeded, "and the most remarkable feature was the ridiculous softness of the job. Billington was a silly fool. He had an important collection of jewellery, which is a stupid thing in itself. No man ought to keep in a private house a collection of property of such value – and portable property, too – as to offer a continual temptation to the criminal class. But he did; and what is more, he kept the whole lot of jewels in a set of mahogany cabinets that you could have opened with a pen-knife. It is astonishing that he went on so long without a burglary.

However, he got what he deserved at last. He had gone across to Paris, to buy some more of the stuff, I believe, when, some fine night, some cracksmen dropped in and did the job. It was perfectly simple. They just let themselves in, prised the drawers open with a jemmy, cleared them out and went off quietly with the whole collection. Nobody knew anything about it until the servants came down in the morning and found the drawers all gaping open.

"Then, of course, there was a rare philaloo. The police were called in and our people made a careful inspection of the premises. But it had been such an easy job that anybody might have done it. There was nothing that was characteristic of any known burglar. But, on taking impression of the jemmy-marks and a few other trifles, we were inclined to connect it with one or two other jobs of a similar type in which jewels had been taken. But we had not been able to fix those cases on any particular crooks, though we had a growing suspicion of two men who were also suspected of receiving. Of those two men, one was Jonathan Crabbe and the other was a man named Wingate. So we kept those two gentlemen under pretty close observation and made a few discreet inquiries. But it was a long time before we could get anything definite; and when, at last, we did manage to drop on Mr Crabbe, it was only on a charge of receiving. The Billington job still remained in the air. And that's where it is still."

"And what about Wingate?" asked Thorndyke.

"Oh, he disappeared. Apparently he rumbled the fact that he was getting a bit of attention from the police, and didn't like it. So he cut his connection with Crabbe and went away."

"And have you lost sight of him?" Thorndyke asked.

"Yes. You see, we never had anything against him but his association with Crabbe, and that may have been a perfectly innocent business connection. And our inquiries seemed to show that he belonged to quite a respectable family, and the man, himself, was of a decidedly superior type; a smart, dressy sort of fellow with a waxed moustache and an eye-glass. Quite a toff, in fact. The only thing about him that seemed at all fishy was the fact that he was using an assumed name. But there was not so very much even in that, for we ascertained that he had been on the stage for a time, and he had probably taken the name of Wingate in preference to his family name, which was rather an odd one – Deodatus Pettigrew."

"You never traced any of the proceeds of the robbery?" Thorndyke suggested.

"No. Of course, jewellery is often difficult to trace if the stones are taken out of their settings and the mounts melted down. But these jewels of Billington's ought to have been easier than most to trace, as a good many of them were quite unusual and could only have been disguised by re-cutting, which would have brought down their value a lot. And there was one that couldn't have been disguised at all. I remember the description of it quite well. It was rather a famous piece, known as the Jacobite Jewel. It consisted principally of a lump of black opal matrix with a fire opal in the centre, and on this fire opal was carved a portrait of the Old Pretender, who called himself James the Third. I believe there was quite a little history attached to it. But the whole collection was rather famous. Billington was particularly keen on opals and I believe that his collection of them was one of the finest known."

"Had you any inkling as to what had become of this loot?" Thorndyke asked. "The thieves could hardly have been able to afford to put the whole of it away into storage for an indefinite time."

"No." agreed Miller. "They would have had to get rid of the stuff somehow. We thought it just possible that there might be some collector behind the affair."

"But," I objected, "a collector would probably know all about the specimens in other collections and particularly a famous piece like this Jacobite Jewel. And he would be almost certain to have heard of the robbery. It would be a matter of special interest to him."

"Yes, I know," said Miller. "But collectors are queer people. Some of them are mighty unscrupulous. When a man has got the itch to possess, there is no saying what he will not do to gratify it. Some of the rich Americans who have made their fortunes by pretty sharp practice, are not above a little sharp practice in spending them. And your millionaire collector is dead keen on getting something that is unique; something of which he can say that it is the only one of its kind in the world. And if it has a history attached to it, so much the better. I shouldn't be at all surprised if that Jacobite Jewel had been smuggled out of the country together with the great collection of opals. It is even possible that Crabbe had negotiated the sale before the robbery was committed; but, of course, it is also possible that I may be mistaken and that Crabbe may have had nothing to do with the robbery. We are all liable to make mistakes."

Here the superintendent, having come to the end of his story, emptied his glass, relit his cigar and looked at his watch.

"Dear me!" he exclaimed, "how the time does go when you are enjoying intellectual conversation – especially if it is your own. It's time I made a move. No, thank you; not another drop. But, well, yes, I will take another of these excellent cigars. You have listened very attentively to my yarn, and I hope you have picked up something useful from my chatter."

"I always pick up something useful from your chatter, as you call it," replied Thorndyke, rising as the superintendent rose to depart; "but on this occasion you have given me quite a lot to think about."

He walked to the door with Miller and even escorted him out on to the landing; and meanwhile, I occupied myself in restraining, with exaggerated hospitality, a strong tendency on the part of our guest to rise and follow the superintendent. For I could not let him go until I had seen what Thorndyke's next move was to be.

The superintendent's narrative had given me a very curious experience, in respect of its effect on Lockhart. At first, he had listened with lively interest, probably comparing the Billington collection with that of Penrose. But presently be began to look distinctly uncomfortable and to steal furtive glances at Thorndyke and me. I kept him unobtrusively under observation, and Thorndyke, I know, was watching him narrowly, as though no one who did not know him would have suspected it, and we both observed the change of manner. But when Miller mentioned the Jacobite Jewel and went on to describe its appearance, the expression on Lockhart's face was unmistakable. It was that of a man who has suffered a severe shock.

Having seen the last of the superintendent, Thorndyke closed both doors and went back to his chair.

"That was a queer story of Miller's," he remarked, addressing Lockhart. "One does not often hear of a receiver including burglary in his accomplishments. I am disposed to think that Miller's surmise as to the destination of the swag from the Billington robbery is about correct. What do you think, Lockhart?"

"You mean," the latter replied, "that it was smuggled out of the country."

"No," said Thorndyke, "I don't mean that, Lockhart, and you know I don't. What I am suggesting is that the Billington opals, including the Jacobite Jewel, are, or were in Penrose's possession; that they were in the cupboard in the small room and that you saw them there."

Lockhart flushed hotly, but he kept his temper, replying with mild facetiousness:

"Now, you know, Thorndyke, it's no use for you to try the suggesting dodge on me. I am a practising barrister, and I have used it too often myself. I have told you that I gave an undertaking to

Penrose not to discuss his collection with anybody and I intend to honour that undertaking to the letter and in the spirit."

"Very well, Lockhart," Thorndyke rejoined, "we will leave it at that. Probably, I should adopt the same attitude if I was in your position, though I doubt if I should have given the undertaking. We will let the collection go, unless you would consider it admissible to discuss the source of some of the things in the big room, which we all saw. The question as to where he got some of those things has a direct bearing on the further question as to where he is lurking at the present moment."

"I don't see the connection," said Lockhart, "but if you do, that is all that matters. What is it that you want to know?"

"I should like to know," Thorndyke replied, "what his methods of collection are. Has he been in the habit of attending farmhouse auctions, or prowling about in labourers' cottages? Or did he get his pieces through regular dealers?"

"As to that," said Lockhart, "I can only tell you what he told me. He professed to have discovered many of his treasures in cottage parlours and in country inns and elsewhere, and to have practised on quite an extensive scale what he called 'resurrectionist activities,' but he was mighty secret about the actual localities. My impression is that his explorations were largely bunkum. I suspect that the bulk of his collection came from the dealers, and particularly from the antique shop that I mentioned to you. In fact, he almost admitted as much, for he told me that when his explorations drew a blank, he was accustomed to fall back on the Popinjay."

"The Popinjay?" I repeated.

"The proprietor of the antique shop was a man named Parrott, but I need not say that Penrose never referred to him by that name. He was always 'our psittacoid friend,' or 'Monsieur le Perroquet' or 'the Popinjay.' You will even find him referred to in those terms in the catalogue."

"That is useful to know," said Thorndyke. "I met with some entries containing the words, 'Psitt', 'Perro' and 'Pop' and could make nothing of them. Now I realise that they represented purchases from Mr Parrott. And there was an entry, 'Sweeney's resurrection.' That, I suppose, had a similar meaning. Do you know who Sweeney is?"

Lockhart laughed as he replied: "No I have never heard of him, though I remember the entry. The only thing that I feel sure of is that his name is not Sweeney. Possibly it is Todd; and he is probably a dealer in antiquities. The piece, I remember, is an Anglo-Saxon brooch; and we may guess that Mr Sweeney Todd got it from a Saxon burial ground in the course of some unauthorised excavations."

"That seems likely," said Thorndyke. "I must look up the list of dealers in antiquities in the directory and see if I can find out who he is."

"But does it matter who he is?" asked Lockhart. "If you are trying to discover the whereabouts of our elusive friend, I don't quite follow your methods."

"My dear Lockhart," Thorndyke replied, "my methods are of the utmost simplicity. I know practically nothing about Penrose, his habits and his customs, and I am out to pick up any items of information on the subject that I can gather, in the hope that some of them may prove to have some bearing on my quest. After all, it is only the ordinary legal method which you, yourself, are in the habit of practising."

"I suppose it is," Lockhart admitted. "But, fortunately for me, I have never had a problem of this kind to deal with. I can't imagine a more hopeless task than trying to find a very artful, secretive man who doesn't mean to be found."

At this moment, I heard the sound of a key being inserted in the outer door. Then the inner door opened and Polton entered with an apologetic crinkle.

"I have just looked in, sir," he announced, "to see if there is anything that you wanted before I go out. I shall be away about a couple of hours."

"Thank you, Polton," Thorndyke replied. "No, there is nothing that I shall want that I can't get for myself."

As Thorndyke spoke, Lockhart looked round quickly then stood up, holding out his hand.

"This is a very unexpected pleasure, Mr Polton," said he. "I didn't know that you were a denizen of the Temple; and I was afraid that I had lost sight of you for good, now that Parrott's is no more." He shook hands heartily with our ingenious friend and explained to us: "Mr Polton and I are quite old acquaintances. He, also, was a frequenter of Parrott's establishment, and the leading authority on clocks, watches, hallmarks and other recondite matters."

"You speak of Parrott's shop," said Thorndyke, "as a thing of the past. Is our psittacoid friend deceased, or has he gone out of business?"

"Parrott is still to the good, so far as I know," replied Lockhart, "but the business is defunct. I suspect that it was never more than half alive. Then poor Parrot had a double misfortune. Penrose, who was by far his best customer, disappeared; and then his cabinet-maker – a remarkably clever old man named Tims – died and could not be replaced. So there was no one left to do the restorations which were the mainstay of the business. I was sorry to find the shop closed when I came back from my travels on circuit. It was quite a loss, wasn't it, Mr Polton?"

"It was to me," replied Polton, regretfully. "Many a pleasant and profitable hour have I spent in the workshop. To a man who uses his hands, it was a liberal education to watch Mr Tims at work. I have never seen any man use wood-working tools as he did."

With this, Polton wished our guest "Good evening!" and took himself off. As the outer door closed, Lockhart asked:

"If it is not an impertinent question, what is Mr Polton's connection with this establishment? He has always been rather a mystery to me."

"He is rather a mystery to me," Thorndyke replied, with a laugh. "He says that he is my servant. I say that he is my faithful friend and Jervis'. Nominally, he is our laboratory assistant and artificer. Actually, since he can do or make anything and insists on doing everything that is to be done, he is a sort of universal fairy godmother to us both. And I can assure you that he is not unappreciated."

"I am glad to know that," said Lockhart. "We all – the frequenters of Parrott's, I mean – held him in the greatest respect, and none more so than Penrose."

"Oh, he knew Penrose, did he?" said I, suddenly enlightened as to Polton's interest in our conversations respecting the missing man. "He has never mentioned the fact."

"Perhaps you have never given him an opening," Lockhart suggested, not unreasonably. "But they were quite well acquainted; in fact, the very last time that I saw Penrose, he and Mr Polton were walking away from the shop together, carrying a lantern clock that Mr Polton had been restoring."

We continued for some time to discuss Polton's remarkable personality and his versatile gifts and abilities, in which Lockhart appeared to be deeply interested. At length the latter glanced at his watch and rose.

"I have made an unconscionably long visit," said he, as he prepared to depart; "but it is your fault for making the time pass so agreeably."

"You certainly have not outstayed your welcome," Thorndyke replied, "and I hope you will stay longer next time."

With this exchange of civilities, we escorted our guest out to the landing and, having wished him "Good night!" returned to our chambers to discuss the events of the evening.

CHAPTER ELEVEN

Re-Enter Mr Kickweed

When I had closed the door and drifted back towards my chair, I cast an expectant glance at Thorndyke; but as he maintained a placidly reflective air, and thoughtfully refilled his pipe in silence, I ventured to open the inevitable discussion.

"May I take it that my revered senior is satisfied with the evening's entertainment?"

"Eminently so," he replied; "in fact, considerably beyond my most sanguine expectations. We have made appreciable progress."

"In what direction?" I asked. "Does Miller's story throw any light on the case?"

"I think so," he answered. "What he told us, in conjunction with what Lockhart refused to tell us, seems to help us to this extent; that it appears to disclose a motive for the burglary, or the attempt."

"Do you mean that it establishes the probability that there was something there worth stealing and that somebody besides Penrose knew of it?"

"No," he replied, "though that also is true. But, what is in my mind is this: When Penrose disappeared, either for good or for some considerable time, there arose the probability that, sooner or later, the cupboard in the small room would be opened for inspection by Horridge or some other person claiming authority. But if that cupboard contained – as I have no doubt it did – a

116

quantity of stolen property, the identifiable proceeds of a known robbery, a very awkward situation would be created."

"Yes," I agreed, "it would be awkward for Penrose when Miller caught the scent. There would be a hue and cry with a vengeance. And it might be unpleasant for Mr Crabbe if any connection could be traced between him and Penrose. I suppose there can be no doubt that the stuff was really there?"

"It is only an inference," Thorndyke replied, "but I am convinced that the Billington jewels were in that cupboard and that Lockhart saw them there. Everything points to that conclusion. You saw how intensely uncomfortable Lockhart looked when Miller described the stolen jewels; and you must have noticed that he was perfectly willing to discuss the general collection. From which we may reasonably infer that his promise of secrecy referred only to the contents of the small room. Besides, if the stolen jewels had not been there, or he had not seen them, he would certainly have said so when I challenged him. The denial would have been no breach of his promise."

"No," I agreed, "I think you are right in assuming that he saw them, though how Penrose could have been such an idiot as to show them at all is beyond my comprehension – that is if he knew that they were stolen goods, which I gather is your opinion."

"It is not by any means certain that he did," said Thorndyke. "Evidently he is quite ignorant of the things that he collects. The promise may have been only a manifestation of his habitual secrecy, accentuated by the knowledge that he had acquired the jewels from some rather shady dealer. The evidence seems a little contradictory."

"At any rate," said I, "it was a lucky chance that Miller happened to drop in this evening. Or wasn't it a chance at all? There was just a suspicion of arrangement in the way things fell out. Did you know that Miller would select this evening for his call?"

"In effect, I may say that I did. I had good reason to believe that he would call this evening, and, as you suggest, I made my arrangements accordingly. But those arrangements did not work out according to plan, for I knew nothing of the Billington robbery. Miller's disclosure was a windfall and it made the rest of my plan unnecessary."

"Then what had you proposed to do?"

"My intention was," Thorndyke replied, "to demonstrate to Lockhart that there had been transactions between Crabbe and Penrose. Of course, I could have done this without Miller's help, but I thought that if he heard of Crabbe's misdeeds from a police officer he would be more impressed and, therefore, more amenable to questions. But, as I said, Miller's story did all that was necessary."

"Then," said I, "there was a connection between Crabbe and Penrose, and that connection was known to you. How did you find that out? And, by the way, how did you come by your knowledge of Mr Crabbe? I had never heard of him until you mentioned his name."

Thorndyke chuckled in his exasperating way. "My learned friend is forgetting," said he. "Are we not decipherers of crossword puzzles and interpreters of dark sayings?"

""I am not," said I, "So you may as well come straight to the point."

"You have not forgotten the scrap of paper with the cryptic inscription which was found in the small room?"

"Ha!" I exclaimed, suddenly recalling the ridiculous inscription, "I begin, as Miller would say to 'rumble you.' But not very completely. The inscription read: 'Lobster (*Hortus petasatus*.)' But I still don't see how you arrived at it. Crabs are not the only crustaceans – besides lobsters."

"Very true, Jervis," said he. "Lobster ambiguous as to its possible alternatives. Evidently, the more specific character was contained in the other term, '*hortus petasatus.*' Now, the learned Dr Smith translates *petasatus* as 'wearing, or having on, a travelling-cap; ready for a journey.' But the word *petasus* means either a cap or a hat, so the adjective, *petasatus*, may be rendered as 'hatted' or 'having a hat on.' "

"Yes, I see," said I, with a sour grin. "So *hortus petasatus* would be a hat-on garden. But what puerile balderdash it is. That man, Penrose, ought to be certified.

"Still," said Thorndyke, "you see that it was worth while to study his jargon, for, when I had deciphered the inscription so far, the rest of the inquiry was perfectly simple. I looked up Hatton Garden in the directory and ran through the names of occupants in search of one that seemed related to the term 'lobster.' Among them I found the name of Jonathan Crabbe (the only one, in fact, who answered the description); and, as he was described as a diamond broker and dealer in precious stones, I decided that he was probably the man referred to by Penrose. Accordingly, I paid a visit to Hatton Garden and made a few discreet inquiries, which elicited the fact that Mr Crabbe was absent from his premises and was in some sort of trouble in connection with a charge of receiving. Whereupon I made arrangements to give Lockhart a shock."

"And very completely you succeeded," said I. "He is in a deuce of a twitter, and well he may be, knowing quite well that he is making himself an accessory after the fact."

"Yes," Thorndyke agreed, "he is in a very unpleasant dilemma. But I don't think we can interfere, at least for the present. He is a lawyer and knows exactly what his position is, and, meanwhile, his reticence suits us well enough. I don't want a premature hue and cry raised."

Here the discussion appeared to have petered out; but it seemed that the evening's experiences were not yet finished for, in the silence which followed Thorndyke's rejoinder, there came to my ear the sound of soft and rather stealthy footsteps ascending the stairs, and at the same moment I suddenly remembered that I had not shut the outer door when we came in after seeing Lockhart off.

The steps continued slowly to ascend. Then they crossed the landing and paused opposite our door. There was a brief interval followed by a very elaborate flourish, softly and skilfully executed, on the little brass knocker of the inner door, very much in the style of the old-fashioned footman's knock. I rose, and, striding across the room, threw open the door, when my astonished gaze encountered no less a person that Mr Kickweed. He broke out at once into profuse apologies for disturbing us at so untimely an hour. "But," he explained, "the matter seemed to me of some importance, and I thought it best not to call in the daytime in case you might not wish my visit to become known."

This sounded rather mysterious, so, in accordance with his hint, I closed both the doors before ushering him across the room to the chair lately vacated by Mr Miller.

"You needn't be apologetic, Mr Kickweed," said Thorndyke, as he shook his visitor's hand. "It is very good of you to turn out at night to come and see us. Sit down and mix yourself a whisky and soda. Will you light a cigar as an aid to business discussion?"

Kickweed declined the refreshments but was obviously gratified by the manner of his reception; and, having expressed his thanks, he came at once to the object of his visit.

"I am the bearer of news, sir, which I think you will be glad to hear. I have received a letter from Mr Penrose."

There did not, to me, appear to be anything particularly surprising in this statement. But it was evidently otherwise with Thorndyke, for he received the announcement with more astonishment that I had ever known him to show; though, even so, it needed my expert and accustomed eye to detect his surprise.

"When did you receive the letter? he asked.

"It came by the first post this morning," Kickweed replied. "I thought you would like to know about it, and, perhaps, like to see it, so I have brought it along for your inspection."

He produced from his pocket a bulging letter-case from which he extracted a letter in its envelope and handed it to Thorndyke, who took out the letter, opened it and read it through. When he had finished the reading, he proceeded, according to his invariable custom when dealing with strange letters, to scrutinise its various parts, especially the signature and the date, to examine the paper, holding it up to the light, and, finally, to make a minute inspection of the envelope.

"The letter, I see," said he, "is dated with yesterday's date but gives no address; but the postmark is Canterbury and is dated yesterday afternoon. Do you suppose Mr Penrose is staying at Canterbury?"

"Well, no sir," replied Kickweed, "I do not, though he used rather frequently to stay there. But, from my knowledge of Mr Penrose, I don't think he would have posted the letter in the town where he was staying. Still, he can hardly be far away from there. I think he knows that neighbourhood rather well."

"Does anyone else know about this letter?"

"No, sir. I took it from the letter-box myself, and I have not spoken of it to anybody."

"I think," said Thorndyke, "that Mr Brodribb ought to be told. In fact I think that the letter ought – with your consent – to be handed to him for safe keeping. You probably realise that it may become of considerable legal importance."

"Yes, sir, I realise that and that it ought to be taken great care of. What I proposed was to hand it to you, if you will take custody of it. Of course, you will dispose of it as you think best, but I brought it to you because you seemed to take a more sympathetic view of poor Mr Penrose than anyone else has done. And I may say, sir, that I should be more happy if you would keep it in your possession for the present. I shouldn't like it to be used to help the police to worry Mr Penrose by searching in his neighbourhood."

"Very well, Mr Kickweed," said Thorndyke. I will keep the letter for the present on the understanding that it shall be produced only if circumstances should arise which would make its production necessary in the interests of justice. Do you agree to that?"

"Oh, certainly, sir," replied Kickweed. "You will, of course make any use of it that you think proper and necessary, other than the one I mentioned."

"You may take it," said Thorndyke, "that no attempt will be made by me, or with my connivance, to harass Mr Penrose and that you may safely leave the letter in my custody. And I may say that I am greatly obliged to you for letting me have it and for having taken the trouble to report the matter to me."

Kickweed mildly deprecated these acknowledgements, and Thorndyke continued: "On reading this letter I am struck by certain peculiarities on which I should like to hear your opinion. It is a rather odd letter."

"It is," Kickweed admitted, "but then you know, sir, Mr Penrose is a rather odd man, if I may venture to say so.

Here Thorndyke handed me the document and I rapidly read it through. It was certainly a very odd letter. Secretly, I pronounced it the letter of a born fool or a lunatic, but I made no audible comments. Its precious contents were as follows:

"26th March, 1935.

"CERASTIUM VULGATUM, ESQ.

"RESPECTED CER,

"These presents are to inform you that, some time after my departure from Her Deceased Majesty's Equilateral Rectangle, I dish-covered that the key of the small room was not in my pocket. Thereupon I reflected, and after profound cogitation decided that it must be somewhere else. Peradventure, when I sarahed forth on that infelicitous occasion, I may have left it in the door, where it may have presented itself to your penetrating vision and been taken into protective custardy. This is my surmise; and if I have reason and you are now seised or possessed of the said key, I will ask you to convey the same to my bank and deliver it into the hand of the manager, in my name, to have and to hold until such time as I shall demand it from him. But first, fasten the window and lock the door. The room contains nothing but a few unconsidered trifles of merely scentimental value, but I wish it to remain undisturbed until I shall return carrying my sheaves and ready to do justice to the obese calf.

"Hoping that you are in your usual boisterous spirits,

"Yours in saecula saeculorum,

"DANIEL PENROSE."

"You will agree with me, Jervis," said Thorndyke, when I returned the document, "that this is a very odd letter?"

I agreed with him in the most emphatic and unmistakable terms.

"We are all, by now," he continued, "accustomed to Mr Penrose's oddities of speech. But this seems to go rather beyond even his usual eccentricity. What do you think, Mr Kickweed?"

"I am disposed to think you are right, sir," replied Kickweed a little to my surprise; for the letter contained just the sort of twaddle that I should have expected from Penrose.

"I think," said Thorndyke, "that you mentioned, when we last met, having noticed a gradual change in Mr Penrose; a growing tendency to oddity and obscurity of speech."

"I think I did say," replied Kickweed, "that the habit of jocularity had been growing and becoming more confirmed. But habits usually do tend to grow and I don't know that he was changed in any other respect. And as to this letter, we must bear the circumstances in mind. He is probably very much upset and he may have been a little more facetious than usual by way of keeping up his spirits."

"Yes," said Thorndyke, "that has to be considered. But a tendency to increasing eccentricity is a very significant thing, especially in the case of a man who has rather unaccountably disappeared. Any recent change in Mr Penrose's mental condition might have an important bearing on his recent conduct, and I am inclined to believe that there has been some such change. Now, take this letter. Is it the kind of letter that you have been in the habit of receiving from him?"

"Well, no, sir," Kickweed admitted. "He did not often have occasion to write to me, and when he did, his letters were usually quite short and to the point. They were not written in a jocular vein."

"In this letter," Thorndyke continued, "he addresses you by the style and title of Cerastium Vulgatum, Esq. Has he ever done that before?"

"No, sir; and it doesn't convey much to me now."

"*Cerastium vulgatum*," said Thorndyke, "is the botanical name of the common chickweed."

"Oh, indeed," said Kickweed, with a sad and rather disapproving smile. "I supposed it was some kind of a joke but I did not connect it with my somewhat unfortunate name."

"Has Mr Penrose ever before made any kind of joke on your surname?" Thorndyke asked.

"No, sir," Kickweed replied, promptly and emphatically. "Mr Penrose has his oddities, but he is a gentleman, and in all his dealings with me he has always been scrupulously correct and courteous. I am almost disposed to think that you may be right, sir, after all, in believing that his troubles have affected his mind."

Evidently, the botanical joke had produced a profoundly unfavourable impression.

"By the way," said Thorndyke, "have you delivered the key to the bank manager?"

"Not yet," replied Kickweed. "Of course, I must carry out Mr Penrose's instructions, but I don't at all like the idea of having a locked room – possibly containing valuable property – with no means of access in case of an emergency."

"No," said Thorndyke, "it is a bad and unsafe arrangement. I suppose you have kept the key in your own possession?"

"Always," was the reply, "excepting on one occasion when I let Mr Horridge have it for a few minutes to examine the window of the room. I was just going out to post a letter when he asked for it, and he gave it back to me when I returned from the post."

"I certainly think," said Thorndyke, "that you ought to have the means of access to that room. Do you happen to have the key about you?"

By way of reply, Kickweed thrust his fingers into his waistcoat pocket and withdrew them holding a key, which he held out to Thorndyke, who took it from him and inspected it.

"An extraordinarily simple key," he remarked, "for the lock of so important a room. It looks very like the key of my office cupboard. Would you mind if I tried it in the lock?"

"Not in the least," replied Kickweed; whereupon Thorndyke bore the key away to the office, the door of which he closed after him; a proceeding that somehow associated itself in my mind with the idea of moulding wax. In a couple of minutes he returned, and, handing the key back to Kickweed, announced:

"It fits the lock quite fairly; which is not surprising as it is of quite a common pattern. But it is a fortunate circumstance, for now, if the need should arise, I could supply you with a key that would open the small room door."

"That is very kind of you, sir," said Kickweed, "and I will bear your offer in mind. And now I mustn't detain you any longer. It is exceedingly good of you to have given me so much of your time."

With this he rose, and once more declining our offer of refreshment, took up his hat and stick and was duly escorted out on to the landing. When he had gone, and we were once more within closed doors, I delivered myself of a matter that had rather puzzled me.

"There seems to be something a little queer about that key. You haven't forgotten that Horridge had it – or a duplicate – in his possession when he showed us the small room?"

"I remember that he had a key," replied Thorndyke; "and the feeble and clumsy efforts that he made to keep it out of sight made me suspect that it was a duplicate. Now we know that it was.

"I presume that you took a squeeze of Kickweed's key?"

"Yes," he replied, "and I shall ask Polton to make a key from the pattern. If it is good enough for Horridge to have a duplicate, it is good enough for us to have one, too."

"Why do you suppose Horridge had his made?"

"It is difficult to say. Horridge, as you observed is convinced that the mysterious cupboard contains something of enormous value – which it undoubtedly did at one time, and may still – and he is highly suspicious of Kickweed. He may want to try the cupboard lock at his leisure, or he may simply want to see that Kickweed does not. I doubt whether he has any very definite purpose."

"You seem," said I, "to be pretty confident that the Billington jewels were in that cupboard and that they are not there now. Have you formed an opinion as to who the burglar was?"

"We haven't much to go on," he replied. "We know that Crabbe could not have been the man, as he was in prison when the burglary occurred; and we know – or may fairly assume – that the Chubb key was in Penrose's possession. Those are all the facts that we have, and they lead to no certain conclusion. But now we have another problem to consider."

"You mean that idiot Penrose's letter. But what is its importance, apart from the internal evidence that the writer is certainly a fool and possibly a lunatic?"

"That is precisely what we have to discover. How important is it? Perhaps we had better begin with the obituary columns of *The Times*."

We did not keep a complete file of *The Times* on account of its enormous bulk, but it was our custom to retain our copies for three months, which usually answered our purpose. And it did on this occasion; for on opening the file and scanning the obituary columns, we presently came upon a notice announcing that Oliver Penrose passed away peacefully in his sleep on the 16th of March, a few days before his ninetieth birthday.

"There," said Thorndyke, carefully replacing the papers and closing the file, "you have the answer to our question. Penrose's letter is dated – and was posted – ten days after his father's death.

That is a fact of cardinal importance. It anticipates any possible question of survivorship. If Penrose should never be heard of again; if he should die and neither the time nor the place of his death should ever be known, this letter could be produced as decisive proof that he was alive ten days after his father's death. Its immediate effect is to enable Brodribb to deal with Oliver's estate. If there is a will, it can be proved and administered; if there is no will, the intestacy proceedings can be set going."

"Yes," I said, "it is a mighty important letter in spite of its ridiculous contents, and its arrival will be hailed with profound relief by Brodribb. But it is a remarkably opportune letter, too. Doesn't it strike you as rather singularly opportune?"

"It does," he replied. "That is what immediately impresses one. So much so that one asks oneself whether its arrival can be no more than a coincidence."

"To me," said I, "it suggests that Penrose is not such a fool as his letter would imply. He has been keeping his eye on obituary columns of *The Times,* and, when he read the notice of the old gentleman's death, he made a pretext to write to Kickweed and thus put it on record that he was alive. That is how it strikes me. And that view is supported by the letter, itself. It was a perfectly unnecessary letter. Kickweed had had the key for months and there was no reason why he should not have continued to keep it, and every reason why he should. It looks as if the key had been a mere pretext for writing a letter. Don't you agree with me?"

"I do," he replied, "so far as the character of the letter is concerned. But we have to remember that when Penrose went away, his father was quite well, so that there was no need for him to watch the obituary columns. However, this is all rather speculative. The material fact is that the letter has arrived, and that fact will have to be communicated to Brodribb. I shall take the letter round and show it to him tomorrow morning."

CHAPTER TWELVE

Mr Elmhurst

Between Thorndyke and me there existed a rather queer convention, which the reader of this narrative may have noticed. In the cases on which we worked together, he was always most scrupulous in keeping me informed as to the facts, and making me, if possible, a partner in the investigation by which they were ascertained. But he expected me to make my own inferences. Any attempt of mine to elicit from him a statement of opinion, or of his interpretation of the facts that were known to us both, met with the inevitable response: "My dear fellow, you know as much about the case as I do, and you have only to make use of your excellent reasoning faculties to extract the significance of what is known to us." The convention had been established when I first joined Thorndyke as his partner or understudy, as part of my training in the art and science of medico-legal investigation. But, apparently, my education was to continue indefinitely, for Thorndyke's attitude continued unchanged. He would tell me everything that he knew, but he was uncommunicative, even to secretiveness as to what he thought.

But a habit of secretiveness sets up certain natural reactions. If Thorndyke would not tell me what he thought, it was admissible for me to find out, if I could; and I occasionally got quite a useful hint by observing the books that he was reading. For, unlike most lawyers, he dealt comparatively little in legal literature. His peculiar type of practice demanded a wide range of knowledge other than legal; and frequently it happened that his knowledge required amplification on some particular point. But, by observing the direction in which he was seeking to enlarge his knowledge, I was able, at least, to judge which of the facts seemed to him the most significant.

Now, I had noticed, of late, the appearance in our chambers of a number of books on prehistoric archaeology, a subject in which, so far as I knew, Thorndyke was not specially interested. There was, for instance, Jessup's *Archaeology of Kent*, into which I dipped lightly; and there was a copy of the *Archaeological Journal*, containing a paper by Stuart Piggott on the Neolithic Pottery of the British Isles." In this a slip of paper had been inserted as a book-mark, and, on opening it, I found that it was marked at the section headed "Pottery of the Windmill Hill Type," and opposite, a page of drawings representing the characteristic forms of vessels and their decorative markings. And there were others of different characters, but all agreeing in giving descriptions and illustrations of Neolithic pottery.

From these facts it was evident to me that Thorndyke's attention was still occupied by the ridiculous fragment of pottery that we had found in the pocket of Penrose's raincoat, and the object of his researches was, I had no doubt, the discovery of some likely place from which that fragment might have come. But why he wished to discover that place or what light it would throw, if found, on the present whereabouts of Daniel Penrose, I was utterly unable to imagine. That the question was one of importance I did not doubt for a moment. Thorndyke was not in the least addicted to the finding of mare's nests or the pursuit of that interesting phenomenon, the will-o'-the-wisp. He wanted to discover the place which had been the starting-point of that wild journey in the motor car. Therefore, the identity of that place had some profound significance; and for several days I continued, at intervals, to cudgel my brains in a vain effort to reason out its bearing on our quest.

About a week after the receipt of the mysterious letter from Mr Penrose, our inquiry entered on a new stage. Hitherto, Thorndyke's attitude had been mainly that of a passive observer. The visit to Queen Square, the examination of the coat and the pottery fragment, and the unearthing of Mr Crabbe were the only instances of anything like active investigation. Otherwise, he had listened to the reports from Brodribb, Miller and Lockhart, and, while he had, no doubt, turned them over thoroughly in his mind, had made no positive move. But now he showed signs of a kind of activity which I associated, by the light of experience, with a definite objective.

I became aware of the change when, on a certain evening, coming home after a long day's work, I found a visitor seated by the fire, apparently in close consultation with Thorndyke. A glance at the little table with the decanter, wine glasses and box of cigars told me that he was certainly a welcome and probably an invited guest; and a sheet of the six-inch ordnance map, on which lay the pottery fragment, hinted at the nature of the consultation.

The visitor, who rose as I entered, was a young man of grave and studious aspect, whose face – adorned with an impressive pair of tortoise-shell rimmed spectacles – seemed familiar, but yet I could not place him until Thorndyke came to my aid.

"You haven't forgotten Mr Elmhurst, surely, Jervis?" said he.

"Of course, I haven't," I replied, as we shook hands. "You are the dene-hole gentleman and the discoverer of headless corpses."

Mr Elmhurst did not repudiate the dene-hole, but protested that he had not actually made a habit of discovering headless corpses, at least in the recent state. "The corpses that come my way," he explained, "are usually prehistoric corpses, in which the presence or absence of the head is of no special significance."

"In short," said Thorndyke, "Mr Elmhurst is an archaeologist who is kindly allowing us to benefit by his special knowledge, as we did in the case of the dene-hole."

"That," said Elmhurst, "is very nicely put, but it gives me undeserved credit. I am not an altruist at all. I am agreeing to do something that I have long wanted to do, but have been deterred by the cost. But now Dr Thorndyke wants this thing done and is prepared to bear the expense, or at least part of it. You see, it is a case of enlightened self-interest on both sides."

"And what is this job?" I asked. "Something in the resurrection line, I suspect."

"Yes," said Elmhurst, "it is an excavation. The doctor has here a fragment of what seems to have been a Neolithic pot of the Windmill Hill type, as it is usually described. He thinks it possible that this fragment was found in a certain long barrow in Kent. I don't know why he thinks so, but it is not improbable that he is right. At any rate, if that barrow contains any pottery, it is pretty certain to be of this type."

"That doesn't carry you very far," said I. "Supposing you found some pottery of this kind in the barrow, would that enable you to say that this fragment must have come from that barrow?"

"No," he replied. "It would only enable one to say that this fragment was of the same type as that found in the barrow."

"But you know that already," said I.

"Believe," Elmhurst corrected.

"You said it was pretty certain to be of this type; and if you would repeat that on oath in the witness-box, I should think it would be sufficient. The excavation seems to be unnecessary."

"Oh, don't say that!" exclaimed Elmhurst. "You would degrade me from the rank of an investigator to that of a mere expert witness."

"My learned friend," said Thorndyke, "in spite of his great experience in court, seems to fail to appreciate the vast difference, in their effects on a jury, between an expert opinion – and a qualified one at that – and a pair of exhibits which the expert can declare, and the jury can see for themselves, are identically similar."

"Still," I persisted, "even if you could prove them to be identically similar, that would not be evidence that they came from the same barrow. You admit that, Elmhurst?"

"I admit nothing," he replied. "You know more about evidence than I do. But Dr Thorndyke wants that barrow excavated and I want to do the excavation. And I may say that all the necessary preliminaries have been arranged. As the barrow is scheduled as an Ancient Monument, I have had to apply for, and have been granted by the Office of Works, a permit authorising me to excavate and examine the interior of the tumulus situated by the river Stour near Chilham in Kent and commonly known as Julliberrie's Grave."

"Whose grave?" I demanded with suddenly-aroused interest; for as he pronounced the name there flashed instantly into my mind the words of Penrose's ridiculous entry: "Moulin-à-vent; Julie: Polly."

Elmhurst cast a quick, inquisitive glance at me and then proceeded to explain:

"Julliberrie's. There is a local tradition that the mound is the burial-place of a more-or-less mythical person named Jul Laber, or Julaber, said to have been either a witch or a giant. If he was a giant we may be able to confirm that tradition, but I am afraid that a witch – in the fossil state – would defy diagnosis."

"And has this mound never been excavated, so far as you know?" I asked.

"It was excavated tentatively," he replied, "in 1702 by Heneage Finch, whose report is extant; but it appears that nothing was found beyond a few animal bones. Then an aerial photograph, taken only a week or two ago, shows signs of some more recent disturbance of the surface. Apparently someone has been doing a little unauthorised digging, which may account for this fragment of the doctor's. But still, we hope to find the burial chamber intact."

I reflected on the possible means by which Thorndyke had managed to locate this barrow and once more speculated on his inexplicable interest in this locality. And then suddenly I recalled Penrose's mysterious letter and the postmark on it.

132

"You say," said I, "that this mound is near Chilham. Isn't that somewhere in the Canterbury district?"

"Yes," he replied. "Quite near. Not more than half a dozen miles from Canterbury."

This began to be a little more understandable, though I was still unable to make out exactly what was in Thorndyke's mind. But I now had something like a clue which I could consider at my leisure; and meanwhile I returned to the subject of the excavation.

"I gather," said I, "that you are practically ready to begin operations. Is the date of the expedition fixed?"

"That is what we were discussing when you came in," replied Elmhurst. "Of course, there is no need for the doctor or you to attend the function. I can let you know if any pottery is found, and produce it for your inspection. But I hope you will both be able to come at least once while the work is in progress. One doesn't often get the chance of seeing a complete excavation of a virtually intact long barrow. If you can only make one visit, I would recommend you to wait until we are ready to expose the burial chamber. That is the most thrilling moment."

"It sounds like quite a big job," I remarked. "How long do you think it will take?"

"I should say from three to four weeks," he replied.

"My word!" I exclaimed. "Four weeks! Why, it will cost a small fortune. Of course, you will have to employ a gang of labourers."

"We shall want five men," said he, "in addition to the volunteers, and I reckon that sixty pounds will cover it easily."

I whistled. "I suspect, Thorndyke," said I, "that you will have to find that sixty pounds yourself. You won't get Brodribb to include archaeological researches in the costs. But do you tell me, Elmhurst, that this colossal work is necessary just to find out what sort of pottery there is in the barrow?"

"Perhaps not," he replied. "But, you see, the position is this: Julliberrie's Grave is scheduled as an Ancient Monument. No one may − lawfully − disturb it without a permit from the Office of Works. Now, they are perfectly willing to grant a permit to genuine archaeologists who are known to them as such, but subject to very rigorous conditions. They won't grant permits for mere casual digging. Their conditions are that, if you want to excavate, you must excavate completely and exhaustively so that the mound need never be touched again. All finds must be preserved and labelled and a detailed account of the excavation must be published; and when the work is finished, the barrow must be restored completely to its original condition. I explained all this to the doctor."

I must confess that I was staggered. The means seemed to be so disproportionate to the end. But Thorndyke seemed quite satisfied to pay sixty pounds for a few specimens of pottery and Elmhurst made no secret of his unholy joy at the prospect of a first-class "dig".

"Are you proposing to take part in this super-resurrection, Thorndyke?" I asked sourly.

"I am not proposing to join the diggers," he replied, "but I shall take the opportunity to see how a thorough excavation is done. I want to see the burial chamber opened, but I am also rather curious to see how the work is begun, and what the barrow looks like when the turf is removed and the mound exposed as it appeared when it was newly made. When do you reckon that you will have the barrow uncovered?"

"I expect," Elmhurst replied, "that we shall begin skinning off the turf on Thursday. We start operations, as I told you, on Tuesday morning, and there will be a full two days' work on the preliminaries – pegging out the site, putting up an enclosing fence and preparing the dumps. I think, if you come down on Thursday – not too early – I can promise you that you will see the barrow as its builders saw it. I could, if you liked, meet you at Maidstone or Canterbury and personally conduct you to the scene of the operations."

"That isn't necessary," said Thorndyke. "We have the map, and you will want to be early at work. Moreover, I think I shall take the opportunity to do some prospecting on my way and I may be a little late in arriving at the barrow."

"That will be all to the good," said Elmhurst. "The later you arrive the more we shall have ready to show you."

This brought the discussion on ways and means to an end; and shortly afterwards our guest, having a train to catch, rose and took his leave.

During the week that intervened, very little was said either by Thorndyke or me on the subject of the expedition. Not that I was not keenly interested; for Thorndyke's reference to his "prospecting" intentions made it clear to me that he had something in his mind beyond the mere search for pottery. It seemed that now, for the first time, he was going to take some active measures to locate the elusive Penrose. But I asked no questions. I was going to take part in the prospecting operations and I hoped that their nature would throw some light on the methods by which Thorndyke proposed to attempt what looked like an impossibility.

One discovery I made, however; which was that Polton had in some way managed to attach himself to the expeditionary force. The fact was revealed to me when I found him in the act of pasting a couple of sheets of the six-inch ordnance map on thin mounting board. Observing that one of them included Chilham and our tumulus on Julliberrie Downs, I ventured to make inquiries.

"Why are you mounting them, Polton?" I asked. "You are not proposing to frame them and hang them on the wall?"

"No, sir," he replied. "When they are dry, I am going to cut them up into sections nine inches by six, that is four sections to a sheet. Then I shall number them and make a case to carry them in. You see, sir, a map is awkward to carry, even if you fold it, and most inconvenient to use out of doors, if there is any wind. But by this method you can just take out the one or two sections that you are using, and the whole lot will go easily into my poacher's pocket, or the doctor's either, for that matter. I'm getting them ready for our little trip next Thursday."

"Oh!" said I, "you are coming with us, are you?"

"Yes, sir," he replied, with a complacent crinkle. "The doctor mentioned to me that he was going down into Kent on some sort of exploring job, so I persuaded him to let me come and lend a hand. I understood him to say that they were going to dig up that old grave that is marked on the map – Jullieberrie's Grave."

"That is quite correct, Polton," I assured him.

"Ah!" said he, with a crinkle of ghoulish satisfaction. "That will be very interesting. Do you happen to know when the party was buried?"

"I understand," I replied, "that the burial took place at some time from four to ten thousand years ago."

"Good gracious!" exclaimed Polton. "Ten thousand years! Well, well! I should have thought that if he has been there as long as that they might have let him stay there. There can't be much of him left.

"That is what we are going to find out," said I; and with this I retired, leaving him to his pasting and his reflections.

CHAPTER THIRTEEN

The Track of the Fugitive

In the course of my long association with Thorndyke, I had often been impressed by the number of things that he appeared to carry in his pockets. He reminded me somewhat of The White Knight. But there was this essential difference; that whereas that unstable equestrian was visibly encumbered with a raffle of things that he could never possibly want, Thorndyke was invisibly provided with the things that he did want. If the need arose for an instrument, appliance or material, forthwith the desiderated object was produced from his pocket even as the parlour magician produces the required guinea-pig or goldfish. So, after all, the appearances may have been illusory; they may have been due, not to the gross quantity of things carried, but to an accurate prevision of the probable requirements.

The matter is recalled to my mind by the astonishing stowage capacity that Polton developed on the morning of our expedition to Chilham. Not only did the special outfit for the day's work – six-inch map, one-inch map, prismatic compass, telescope, surveyor's tape and other oddments, laid out for Thorndyke's inspection – vanish into unsuspected pockets, leaving no trace, but, as appeared later, his lading included a substantial meal, a big flask of sherry and a nest of aluminium drinking cups. And even then he didn't bulge perceptibly.

Of the details of our travels on that day I have but a confused recollection. It was all very well for Thorndyke, who had apparently transferred the six-inch map bodily to his consciousness; he knew exactly where he was at any given moment. But to me, when once we had left the plain high road, all sense of direction was lost and I was aware only of a bewildering succession of abominably steep lanes, cart-tracks and footpaths, which we scrambled up or stumbled down until we became finally and hopelessly submerged in a wood.

However, I will make an effort to give an intelligible account of this "prospecting" expedition, with apologies in advance for the somewhat nebulous topography. From Charing Cross we proceeded uneventfully to Ashford, where we got out of the train and took our places in a motor omnibus which was lurking in the vicinity and which was bound for Canterbury. Apparently it had been awaiting the arrival of the train, for as soon as we and one or two other train passengers had settled ourselves, the conductor, having taken a last fond look at the station, gave the signal to the driver, who thereupon started the vehicle with a triumphant hoot.

We rumbled along the main road for about six miles (as I afterwards ascertained) and then, shortly after crossing a small river, drew up at a village which the conductor announced as Godmersham. Here we got out and walked forward until we came to the cross-roads beyond the village, where Thorndyke turned to the right and led the way along the by-road. Presently we passed under a railway line and then, as the road made a sharp turn to the right, followed it along the bottom of a valley nearly parallel to the railway. About half a mile farther on, another by-road led off to the left, and, as Thorndyke turned off into it, my sense of direction began to get somewhat confused. It was quite a good road and fairly level, but its windings made it difficult to keep a "dead reckoning," and when, half a mile along it, yet another by-road led off from it to the left at right angles – into which Thorndyke turned confidently – and then made a right-angle turn to the right, I abandoned all attempts to keep count of our direction.

Along this road we trudged for three-quarters of a mile, still keeping fairly on the level, but then the ground began to rise sharply and the road zigzagged more than ever. A mile or so farther on we passed through a village, and I found myself casting a slightly wistful glance at a couple of rustics who were seated on a bench outside the inn, sustaining themselves with beer and conversation. But Thorndyke plodded on relentlessly, and when, a few hundred yards beyond the village, we came to yet another cross-roads, he finished me off by taking the turning to the left.

"I suppose, Thorndyke," said I, when we had toiled up this road for about half a mile and he halted to look around, "you know where you are."

"Oh, yes," he replied. "That village that we passed through just now is Sole Street. I will show you on the map where we are. Let us have the six-inch, Polton."

The latter dived into the interior of his clothing, whence he produced the case of mounted sections and handed it to his principal.

"Here we are," said Thorndyke, when he had picked out the appropriate card. "That is the village at the bottom and this is the road we are on. You see that it peters out, more or less, when it enters the wood."

I compared the section of map with the visible objects and was able to identify a farm-house across the fields on our right and a considerable wood which we were approaching.

"Yes," I said, "it is clear enough so far, though it doesn't mean much to me. What is the significance of that pencilled cross by the roadside?"

"That," he replied, "marks the spot, as nearly as I could locate it from the evidence at the inquest, where the old woman was killed."

"Indeed!" I exclaimed. "So this is where the chapter of accidents began, or, at least, a few yards farther up. Then I may assume that the purpose of this prospecting expedition is to trace the route of Penrose's car?"

"That is so," he admitted; "and presently we must begin to look for traces. At the moment, we don't need them, as there seems to be no doubt that the car came down this road. It was seen – or, at least, *a* car was seen – to come flying round the corner into the village and past the inn. Of course, it may not have been Penrose's car. But the time, the outrageous speed and the wild manner in which it was being driven, all seem to connect it with the disaster."

"But," I objected, "even if it *was* the car that killed the woman, that is no evidence that it was Penrose's car. It seems to me that the argument against Penrose moves in a circle, Penrose is proved to have killed the old woman by the fact that he was on the road where she was killed; and he is proved to have been on that road by the fact that he killed the old woman. I respectfully suggest that my learned senior may possibly be tracing, laboriously and with characteristic skill, the movements of a motor car in which we are not interested at all."

Thorndyke chuckled appreciatively. "Admirably argued, Jervis; and the point that you make is clearly realised by the police. There is very little doubt that it was Penrose's car, but there is no positive evidence that it was. And the police know, and we know, that you can't secure a conviction on mere probabilities. That is a further purpose of the prospecting expedition; not only to ascertain which way, and from whence, the car was travelling, but also, if possible, to establish what car it was."

As we continued to toil upward towards the wood, I cogitated on this statement with considerable surprise. It seemed inconsistent with what I had supposed to be Thorndyke's object and especially with his assurance to Kickweed that no action was contemplated which might compromise Penrose or menace his safety. Yet, here he was, by his own admission, industriously searching for the one missing item of evidence which could secure Penrose's conviction. Unless, indeed, he had any reason to believe that the wrong car had been identified; which his words did not in the least suggest. Incidentally, I was utterly unable to imagine how he proposed to identify a car which had passed down the road months ago, or even pick up its tracks. The road was extraordinarily unfrequented. We had met not a single car, and only one farm cart, since we had passed under the railway. But still it was a metalled road, showing only slight traces of the carts and wagons that had passed over it; and obviously none of those traces had anything to tell us.

When we entered the wood, I noticed that Thorndyke kept a close watch on the borders of the road though he did not slacken his pace.

"I presume," said I, "that you are looking for the tracks of the car. But isn't that rather hopeless, seeing that it is about six months since Penrose passed down this road – if he ever did actually pass down it?"

"Of course," he replied, "it would be futile to look for tracks on the road, or even on the margins. But what I am looking for – though I don't expect to find it here – is some sign of a car having driven or backed off the road into the wood and along one of the footpaths. The marks made by a car entering the wood over the soft soil would be deep and they would remain visible for years. Moreover, they would be unique. They would not be confused with other tracks, as in the case of any kind of road."

"You have reasons, then, for believing that Penrose backed his car into the wood?"

We have reasons, Jervis," he replied. "You saw the car and the dead leaves and earth on the wheels; and you will remember that the earth was of the same type as the surface soil here; a loam of the Thanet Sands type. Besides, there is the fact that, if Penrose was engaged, as the evidence suggests, in digging in the barrow, he must have left the car somewhere. But it appeared at the inquest that nobody had seen the car until it passed through Sole Street."

"There isn't much in that," said I. "We seem to have this tract of country all to ourselves. A car might remain parked by the side of this road for hours without being noticed."

He admitted the truth of this, "but," he added, "don't forget the state of the car, or the fact that Penrose was engaged in an unlawful act."

"And have you any idea," I asked, "where the car was probably left?"

"I have settled on a spot which seems likely," he replied. "But it is little more than a guess; and if I am wrong we shall have to give up the quest. We can't search the whole area of woodland."

Half a mile farther on, we came to a fork in the road, the left-hand branch being little more than a cart-track. Into this Thorndyke turned unhesitatingly; and by the care with which he scrutinised the margins, I judged that we were approaching the "likely spot." But the issue was rather confused by the fact that the rough, unmetalled road was fairly deeply rutted, having evidently been used by various carts and wagons. This road, however, after crossing a considerable open space, took a sharp, right-angle turn to the left opposite a pair of cottages, but its original direction was continued by a broad footpath. Thorndyke first followed the road in its new direction where it entered and crossed a narrow strip of wood, but, after a careful examination of the ruts in the wood, he came back and explored the footpath. And here it was that we struck the first trace of what might have been a car-track.

The footpath passed along the front of the cottages, still in the open, but presently it skirted the edge of the wood. It was an old path, never disturbed by the plough, and its surface was trodden down hard by years of use. Moreover, its margins showed faint impressions of wheels, which had been nearly obliterated by the feet of the wayfarers who had walked over them.

"They don't look to me like the tracks of a car," I remarked as we all stooped to examine them.

"No," he agreed, taking a rough measurement with his stick. "The gauge is much too wide. Probably they are the tracks of some woodman's cart or timber-carriage. But a hard path like this would scarcely show an impression of a pneumatic tyre excepting after heavy rain."

We continued our progress slowly for another hundred yards, keeping a close watch on the faint ruts beside the path. Then we all halted simultaneously. For here we could see the faint, but clearly distinguishable, tracks of some wheeled vehicle which had turned off the path on to the rough turf of the open field.

"This looks more likely," I remarked; and Polton supported me with the opinion that "the Doctor's got him this time, as I knew he would."

Thorndyke made no comment but, producing from his pocket a steel tape, carefully measured the space between the wheel-marks.

"The measurement is correct," he announced, "but that is only an agreement. It would apply to thousands of other cars. However, we will see whither these tracks lead us."

We followed the tracks, not without difficulty, across the wide meadow until we reached another belt of woodland. Here the tracks entered the wood by a footpath and were easy enough to follow on the soft earth. The path continued for about a furlong and then emerged into the open, where it crossed a small grass-covered space; and, following it, we were still able to distinguish the wheel-tracks by its sides. When it reached the edge of the wood, the footpath turned sharply to the right, keeping in the open. But here the tracks left the path and plunged straight into the wood, which was fairly free from undergrowth. Following the comparatively deep ruts which the wheels had made in the soft leaf-mould, we advanced by a rather tortuous route about a couple of hundred yards into the wood. And then, once more we halted; for we had apparently come to the end of the tracks.

There seemed to be no doubt about it; but, as the last year's leaves lay here more deeply, and the undergrowth had suddenly grown denser, I went on a few yards to make sure that the tracks did not reappear beyond the place where they had seemed to end. With difficulty I forced my way through the bushes and was further impeded by the brambles and spreading roots; and I had not gone more than a few yards when my foot was caught by some hard, angular object – obviously not a root or a bramble – whereby, after staggering forward a pace or two, I fell sprawling among the tangle of vegetation.

At the sound of the fall, and the accompanying pious ejaculations, Thorndyke hurried towards me to see what had happened. I picked myself up, and having wiped my hands, proceeded to search for the object which had tripped me up. Cautiously probing with my foot in a clump of nettles, I brought to light what looked like the haft of an axe; but, when I seized it and drew it out, it proved to be a trenching tool.

It was at this moment, as I stood with it in my hand, trying to connect it with some vague stirring of memory, that Thorndyke appeared through the bushes.

"I hope you are not hurt, Jervis," he said, anxiously. "That would be a nasty thing to fall upon."

I assured him that I had come to no harm beyond a few scratches. "But," I added, "I am not quite clear about the significance of this thing. I have a vague idea that something was said by somebody about a trenching tool, but I can't remember what or who it was."

"The somebody," he replied, "was Kickweed. Don't you remember our interview in the garage when he told us, among other items, that he had a vague collection of having seen a trenching tool there?"

"Yes, of course, I remember now. Then it is quite possible that this is the very tool he was speaking of?"

By way of answer, he took the tool from me, and, having run his eye along the handle and turned it over, placed his finger on a spot near to the blade and held it out to me. Looking at it closely, I was able to make out in very faded lettering the name "D Penrose," apparently printed with a rubber stamp.

I must confess that I was profoundly impressed. Once more Thorndyke had achieved what had seemed to me an impossibility. Not only had he traced the route that the car had followed, but he had clearly established the identity of the car. Moreover, he had settled the place from which the car started in a country which he had never seen, working by inference and aided only by the map. It was a remarkable performance even for Thorndyke.

But here my reflections were interrupted by a hail from Polton in a tone of high excitement. For he, too, had been "prospecting"; and as we returned to the end of the track, he met us, fairly bubbling with exultation and carrying his treasure trove in the form of a small spade and leather case.

"Here is an astonishing thing, sir!" he exclaimed. "I found these in the bushes, and they've both got Mr Penrose's name stamped on them. I could hardly believe my eyes. But there," he added, "I don't suppose, sir, that you are surprised at all. I expect you knew they were there before we started from home."

Thorndyke smilingly disclaimed the omniscience with which his admiring henchman credited him (though, in fact, Polton was not so very wide of the mark), and taking from him the spade and case, looked them over and verified the marks of ownership.

"You notice, Jervis," said he, "that these things correspond exactly with Kickweed's description; a small, light spade pointed at the end, and a leather sheath or case to protect the point. The spade and the trenching tool appear to have been Penrose's equipment for his clandestine digging expeditions."

"Yes," I said, "and their presence here demonstrates that you were right in your inference as to the place where he parked his car. By the way, how did you arrive at it?

"I can hardly say that I arrived at it," he replied. "As I said it was little more than a guess. I started with the hypothesis – a very well-supported one – that Penrose went forth that day with the intention of digging in Julliberrie's Grave, and that he did dig there. If that were so, he would park his car as near to the place as possible; and the more so since he knew that he was committing an unlawful act and might have to clear out of the neighbourhood in a hurry. For the same reason he would wish to leave his car where it would not be seen. But examination of the map showed this excellent place of concealment, less than half a mile from the barrow."

"Yes," I said, "it looks perfectly simple and obvious now that you have explained matters. But these tools, thrown away in the bushes, seem to suggest that the contingency that you mentioned did actually arise. Apparently, he did have to clear out of the neighbourhood in a hurry. Probably he was spotted in the act of digging and had to do a bolt, which would account for his having got rid of the incriminating tools. At any rate it looks as if the panic had started here and not after the accident."

"Exactly," Thorndyke agreed. "The killing of the old woman was not the cause but the consequence of the panic. And now, as we have finished this part of our quest, we may as well move on and see how Elmhurst is progressing – unless there is anything more that you would like to see."

"There is," I replied with emphasis. "What I should like to see, above all other things in the world, is a good hospitable pub with oceans of beer and mountains of bread and cheese. As you seem to have memorised the whole neighbourhood, perhaps you know where one is to be found."

"I am afraid," said Thorndyke, "that there is nothing nearer than the Woolpack at Chilham."

But here Polton, crinkling ecstatically, proceeded to unbutton his coat.

"No need for a pub, sir," said he. "We're provided. And we can do something better than bread and cheese and beer."

With this he fished out of his inexhaustible pockets a flat parcel – found to contain a veal and ham pie – a large flask of sherry, a nest of three aluminium drinking-cups and a shoemaker's knife in a leather sheath wherewith to carve the pie. There were no forks but the need of them was not felt as the thickness of the flat pie had been thoughtfully adapted to the dimensions of a moderately-opened human mouth. Joyfully, we selected a place as free as possible from brambles and nettles and there seated ourselves on the ground; and while Polton, by his unerring craftsman's eye, divided the pie into three equal parts, Thorndyke and I filled our cups and toasted the giver of the feast.

When the banquet was finished and the empty flask, the cups and the knife had vanished into the receptacles whence they came, Polton thriftily utilised the wrapping-paper to disguise the naked form of the trenching tool. Then, with the aid of the compass, Thorndyke led the way through the wood and presently brought us out on to a stretch of rough pasture where, some three hundred yards away, we could see the excavators at work.

CHAPTER FOURTEEN

Julliberrie's Grave

The scene on which I looked as we came out of the wood rather took me by surprise; though, to be sure, Elmhurst's lucid and detailed account of the proposed operations ought to have prepared me. But to an uninformed person like myself, excavation is just a matter of digging, and I had hardly taken in the elaborate preliminaries that exact scientific procedure demands.

Looking along the brow of the steep hill-side, one could see the barrow – a long, oval, grassy mound about fifty yards in length – standing out plainly against a background of trees that were just about to burst into leaf. Past it, to the left, down in the river valley, rose the tall white shape of Chilham Mill, while farther to the left and more distant was the town or village of Chilham. At ordinary times it must have been a rather desolate and solitary place, for no habitation was visible nearer than the distant mill, but now it was a scene of strenuous activity, peopled by busy workers.

The preparatory operations had apparently been nearly completed. The barrow was surrounded by a substantial spile fence – evidently new – which marked off a rectangular enclosure. Inside this, two rows of surveying pegs had been driven into the ground and a theodolite stand set up over one of them suggested a survey in progress. Outside the enclosure was a methodically spread dump of turf, and a trackway of planks was being laid to another spot, apparently the site of a dump for the chalk and earth which would be removed from the mound as the excavation proceeded. There was also a stack of half a dozen metal wheelbarrows, and, hard by, a small shepherd's hut, in which a stoutly-built gentleman, apparently the surveyor, was at the moment depositing what looked like a theodolite case; which he did carefully, with a proper respect for the instrument, and then, having shut the door of the hut, strode away briskly down the hill towards the village.

We seemed to have timed our arrival rather fortunately, for the work of uncovering the barrow had already commenced. Within the fenced enclosure two parties of workers were engaged, from opposite sides, in cutting out strips of turf and rolling them up like lengths of stair carpet. Of the two parties, one consisted of four labourers, who went about their work with the leisurely ease born of long experience, while the other party was, with the exception of one labourer, evidently composed of volunteers, among whom I distinguished, with some difficulty, our friend Elmhurst, transformed into the likeness of a coalminer with leanings towards tennis.

We halted near the edge of the wood to observe the procedure without interrupting the work. Presently, Elmhurst, having accumulated a goodly heap of turf-rolls, loaded them into a wheelbarrow, which was promptly seized by one of his two assistants – a fair-haired young Viking in a blue jersey and a pair of the most magnificent orange-red trousers of the kind known by fishermen as "fear-noughts" – who trundled it off through an opening in the fence and unloaded it neatly on to the turf dump on top of the already considerable stack that occupied it. Then he returned at a brisk trot, and, having set down the empty wheelbarrow, picked up his spade and fell to work again on the cutting out of a fresh load.

It was at this moment that Elmhurst, happening to glance in our direction, not only observed our presence but evidently recognised us, for he laid down his spade and began to walk towards us; whereupon we hurried forward to meet him. As he approached, I noticed that he cast an inquisitive eye on the tools which Polton was carrying, and, as soon as we had exchanged greetings, he inquired:

"Are you proposing to take an active part in the proceedings? I see that you are provided with the necessary implements."

"The appearance is illusory," Thorndyke replied. "We did not bring these tools with us. They are the products of our prospecting activities in the wood hard by. And they are not going to be used on this occasion. It seems advisable to preserve them in the condition in which they were found."

Elmhurst regarded the tools with intelligent interest and, I thought, with some disfavour.

"I see," he said reflectively; "you connect those tools with the piece of pottery that you showed me?"

Thorndyke admitted that the connection seemed to be a reasonable one.

"Yes," said Elmhurst. "A pick and a spade do certainly seem to connect themselves with traces of unlawful digging in the neighbourhood. And they are quite workmanlike tools, especially the spade. I only hope that your friends have not been too workmanlike. In one respect they certainly have not. They have made a very poor job of replacing the turf."

"Then," said Thorndyke, "you have found evidence that the mound has really been dug into?"

"Yes," was the reply. "There is no doubt whatever. But they seem only to have made a short, irregular trench, and, as they were nowhere near the burial chamber, I am still hopeful of finding that intact. But we shall see better how far they went when we get the turf off. As you see, we have got all the margin un-turfed and we are just starting on the mound itself. We shall soon get that done with eight workers besides myself; and, meanwhile, I can take you round and show you the arrangements for excavating a barrow."

"You mustn't let us waste your time," said Thorndyke, "and leave your colleagues to do all the work; though I must say, they seem to enjoy it."

"Yes, by Jove!" I agreed. "They are proper enthusiasts. I have been watching that sea rover in the decorative trousers and wondered what those labourers think of him. But perhaps they are not Union men."

Elmhurst smiled a cryptic smile but expressed complete satisfaction both with the labourers and his volunteer assistants. "I think," he added, "that my friends would like to make the acquaintance of the benefactor who has given us this very great pleasure."

Accordingly we proceeded towards the fenced enclosure and entered it by one of the openings left for the wheelbarrows to pass in and out.

"You notice," said Elmhurst, "that we have driven in a new row of pegs all around the tumulus to define its edges. Those are for use in marking our plan and to guide us when we come to rebuild the mound. It has to be restored exactly to its original shape and size."

"You speak of rebuilding the mound," said I. "You don't mean that you are going to move the entire structure?"

"Certainly we are," he replied. "The essence of a complete excavation is in the thorough examination of every part of it. The whole of it will be moved excepting a narrow longitudinal wall, or spine, along the middle, which has to be left to preserve the contour and serve as a guide to build up to. We shall move one half at a time and the earth – or chalk rubble, as it will be in this case – that we take out will be carefully deposited in one of those dumps. Each dump will have a revetment of chalk blocks to prevent the piled earth from slipping away and getting scattered."

"Yes," said Thorndyke, "it is all very thorough and methodical; a very different thing from the slovenly methods of the casual digger. By the way, which side do you propose to begin with?"

"The right-hand side," replied Elmhurst. "That is the side on which your friends operated, and we are rather anxious to settle once for all what they really did in the way of excavation and how much damage they have done. My colleagues are now beginning to peel off the turf from the side of the mound."

As he spoke we rounded the end of the barrow and came in sight of the two volunteers and the labourer, all busily engaged in cutting lines in the turf with implements like cheese-cutters set on long handles. As we approached, the owner of the fear-noughts looked up and rather disconcerted me by disclosing an extremely comely feminine countenance; which accounted for Elmhurst's cryptic smile and caused me hurriedly to re-examine the other "gentleman," only to discover that the breeches which I had innocently accepted as diagnostic of masculinity, appertained to a lady.

The introductions, effected by Elmhurst with a ceremonious bow and a grin of malicious satisfaction, informed us that the two ladies were, respectively, Miss Stirling – the wearer of the nautical garments and Miss Bidborough, and that both were qualified and enthusiastic archaeologists (this was Elmhurst's statement, and neither denied it on behalf of the other); and that both were profoundly grateful to Thorndyke.

"It is the chance of a life-time," said Miss Stirling, "to carry out a complete excavation of a Neolithic barrow; and such a famous one, too. I have often come here and looked at Julliberrie's Grave and thought how interesting it would be to turn it out thoroughly and see what it really contained. But we are in an awful twitter about those tomb-robbers who have been hacking at the ground. It will be a tragedy if they have reached the important part of the barrow."

"Yes," Miss Bidborough agreed, severely. "These clandestine diggers are the bane of scientific archaeology. They confuse all the issues by disturbing the stratification, they break or damage valuable relics, and, worst of all, they sneak off secretly with things of priceless scientific value and never record what they have found. Do you happen to know who these people were, Dr Thorndyke, who broke into this barrow?"

"The only person," replied Thorndyke, "known to me as being under suspicion is an amateur – a very amateur – collector of antiques."

"They usually are," said Elmhurst, gloomily; "and this fellow must have been worse than usual. Just look at the way he put the turf back!"

He pointed indignantly to an irregular area on the side of the mound in which even my inexpert eye could detect the ragged lines which marked the untidy replacement. From my knowledge of the man (and my distinct prejudice against him) it was just what I should have expected; and I was indiscreet enough to say so.

"By the way," said Miss Bidborough, addressing Elmhurst, "I am in hopes that we shall have a visit from Theophilus. He has to come down to Canterbury today, and I think he intends to come on here and see how we are getting on with the work. I hope he will. I know he would like to meet Dr Thorndyke."

Thorndyke looked inquiringly at Elmhurst. "Do I know Mr Theophilus?" he asked.

"His name isn't really Theophilus," Elmhurst explained. "That is only a term of affection among his friends. He is actually Professor Templeton."

"Then I do know him, at least by repute," said Thorndyke. "And now I suggest that we move on and let these ladies proceed with their work and see what enormities the unauthorised diggers have committed."

With this we bowed to the fair excavators, and as they picked up their cheese-cutters to renew their assault on the turf, we resumed our personally conducted tour, passing round the head of the mound (where Elmhurst pointed out to us the probable position of the burial chamber) to inspect the works on the other side. As we came out on to the lower side, whence we could see the whole hill-side and the river valley below, we observed a figure in the distance striding up the steep ascent with a purposeful air suggesting a definite objective.

"Here is Theophilus, himself," remarked Elmhurst (whose power of recognising distant persons did credit to his spectacles). "We may as well go down and meet him and get the introductions over before we come to the scene of the operations."

Accordingly, we proceeded down the hill-side, but at a leisurely pace, as we had to come up again, and, in due course, came within hail of the visitor, who viewed us with undisguised interest; which, indeed, was mutual; for a man who gets called by an affectionate nickname by his juniors probably merits respectful consideration. And this gentleman – a tall, athletic, eminently good-looking man, very unlike the popular conception of a professor – made a definitely pleasant impression.

When we at length met, he shook hands cordially with Elmhurst and then looked at Thorndyke.

"I think," said he, "that I can diagnose the giver of this archaeological feast. You are Dr Thorndyke, aren't you?"

Thorndyke admitted his identity, but protested:

"I am really getting a great deal of undeserved credit for this excavation. Actually, I am greatly indebted to Elmhurst for all the trouble that he is taking, since I am hoping to get some useful information from the opening of the barrow."

Professor Templeton looked at him somewhat curiously.

"Of course," said he, "you know your own business – uncommonly well, as I understand – but I can't imagine what information you expect to get by the excavation that we couldn't have given you without it."

"Probably you are right," Thorndyke admitted, "at least in a scientific sense. But in legal practice, and in relation to a particular set of circumstances, an ascertained fact is usually of more weight than even the most authoritative opinion."

"Yes," said the professor, "I appreciate that. But when Elmhurst told me about the project, I wondered – and am still wondering – whether there might not be some – what shall we say? – some *arrière-pensée,* some expectation that the digging operations might yield some extra-archaeological facts. You see, your reputation has preceded you."

He smiled genially, and Thorndyke was evidently in nowise disconcerted by the implied suspicions; and I was just beginning to wonder, for my part, whether there might not be some justice in those suspicions when my colleague addressed Elmhurst.

"I think," said he, "your presence is required at the diggings. Some rather urgent signals are being made."

We all looked up towards the barrow, and there, sure enough, was a picturesque, red-trousered figure standing on the summit of the mound, beckoning excitedly; and, even as we looked, a labourer came down the hill at a heavy trot, and, when he had arrived within earshot, announced that Miss Stirling asked Mr Elmhurst to return at once.

In compliance with this unmistakably urgent summons, Elmhurst immediately started up the hill at something between a walk and a trot, and we turned and followed at a more convenient pace.

"Those girls have apparently found something out of the common," the professor remarked. "I wonder what it can be. They can't have struck the burial chamber, for they have only begun peeling the turf off; and you don't look for anything important so near the surface."

"We watched Elmhurst run round the end of the mound, where he disappeared for the moment. But in a very short time he reappeared, hurrying in our direction; and, as we, thereupon, quickened our pace, we met within a short distance of the mound.

"My colleagues," he announced in his usual sedate, self-contained manner, though a little breathlessly, "have found something, Doctor, which is rather more in your line than ours. Apparently, there is someone buried just under the surface in the place where the unauthorised digging has been carried out."

"You say 'apparently,'" said Thorndyke. "Then I take it that you have not uncovered a body?"

"No," replied Elmhurst, as we turned to accompany him back. "What happened was this: Miss Stirling was rolling up a strip of turf when she saw what looked like the toe of a boot showing through the surface soil. So she scraped away some of the soil with her spade and uncovered the greater part of a boot; and then the toe of a second boot came into view; whereupon she ran up the mound and signalled for me to come."

"You are sure that they are not just a pair of empty boots?" Thorndyke asked.

"Quite sure," was the reply. "I scraped away the earth enough to see the bottoms of a pair of trousers and then came on to report. But there is no doubt that there are feet in those boots."

Nothing more was said as we walked quickly up the hill, but I caught a significant glance from the professor's eye, and I noticed that Polton had developed a new and lively interest in the proceedings. As to Thorndyke, it was impossible to judge whether the discovery had occasioned him any surprise; but I suspected – and so, evidently, did the professor – that the possibility had been in his mind. Indeed, I began to ask myself if this gruesome "find" did not represent the actual purpose of the excavation.

On arriving at the barrow, we passed round the foot end and came in sight of the scene of the discovery where a broad patch of the chalky soil had been uncovered by the removal of the turf. The two ladies stood close by it, backed by the gang of labourers who had been attracted to the spot by the report of the discovery; and the eyes of them all were riveted on a shallow depression at the bottom of which a pair of whitened boots projected through the chalk rubble.

"Would you like me to get the body out?" Thorndyke asked. "As you said, it is more in my line than yours."

"I didn't mean that," replied Elmhurst, "I'll dig it out. But, as I have had no experience of the exhumation of recent remains, you had better see that I go about it in the right way."

With this, he selected a suitable pick and spade, and, having placed a wheelbarrow close by to receive the soil, fell to work.

We watched him cautiously and skilfully pick away the clammy chalk rubble in which the corpse was embedded, and as each new part became disclosed, attention and curiosity quickened. First the legs, looking almost as if modelled in chalk, then the skirt of a raincoat, and one whitened, repulsive-looking hand. Then, partly covered by the body, an object was seen, the nature of which was not at first obvious; but when Elmhurst had carefully disengaged it from the soil and drawn it out, it appeared as the whitened and shapeless remains of a felt hat, which was at once handed to Thorndyke; who restored it, as far as possible, to a recognisable shape, wiped its exterior with a bunch of turf, glanced into its interior, and then put it down on the side of the mound.

Gradually the corpse was uncovered and disengaged from its chalky bed until, at length, it lay revealed as the body of a stoutish man who, so far as could be judged, was on the shady side of middle age. Naturally, six months of burial in the clammy chalk had left uncomely traces and obscured the characteristics of the face; but when Thorndyke had gently cleaned the latter with a wisp of turf, the chalk-smeared, sodden features still retained enough of their original character to render identification possible by one who had known the man. In fact, it was not only possible. It was actually achieved. For as Thorndyke stood up and threw away the wisp of turf, Polton, who had watched the procedure with fascinated eyes, suddenly stooped and gazed with the utmost astonishment into the dead man's face.

"Why!" he exclaimed, "it looks like Mr Penrose!"

"You think it does?" said Thorndyke, without the slightest trace of surprise.

"Of course, sir," replied Polton, "I couldn't be positive. He's so very much changed. But he looks to me like Mr Penrose; and I feel pretty certain that that is who he is."

"I have no doubt that you are right, Polton," said Thorndyke. "The hat is certainly his hat; and the fact that you recognised the body seems to settle the question of identity. And now another question arises. How is the body to be disposed of? The correct procedure would be to leave it where it is and notify the police. What do you say to that, Elmhurst?"

"You know best what the legal position is," was the reply. "But it won't be very comfortable carrying on the work with that gruesome object staring us in the face. Is there any legal objection to its being moved?"

"No, I think not," replied Thorndyke. "There are competent witnesses as to the circumstances of the discovery, and the soil is going to be thoroughly examined, so that any objects connected with the body are certain to be found."

"Quite certain," said Elmhurst. "The soil will not only be examined. That from this part will be sifted. And, of course any objects found will be carefully preserved and reported. Still, we don't want to do anything irregular."

"I will take the responsibility for moving the body," said Thorndyke, "if you will find the means. But I think it would be as well to send a messenger in advance to the police so they may be prepared."

"Very well," Elmhurst agreed. "Then I will send a man off at once and, if Mr Polton will come and lend me a hand, we can rig up an extemporised stretcher from some of the spare fencing material."

With this he went off, accompanied by Polton, in search of the necessary material; the ladies migrated to the farther end of the mound, where they resumed their turf-cutting operations and the labourers returned to their tasks.

When we were alone, the professor stood for a while looking thoughtfully at the ghastly figure, lying at the bottom of its trench. Presently he turned to Thorndyke and asked:

"Has it occurred to you, Doctor – I expect it has – that the person who buried this poor creature showed very considerable foresight?"

"You mean in selecting a scheduled monument as a burial place?"

"Yes – but I see that you have considered the point. It is rather subtle. According to ordinary probabilities, a scheduled tumulus should be the safest of all places in which to dispose of a dead body. It is actually secured by law against any disturbance of the soil. But for your intervention, this place might have remained untouched for a century."

"Very true," Thorndyke agreed, "but of course, there is the converse aspect. If suspicion arises in respect of a given locality, the very security of a barrow from chance disturbance makes it the likeliest place for a suspected burial."

"I suppose," the professor ventured, "that an ordinary exhumation order would not have answered your purpose?"

"It would not have been practicable," Thorndyke replied. "I did not know that the body was here. I did not even know for certain that there was a dead body; and I don't suppose that either the Home Office or the Office of Works would have agreed to the excavation of a scheduled tumulus to search for a corpse whose existence was purely hypothetical. The only practicable method was a regular excavation by competent archaeologists; which would not only settle the question whether the body was there or not, but, in the event of a negative result, would not have raised any troublesome issues or disclosed any suspicions which might possibly turn out to be unfounded."

"Yes," the professor agreed. "I admire your tact and discretion. You have done a valuable service to archaeology and you have managed very neatly to harness the unsuspecting Elmhurst to your legal chariot."

"I am not sure," said I, "that Elmhurst was quite so unsuspecting as you think. But he also is a discreet gentleman. He wanted to excavate the barrow and was willing to do it and ask no questions. But I fancy that he expected to find something more significant than Neolithic pottery."

Here our discussion was brought to an end by the arrival of Elmhurst and Polton bearing a sort of elongated hurdle formed very neatly by lashing together a number of stout rods. This they deposited opposite the place where the body was lying in readiness to receive its melancholy burden.

"I think, Jervis," said Thorndyke, "that the next proceeding devolves upon us. Will you lend us a hand, Polton? The body ought to be lifted as evenly as possible to avoid any disturbance of the joints.

Accordingly, we placed ourselves by the side of the trench, Thorndyke taking the head and shoulders, I taking the middle, while Polton supported the legs and feet. At the word from Thorndyke, we all very carefully lifted the limp, sagging figure and carried it to the hurdle on which we gently lowered it. As we rose and stood looking down at the poor shabby heap of mortality, Polton, who appeared to be deeply moved, moralised sadly.

"Dear, dear!" he exclaimed, "what a dreadful and grievous thing it is. To think that that miserable, dirty mass of rags and carrion is all that is left of a fine, jovial, happy gentleman, full of energy and enjoying every moment of his life. There is a heavy debt against somebody, and I hope, sir, that you will see that it is paid to the uttermost farthing."

"I hope so, too, Polton," said Thorndyke. That, you know, is what we are here for. Can we find anything to cover the body? It is a rather gruesome object to carry down into the village."

As he spoke, the four labourers who had volunteered as bearers approached carrying a bundle of sacks; and with these laid across the hurdle, the wretched, unseemly remains were decently covered up. Then the four men lifted the hurdle (which, with its wasted burden, must have been quite light) and moved away round the foot of the barrow, watched, not without evident relief by Elmhurst and his two colleagues.

"I suppose," said Elmhurst, as we prepared to follow, "you won't be coming back here?"

"Not today," replied Thorndyke. "But we shall have to attend the inquest, either as witnesses or to watch the proceedings, so we shall have an opportunity to see your work in a more advanced stage. Don't think our interest in it is extinct because we are no longer concerned with Neolithic pottery."

With this we took leave of our friends and, starting off down the hill-side, soon overtook and passed the bearers and made our way to the foot-bridge over the river near the mill. A few yards further on, we met our messenger returning in company with a police sergeant, and halted to give the latter the necessary particulars.

"I suppose," he remarked, "you ought, properly, to have left the body where it was and reported to us. Still, as you say, there's nothing in it as the witnesses are available. I'll just note your addresses and those of any other persons that you know of who may be wanted at the inquest.

We accordingly gave our own names and addresses (at which I noticed that the sergeant seemed to prick up his ears), and Thorndyke gave those of Brodribb, Horridge and Kickweed. And this concluded the day's business. Of the spade and the trenching tool Thorndyke said nothing, evidently intending to examine them at his leisure before handing them over to the police.

I may say that the discovery had given me one of the greatest surprises of my life. The idea that Penrose might be dead had never occurred to me. And yet, as soon as the discovery had been made, I began to realise how all the facts that were know to us pointed in this direction, and I also began to see the drift of the many hints that Thorndyke had given me. But, although, over a very substantial tea at the Woolpack Inn, we discussed the various and stirring events of the day, I did not think it expedient to enter into the details of the case in Polton's presence. Not that, in these days, we had many secrets from Polton. But there were certain other matters, as yet undisclosed, that it seemed better to reserve for discussion when we should be alone.

CHAPTER FIFTEEN

What Befell at the Woolpack

The inquest on the body of Daniel Penrose yielded nothing that was new to us. The coroner had been provided by Thorndyke with a brief synopsis of the known facts of the case (which my colleague had, apparently, prepared in advance) to serve as a guide in conducting the inquiry; but he was a discreet man who understood his business and avoided extending the proceedings beyond the proper scope of a coroner's inquest. Nor had we been able to increase our knowledge of the case; for neither the spade nor the trenching tool furnished any information whatever. All our attempts to develop fingerprints failed utterly and the most minute examination of the tools for the traces of hair or blood was equally fruitless. Which was not surprising; for even if such traces had originally existed, six months' exposure to the weather would naturally have dissipated them.

But if the coroner was not disposed to go beyond the facts connected with the discovery, there was another person who was. We had put up for the night at the Woolpack in Chilham in order to be present at the post-mortem (by the coroner's invitation), and were jut finishing a leisurely breakfast when the coffee-room door opened to admit no less a person than Mr Superintendent Miller. He had come down by an early train for the express purpose of getting an outline of the case from Thorndyke to assist him in following the proceedings at the inquest.

"Well, Doctor," he said, cheerfully, seating himself without ceremony at our table, "here we are, and both on the same errand, I take it."

"We are," Thorndyke replied, "if you have come to attend the inquest on poor Penrose."

"Exactly," rejoined Miller. "We have a common purpose, which isn't always the case, Lord, Doctor! What a pleasure it is to find myself, for once in a way, on the same side of the board with you, playing the same game against the same opponent! You won't mind if I ask you a few questions?"

"Not at all," replied Thorndyke. "But the first question is, have you had breakfast?"

"Well, I have, you know," said Miller, "but it was a long time ago. I think I could pick a morsel, since you mention the matter."

Accordingly, Thorndyke rang the bell, and, having given an order for a morsel in the form of a gammon rasher and a pot of coffee, prepared himself for the superintendent's assault.

"Now, Doctor," the latter began, in his best cross-examining manner, "it is perfectly clear to me that you know all about this case."

"I wish it were as clear to me," said Thorndyke.

"There, now, Dr Jervis," exclaimed Miller, "just listen to that. Isn't he an aggravating man? He has got all the facts of the case up his sleeve, as he usually has, and now he is going to pretend – as he usually does – that he doesn't know anything about it. But it won't do, Doctor. The facts speak for themselves. Here were our men traipsing up and down the country, looking for Daniel Penrose to execute a warrant on him, and all the time you knew perfectly well that he was safely tucked away in a barrow – though why the deuce they call the thing a barrow when it is obviously just a mound of earth, I can't imagine."

"That is a wild exaggeration, you know, Miller," Thorndyke protested. "After six months' study of the case, I came to the conclusion that Penrose was probably buried in this barrow. But I was so far from certainty that I had to take this roundabout way of settling the question whether I was or was not mistaken. It happened that my conclusion was correct."

"It usually does," said Miller. "And I expect you have formed some conclusions as to who planted that body in the barrow. And I expect those conclusions will happen to be right, too. And I should very much like to know what they are."

"Really, Miller," I exclaimed, "I am surprised at you. Have you known Thorndyke all these years without discovering that he never lets the cat out of the bag until he can let her right out? No protruding heads or tails for him. But, when everything is finished and the course is clear, out she comes."

"Yes, I know," said Miller, gloomily, "I know his beastly secret ways. I think that, in some previous state of existence, he must have been an oyster. Still, Doctor, you needn't be so close with an old friend."

"But my dear Miller," protested Thorndyke, "you are entirely mistaken. I am withholding nothing that I could properly tell you. What Jervis has said, though crudely put, is the strict truth. If I knew who had committed this crime, of course I should tell you. But I don't know. And if I have any half-formed suspicions, I am going to keep them to myself until I am able to test them. In short, Miller, I will tell you all I know. But I tell nobody what I think. So now ask me any questions you please."

I must admit that it was not very encouraging for Miller. My experience of Thorndyke was fairly expressed in what he had just said. He would tell you all the facts (which you usually knew already and which were more or less common property) but the general truths which were implicit in those facts he would leave you to discover for yourself; which you never did until the final conclusions emerged; when it was surprising how obvious they were.

"Well, to begin with," said Miller. "There was that chappie at the hospital whom we all supposed to be Penrose. Have you any idea who he really was? You obviously spotted the fact that he was not Penrose."

"No," replied Thorndyke, "I have no idea who he was. My suspicion that he was not Penrose was based on his behaviour, especially on the fact that he appeared particularly anxious to avoid being seen or recognised by anyone who knew Penrose. As a matter of fact, he was not then recognisable at all, and nobody knows what he was really like. But I don't think that there is any utility in going into details of the case at that stage. Remember that my investigations were then concerned with the questions: Is Penrose alive or dead? And, if he is dead, what has become of his body? Now, I have settled those questions and their solution has evolved the further questions: Was he murdered? And, if so, who murdered him? The first question will be answered at the inquest – pretty certainly in the affirmative; and we shall then address ourselves to the second. And, as you say, we have a common purpose and shall try to be mutually helpful.

"Now, I have given the coroner a synopsis of the case from the beginning, and I have a copy of it which I am going to hand to you. I suggest that you study it, and then, if anything occurs to you in connection with it, and you like to ask me any questions on matters of fact, I will give you all the information that I possess. How will that do for you?"

I suspected that it was not at all what Miller would have liked; but he saw clearly, as I did, that Thorndyke was not going to disclose any theories that he might have formed as to where we might look for the possible murderer. Accordingly, he accepted the position with as good a grace as he could, and, when he had finished a very substantial breakfast, he demanded the synopsis, which Thorndyke fetched from his room and placed in his hands.

"Are you coming to watch the post-mortem, Jervis?" my colleague asked.

"No," I replied. "I shall hear all about it at the inquest, so I think I shall improve the shining hour by taking a walk up to the barrow to see how the work is progressing."

"Ha!" said Miller. "Then perhaps you wouldn't mind my walking with you. I have never seen a barrow. Never heard of one until I read the report in the paper."

Of course, I had to agree; nor unwilling, in fact, for I liked our old friend. But I knew quite well what the proposal meant. As nothing was to be got out of Thorndyke, Miller intended to apply a gentle squeeze to me. And to this also I had no objection, for I was still in the dark as to how Thorndyke had reached his very definite conclusions and was quite willing to have my memories of the investigation stirred up.

The process began as soon as we were fairly outside the inn.

"Now, look here, Dr Jervis." said the superintendent, "it's all very well for the doctor to pretend that he hasn't anything to go on, but there are certain obvious questions that arise when a well-to-do man like Penrose gets murdered. The first is: Who benefits by his death?"

"The answer to that," I replied, "is quite simple. Penrose made a will by which practically the whole of his property goes to a man named Horridge."

"Then," said Miller, "it will be worth while to give a little attention to Mr Horridge. Do you know anything about him?"

"Not very much," I replied. "But I know this much; that he is about the most unlikely man in the world to have murdered Penrose."

"Why do you say that?" demanded Miller.

"Because, if Penrose died when we believe he did, Horridge stands to lose something like a hundred and fifty thousand pounds by his death. Penrose was the principal heir of his father, who was quite a rich man. But when Penrose died – if he did die on the date which we are assuming – his father was alive and consequently the father's estate would not pass to him. But Horridge was Penrose's heir and would have inherited the father's property, as well as Penrose's, under the latter's will. So it didn't suit Horridge at all for Penrose to die when he did."

"And is the old man still alive?"

"No. He died quite recently."

"Ha!" said Miller. "Then somebody else benefits by Penrose's death. Do you happen to know who that will be?"

"No." I replied. "I understand, but do not know for certain, that the old man died intestate. In that case, the next of kin will benefit. They will benefit very considerably, as their expectations would have been quite small if Penrose had been alive when his father died. But I have no idea who they are."

"Well, we shall have to find that out," said Miller. "It seems that somebody had a perfectly understandable motive for getting rid of Penrose while the old man was still alive."

As Miller continued his interrogations, asking uncommonly shrewd questions and making equally shrewd comments, I began to feel an unwonted sympathy with Thorndyke in respect of his habitual reticence and secretiveness. For his approach to a criminal problem was quite different from Miller's and there might easily arise some conflict between the two. Miller was evidently on the look-out for a suspect, and he was considering the problem in terms of persons; whereas Thorndyke's practice was to watch, unseen and unsuspected, while he collected and sifted the evidence, and, above all, to avoid alarming the suspected person until he was ready to make the final move.

But our arrival at the top of Julliberrie Downs put an end, for the time being, to Miller's bombardment; for here we came in sight of the barrow, now stripped of its turf and presenting the smooth, white, rounded shape on which its builders had looked a couple of thousand years or more before the coming of the Romans. I explained its nature and its great antiquity to Miller, who was deeply impressed, but who, nevertheless showed a strong inclination to "cut the cackle and get back to the case." But as we approached, the eagle-eyed Elmhurst observed us and came forward to do the honours of the excavation.

Under his guidance we went round to the farther side of the mound which was in the process of being cut away like a gigantic cheese, and the chalk rubble, stored in the dumps, was mounting to the magnitude of a considerable hill. At this point, the superintendent's interest in the barrow awakened surprisingly, for an excavation was more or less in his line, and he took the opportunity to pick up a few technical tips. He was particularly impressed by a builder's sieve which had been set up at the dump.

"I see," he remarked to Elmhurst, "that you don't mean to miss anything. I shall bear your methods in mind the next time I have to direct a search. And speaking of a search, have you turned up anything that seems to be connected with the body that you found?"

"Yes," replied Elmhurst. "We found, near the place where the body was lying, quite an interesting thing, and, I should say, decidedly connected with that body – a small bronze pestle apparently belonging to an ancient drug-mortar. I'll show it to you. Miss Stirling, have you got that pestle?"

As the lady addressed turned round and greeted me with a friendly nod, the superintendent whispered to me in an awestricken tone:

"Good gracious! That young person in the fisherman's trousers is a female! And I believe the other one is too. Well, I never!"

"You would hardly expect them to wear evening dress for a job like this," I remarked; to which the superintendent assented, but continued to watch the ladies furtively and with fascinated eyes.

The pestle was presently produced from the shepherd's hut and offered for our inspection; a smallish pestle of bronze – now covered with a thick green patina – with a bulbous end and a rather elaborately decorated handle surmounted by a bearded head of the classical type which I assumed to represent Aesculapius. Attached to it was a small tie-on label on which was written a note of its precise "find-spot" in the mound.

Miller took it in his hand and executed a warlike flourish with it, by way of testing its weight.

"It's of no great size," he remarked, "but it is quite a formidable weapon. Uncommonly handy, too, and as portable as a life-preserver. Perhaps I had better take charge of it."

He was about to slip it into his pocket when Elmhurst interposed firmly.

"I think I must keep it for the present. I am summoned to give evidence at the inquest and I shall have to produce this. Besides, I am personally responsible to the Office of Works for all objects found during the excavation."

With this he quietly resumed possession of the pestle, which Miller reluctantly surrendered, and as the latter had no further interest in the excavation, and made no secret of the fact, we presently took our leave and resumed our perambulations, with a running accompaniment of interrogation on the part of the superintendent which caused me to hail the luncheon hour with a certain sense of relief.

The superintendent, of course, lunched with us, and even at the table he continued his quest for knowledge, beginning, naturally, with inquiries as to the result of the post-mortem.

"The cause of death is obvious enough," said Thorndyke. "There is a depressed fracture of the skull at the left side and towards the back; not very large, but deep, and suggesting a very violent blow. The shape of the depression – a fairly regular oval concavity – implies a blunt weapon of a smooth, rounded shape."

"Such as a pestle, for instance," Miller suggested.

"Yes," Thorndyke replied, "a pestle would agree with the conditions. But why do you suggest a pestle?"

"Because your excavating friends have found one; a bronze pestle; quite a handy little weapon, and portable enough to go quite easily into an ordinary pocket."

Here he gave a very excellent and concise description of the weapon, to which Thorndyke listened with deep interest.

"So you see," Miller concluded, "that it is a thing that ought to be quite easy to identify by anyone who had ever seen it. Dr Jervis thinks that it would not be likely to be the property of a chemist or apothecary. What do you say to that?"

"I agree with him," Thorndyke replied "That is to say, it does not definitely suggest an apothecary as would have been the case if it had been a Wedgwood pestle. Bronze mortars and pestles are not now in general use; and this is pretty evidently an ancient pestle."

"A sort of curio, in fact," said Miller, "and rather suggestive of a collector or curio-monger?"

Thorndyke agreed that this was so, but he made no further comment, though the connection of a curio with the late Daniel Penrose was fairly significant. But my recent experiences of Miller's eager and persistent cross-examinations enabled me to understand the sort of defensive reticence that they tended to engender. Moreover, the connection, though significant, was not very clear as to its bearing. It would have been more obvious if Penrose had been the murderer.

The inquest was held in a large room at the inn, normally reserved for gatherings of a more festive character, and when we entered and took our places the preliminaries of swearing in the jury and viewing the body had already been disposed of. I looked round the room and noted that in the seats set apart for the witnesses, not only Elmhurst and his two coadjutors were present but also Kickweed and Horridge. Both of the latter showed evident signs of distress, but more especially Horridge. Which rather surprised me. The grief of the lugubrious, red-eyed Kickweed was understandable enough; for not only had he mentioned a genuine affection and loyalty towards his dead master, but the death of Penrose was a very material loss to him. But I could not reconcile Horridge's condition with the callous selfishness that he had shown previously. It is true that the apparent date of the death put an end to his hopes of inheriting the fortune of the lately deceased Penrose senior, but, on the other hand, he stood to gain forthwith the very respectable sum of fifty thousand pounds, for which he might reasonably have expected to wait for years. Nevertheless, he was obviously extremely upset, and it was evident from his pale, haggard face and his restless movements, that this sudden, unforeseen catastrophe had come on him as an overwhelming shock. The first witness called was Miss Stirling, who gave a brief, matter-of-fact description of her discovery, to which the jury listened with absorbed interest. She was followed by Elmhurst, who amplified her statement and described his disinterment of the body and the appearance and position of the latter. He also explained the methods of excavation and the procedure after the body had been removed.

"In the soil which was taken away after the removal of the body," the coroner inquired, "did you find any objects that seemed to be connected with it?"

"Yes," replied Elmhurst. "I found this pestle, which could certainly not have been among the original contents of the barrow."

Here he produced the pestle wrapped in a handkerchief and, having removed the latter, handed the "find" to the coroner, who inspected it curiously and then passed it on to the foreman of the jury.

"This," he remarked, "does not look like a modern pestle. As you are an authority on antiquities, Mr Elmhurst, perhaps you can tell us something about it."

"I am not much of an authority on recent antiquities," Elmhurst disclaimed modestly, "but I should judge that this pestle belonged to a bronze drug-mortar of the kind that was in use in the seventeenth or early eighteenth century."

"You would not regard it as probably part of the outfit of a chemist's shop?"

"No," replied Elmhurst. "I understand that, since the introduction of grinding machinery, the practice of grinding hard drugs in metal mortars is quite extinct."

"Can you form any idea how long this object has been buried?"

"I could not judge the exact time; but, assuming it to have been bright, or at least clean, when it was buried, I should say that it must have been lying in the ground for several months."

That concluded Elmhurst's evidence, and, as he retired to his seat, the name of the medical witness was called.

"You have made an examination of the body of the deceased?" the coroner began, when the preliminaries had been disposed of. "Can you give any opinion as to how long the deceased has been dead?"

"My examination," the witness replied, "led me to the belief that he had been dead at least six months."

"Did you arrive at any conclusion as to the cause of death?"

"The cause of death was an injury to the brain occasioned by a heavy blow on the head. There is a small but deep depressed fracture of the skull on the left side just above and behind the ear, which appears to have been produced by a blunt, smooth weapon with a rounded end."

"Please look at this pestle, which you heard was found near the place where the body had been lying. Could the injuries which you found have been produced by this?"

The doctor examined the pestle and gave it as his opinion that it corresponded completely with the shape of the fracture.

"I suppose that it is a mere formality to ask whether the injuries could have been self-inflicted or due to an accident?" the coroner suggested.

"They certainly could not have been self-inflicted," the witness replied. "As to an accident, one doesn't like to use the word impossible, but I cannot imagine any kind of accident which would have produced the injuries that were found."

This completed the medical evidence proper, but Thorndyke was called to give confirmatory testimony.

"You have heard the evidence of the doctor. Have you any observation to make on it?"

"No," replied Thorndyke. "I am in complete agreement with everything that my colleague has said."

"We may take it," said the coroner, "that you know more about this affair than anybody else. Can you throw any light on the actual circumstances in which the tragedy occurred?"

"No," Thorndyke replied. "My investigations have been concerned with the question whether Daniel Penrose was alive or dead; and, if he was dead, when and where his death occurred. I can make no suggestion as to the identity of the person who killed him."

"As to the date of his death; have you arrived at any conclusion on that point?"

"Yes, I have no doubt that deceased met his death at some time in the evening of the seventeenth of last October. I base that conclusion principally on the fact that his car was seen coming away from the neighbourhood of the place where his body was found, and that it was evidently being driven by some other person."

"And have you formed any opinion as to who that other person may have been?"

"I have not. At present I have no evidence pointing to any particular person."

"Well," said the coroner, "I hope you will now take up this further question, and that your efforts will be as successful in this as in the problem which you have solved in such a remarkable manner. Is there any question that any member of the jury would like to ask?"

Apparently there was not. Accordingly, Thorndyke returned to his seat and the name of Francis Horridge was called. And, as he walked up to the table, I was once more impressed by his extraordinarily agitated and shaken condition. It was noticed also by the coroner, who, before beginning his examination, offered a few words of sympathy.

"This, Mr Horridge," said he, "must be a very painful and distressing experience for you, as an intimate friend of the deceased."

"It is," replied Horridge. "I had not the faintest suspicion that my old friend was not alive and well. It has been a terrible shock."

"It must have been," the coroner agreed, "and I am sorry to have to trouble you with questions. But we have to solve this dreadful mystery if we can, or at least find out as much as possible about it. You have seen the body of deceased. Could you identify it?"

"Yes. It is the body of Daniel Penrose."

"Yes," said the coroner, "there seems to be no doubt as to the identity of the body. Now, Mr Horridge, the medical evidence makes it clear that deceased met his death by the act of some unknown person. It is very necessary to discover, if possible, who that person is. You were an intimate friend of deceased and must know a good deal about his personal affairs. Do you know of anything that might throw any light on the circumstances surrounding his death?"

"No," was the reply. "But I did not know so very much about his personal habits or his friends and acquaintances."

"I understand that deceased had made a will. Do you know anything about that?"

"Yes. I am the executor of his will."

"Then you can tell us whether there was anything in connection with it which might give rise to trouble or enmity. In rough, general terms, what are the provisions of the will?"

"They are quite simple. There is a handsome, but well-deserved legacy to his butler, Kickweed, amounting to two thousand pounds. Beyond that, the bulk of the property is devised and bequeathed to me."

"So you and Mr, Kickweed are the persons who benefit most in a pecuniary sense by the death of deceased?"

"Yes; and I am sure we should both very gladly forgo the benefit to have our friend back again."

"I am sure you would," said the Coroner. "But can you tell us if there are any other persons who would benefit materially in any way by the death of diseased?"

"Yes, there are," replied Horridge. "Quite recently, deceased's father died and left a considerable fortune. If deceased had been alive at that time, the bulk of that fortune would have come to him. As it is, it will be distributed among his next of kin. Consequently, those persons will benefit very considerably by deceased's death if that death occurred on the date given by Dr Thorndyke. I do not know who they are; and, of course, I do not suspect any of them of being concerned in this crime."

"Certainly not," the coroner agreed. "But one naturally looks round for some persons who might have had a motive for making away with deceased. But you know of no such persons? You do not know of anyone with whom deceased was on terms of enmity or who had any sort of grudge against him?"

"No, so far as I know, he had no enemies whatever. He was not likely to have any. He was a kindly man and on pleasant terms with every one with whom he came in contact."

"May the same be said of us all when our time comes," the coroner moralised. "But there is another motive that we ought to consider. That of robbery. Do you know whether deceased was in the habit of carrying about with him – on his person I mean – property of any considerable value?"

"I have no idea," replied Horridge. "He must have done so at times, for he was a great collector and was in the habit of going about the country making purchases. I had supposed that his last journey was made with that object, and I am disposed to think so still. He used to come down to this neighbourhood to visit a dealer named Todd who has a shop at Canterbury."

"You say that he was a collector. What kind of things did he collect?"

"It was a very miscellaneous collection, but I have always believed that, in addition to the oddments that were displayed in the main gallery he had a collection of jewels of much more considerable value which were kept in a small room. That room was always kept locked, and deceased would never say definitely what it contained."

Here Horridge gave a description of the small room as we had seen it on the occasion of our visit of inspection, and he also gave an account of the supposed burglary, to which the coroner – and Superintendent Miller – listened with profound interest.

"This," said the former, "seems to be a matter of some importance. What is the precise date on which the supposed burglary took place?"

"The second of last January."

"That," said the coroner, "would be nearly three months after the death of deceased, if Dr Thorndyke is correct as to the date on which the death occurred. And you say that, if the cupboard was opened, it must have been opened with its own proper key, since the lock is unpickable and the cupboard had not been broken open. Is there any reason to believe that the cupboard was actually opened?"

"I think there is," replied Horridge. "It is certain that someone entered the room on that night, and it is practically certain that he entered the premises by the side gate, as there is no other way of approaching the window. But that gate was always kept locked, and it was found to be locked on the morning after the supposed burglary. So it seems that the burglar must have the key of the gate, at least."

"And who usually had possession of that key?"

"Mr Penrose. It seems that he sometimes used that gate and he kept the key in his own possession. There was no duplicate."

"When you went to the mortuary to identify the body, did you look over the effects of deceased which had been taken from the pockets?

"No; but I asked the coroner's officer if any keys had been found and he told me that there had not."

The coroner nodded gravely and Miller remarked to me in a whisper that we were beginning to see daylight.

"It is unfortunate," the former observed, "that we have no clear evidence as to whether a burglary did or did not take place. However, that is really a matter for the police. But the question is highly significant in relation to the problem of the motive for killing deceased. Do you know whether, apart from this burglary, there were any attempts to rob the deceased?"

"Yes," replied Horridge; "but I think it was only a chance affair. Deceased told me on one occasion that his car had been stopped on a rather solitary road by a gang of men who were armed with revolvers and who made him deliver up what money he had about him. But, apparently, his loss was only trifling as he had nothing of value with him at the time."

This concluded Horridge's evidence; and when the coroner's officer, who turned out to be the police sergeant whom I had met, had deposed to having examined the contents of deceased's pockets and found no keys among them, the name of Edward Kickweed was called.

CHAPTER SIXTEEN

Mr Kickweed Surprises the Coroner

The evidence given by our friend, Horridge, had been listened to with keen interest, not only by the coroner and the jury, but especially by Superintendent Miller. For, though it comprised nothing that we did not already know, it had elicited the important fact that the body of Penrose had apparently been rifled of his keys. But striking and significant as this fact was, it was left to Kickweed to contribute the really sensational item of evidence.

But this came later. The early part of his evidence seemed to be little more than a series of formalities, confirming what had already been proved. When he took his place at the table, his lugubrious aspect drew from the coroner a kindly expression of sympathy similar to that with which he had greeted Horridge, after which he proceeded with his examination.

"You have seen the body which is lying in the mortuary, Mr Kickweed. Were you able to identify it?"

"Yes," groaned Kickweed. "It is the body of my esteemed and beloved employer, Mr Daniel Penrose."

"How long had you known deceased?"

"I have known him practically all his life. I was in his father's service and when he grew up and took a house of his own, he asked me to come to him as butler. So I came gladly and have been with him ever since."

"Then you probably know a good deal about his manner of life and the people he knew. Can you tell us whether there was any one who might have had any feelings of enmity towards him?"

"There was not," Kickweed replied confidently. "Deceased was a rather self-contained man, but he was a kind, courteous and generous man and I am sure that he had not an enemy in the world."

"You confirm Mr Horridge's estimate," said the coroner, "and a very satisfactory one it is, and it seems to dispose of revenge or malice as the motive for killing him. By the way, it is not of much consequence, but do you recognise these objects?"

Here he took from behind his chair the spade and trenching tool which we had found in the wood and laid them on the table for Kickweed's inspection.

"Yes," said the witness, "they belonged to deceased. He used to keep them in the garage. I am not quite sure what he used them for, but I know that he occasionally took them with him when he went out in the country in his car."

"Were you aware that he had taken them with him when he last left home?"

"I was not. But afterwards, when I saw that they were not in their usual place, I assumed that he had taken them with him."

The coroner entered this not very illuminating statement in the depositions and then, noting that the witness' eyes were fixed on the pestle which lay on the table, he picked it up, and, holding it towards him, said:

"I suppose it is needless to ask you if you recognise this object?"

"I do," was the totally unexpected reply. "It belongs to a small bronze mortar which forms part of Mr Penrose's collection."

"This is very extraordinary!" the coroner exclaimed. "You are sure that you recognise it?"

"Perfectly sure," replied Kickweed. "The pestle and mortar stood together on a shelf in the great gallery and I have often, when dusting the things in the collection, given this pestle and the mortar a rub with the cloth. I know it very well indeed."

"Well," the coroner exclaimed, "this is indeed a surprise! The weapon is actually the property of the deceased!"

There was a short interval of silence, in which I could hear Miller cursing softly under his breath.

"There," he muttered, "is another promising clue gone west!"

Then the coroner, recovering from his astonishment, resumed his examination of the witness.

"Can you explain by what extraordinary chance deceased came to have this thing with him on the day when he was killed?"

"Yes. It was his usual custom, when he went out in his car and was likely to be on the road late, to slip the pestle in his pocket before he started. The custom arose after he had been stopped on the road by robbers, as Mr Horridge has mentioned. I urged him to get a revolver or some other means of defending himself. But he had a great dislike to fire-arms, so I suggested a life-preserver. But then he happened to see me polishing this pestle, and it occurred to him that it would do as well as the life-preserver, and, as he said, would be a more interesting thing to carry. So he used to take it with him, and he did on this occasion, as I discovered a few days after he had gone, when I saw the mortar on the shelf without the pestle."

"Well," said the coroner, "there is evidently no doubt that this pestle really belonged to deceased, and that fact may have a rather important bearing on the case."

He paused, and, having entered Kickweed's last statement in the depositions, turned to him once more.

"Apparently, Mr Kickweed, of all the persons who knew deceased, you are the one who last saw him alive. Can you recall the circumstances of his departure from his home?"

"Yes," the witness replied, "very clearly. At lunch-time on the seventeenth of last October, deceased informed me that he should presently be starting for a run in the country in his car. He was not sure about the time when he would return, but he thought he might be rather late; and he directed that no one should sit up for him, but that a cold supper should be left for him in the dining-room. He left the house a little before three to go to the garage, and, about a quarter of an hour later I saw him drive past the house in his car. That would be about three o'clock."

"And after that, did you ever see him again?"

"I never saw him again. I sat up until past midnight, but, of course, he never came home."

"Did you then suspect that any mischance had befallen him?"

"I was rather uneasy," Kickweed replied, because he had apparently intended to come home. Otherwise, I should not have been, as he often stayed away from home without notice."

"When did you first learn that there was something wrong?"

"It was in the afternoon of the twentieth of October. Mr Horridge had called to see him, and we were just discussing the possible reasons for his staying away when a police officer arrived, carrying deceased's raincoat, and told us that deceased had apparently absconded from the hospital at Gravesend. And that was all that I ever knew of the matter until I heard Dr Thorndyke's evidence."

"Then," said the coroner, "to repeat; you saw him drive away on the seventeenth of October and you never saw him or had any knowledge of him, again. Is that not so?"

"I never saw him again. But as to having any further knowledge of him, I am rather doubtful. I received a letter from him."

"You received a letter from him!" the coroner repeated in evident surprise. "When did you receive that letter?"

"It was delivered on the morning of the twenty-seventh of last March."

A murmur of astonishment arose from the jury and the coroner exclaimed in a tone of amazement: "Last March! Why, the man had been dead for months!"

"So it appears," Kickweed admitted; "and I am glad to believe that the letter was not really written by him."

"Why do you say that?"

"Because," Kickweed replied, "it was not a very creditable letter for a gentleman of Mr Penrose's character. It was a foolish letter and not as polite as it should have been."

"Have you that letter about you?"

"No. I handed it to Dr Thorndyke, and I believe he has it still. But I can remember the substance of its contents. It directed me to lock up the small room and deposit the key at Mr Penrose's bank."

"And did you do so?"

"Certainly, I did, though Dr Thorndyke seemed rather opposed to my doing so. But, at the time, I supposed it to be a genuine letter from my employer and, of course, I had no choice but to carry out his instructions."

"Have you formed any opinion as to who might have written that letter?"

"No, I have not the faintest idea. Until I heard Dr Thorndyke's evidence, I still supposed it to be a genuine letter from deceased."

"Well," said the coroner, "it is a most extraordinary affair. I think we had better recall Dr Thorndyke and hear what he can tell us about it."

Accordingly, as Kickweed had apparently given all the information that he had to give, and no one wished to ask him any questions, he was allowed to return to his seat and Thorndyke was recalled.

"Will you tell us what you know about this very remarkable letter that Mr Kickweed received?" the coroner asked.

"I first heard of that letter when Mr Kickweed called at my chambers late in the evening of the twenty-seventh of last March. He then informed me that he had received that letter and gave it to me to read. I read and examined it and at once came to the conclusion that it was a forgery. I took a photograph of it – of which I have a copy here – and carried the original to Brodribb, deceased's solicitor, to whom I handed it for safe custody and to whom I stated my opinion that it was a forgery."

"You decided at once that the letter was a forgery. What led you to that decision?"

"My decision was based on the circumstances and on the character of the letter itself. As to the circumstances, I had by that time formed the very definite opinion that Daniel Penrose was dead and that he had died on the seventeenth of the previous October. The letter itself presented several suspicious features. The matter of it was quite unreasonable and inadequate. The room was already locked up and the key was in the very safe custody of deceased's trusted and responsible servant, and had been for months. The directions in the letter appeared to be merely a pretext for writing and suggested some ulterior purpose. Then the manner of the letter was quite out of character with that of the supposed writer – a gentleman addressing his confidential servant. It was written in a tone of coarse, jocular familiarity with a most ill-mannered caricature of Mr Kickweed's name. It impressed me as a grotesque, overdone attempt to imitate deceased's habitually facetious manner of speech. And, on questioning Mr Kickweed, who was obviously hurt and surprised by the rudeness of this letter, I learned that deceased had always been in the habit of addressing him in a strictly correct and courteous fashion."

"Apart from these inferences, was there anything visible that marked this letter as a forgery?"

"I did not discover anything. Of the handwriting I could not judge as I was not familiar with deceased's writing. But there were no signs of tracing or other gross indications of forgery. But I may say that Mr Brodribb was of opinion that the writing did not look, to him, like that of deceased."

"You say that the matter of this letter suggested to you that a mere pretext had been made for writing and that there was some ulterior purpose. Can you suggest what that ulterior purpose might have been?"

"I suggest that its purpose was to make it appear that deceased was alive."

"That seems to imply that the unknown writer of the letter knew that he was dead, though no one but yourself had any suspicion that he was not still alive. There would seem to be no object in trying to prove that a man was alive when nobody supposed that he was dead. Don't you agree?

"Yes," replied Thorndyke; "that seems to be the natural inference."

"I suppose you cannot offer any suggestion as to who the writer of the letter may have been?

"I cannot. It seems clear that whoever he may have been, he must have been well acquainted with deceased, for the phraseology of the letter, although greatly exaggerated, was a recognisable imitation of deceased's rather odd manner of expressing himself. But I cannot give him a name."

"There was one matter that we overlooked when you were giving evidence. You ascertained in some mysterious manner that deceased was buried in Julliberrie's Grave. But is that the place where he met his death, or was his body brought from some other place?"

"I should say that there is no doubt that he was killed close to the place where his body was found. The implements which we found in the wood and which have been identified as his property suggest very strongly that he came to Julliberrie's Grave of his own accord with the intention of searching for antiquities for his collection. Probably he had actually done some excavation in the mound and the cavity that he had dug offered the facilities for disposing of his body. And the finding of the weapon with which he was apparently killed, near to the body, supports this view."

"Yes," said the coroner, "I think you have made it clear that the death occurred in the neighbourhood of the barrow and that the body was not brought there from a distance. And that, I think, gives us all the evidence that we need."

He bowed to Thorndyke, and as the latter returned to his seat, he began a brief and very sensible summing up.

"The disappearance of Mr Daniel Penrose involves a long and complicated story. But with that story we are not concerned. This is a coroner's inquest; and the function of such an inquiry is to answer certain questions relating to a dead body which has been found within our jurisdiction. Those questions are: Who is the dead person? and where, when and by what means did deceased meet with his death? We are not concerned with the person, if any, who caused the death of deceased unless such person should be plainly and evidently in view. We have to decide whether or not a crime has been committed, but it is not our function to bring that crime home to any particular person. That duty appertains to the police.

"Now, in respect of those questions which I have mentioned, we have no difficulty. The evidence which we have heard enables us to answer them quite confidently. The body has been identified as that of a gentleman named Daniel Penrose; and it has been clearly proved that he met his death at a place called Julliberrie's Grave on the seventeenth of last October and that his death was caused by violence inflicted by some unknown person. These are matters of fact which have been proved; and the only question which you have to decide is that of the nature of the act by which the death was caused. Deceased was killed by a heavy blow on the head inflicted with a bronze pestle. The person who struck that blow killed deceased and, therefore, undeniably committed an act of homicide. But there are many kinds of homicide, varying in their degree of culpability. A man may justifiably kill another in defence of his own life. Then there is no crime. Or he may kill another quite accidentally when again there is no crime. Or he may kill another in the course of a struggle, by violence which was not intended to cause death. Here the act of homicide amounts only to manslaughter; and the degree of criminality will depend on the particular circumstances. Again, a man may kill another with the deliberate and considered intention of killing him – that is with what the law calls malice. Such deliberate and premeditated killing constitutes wilful murder.

"Now, in the present case, we have to consider the circumstances in which the death of deceased occurred; and of those circumstances we have very imperfect knowledge. A striking fact is that the weapon with which deceased was killed was his own property and must, apparently, have been brought to the place by himself. We have learned, also, that he habitually carried this weapon for the purpose of self-defence. There is thus the suggestion that he may have so used it on the occasion when he was killed. That is to say, there is a distinct suggestion of a struggle, and the actual possibility that deceased may have been the aggressor, killed by the unknown in self-defence.

"On the other hand, the unknown, having killed deceased buried the body secretly and hurried away from the place – incidentally killing another person on his way – and has since given no information and made no sign, unless we assume that the very mysterious letter that Mr Kickweed received emanated from him. And it is, perhaps, worth while to give that letter a brief consideration, as it seems to have some bearing on the question which we are trying to decide.

"Who was the writer of that letter and for what purpose was the letter written? From Dr Thorndyke we learn that the writer must have been some person who was well acquainted with deceased. That is an important matter, but we are not concerned with the actual identity of the writer. We are concerned with his connection with the death of deceased and that connection seems to be suggested by the purpose of the letter. That purpose seems to be indicated quite clearly by Dr Thorndyke. It was to create the belief that deceased was still alive. But nobody – excepting the doctor – had any doubt that he was alive. No suggestion had been made by anybody that he might be dead. Then why should the writer of this letter have sought to create a belief which was already universally held? The only possible answer seems to be that he, himself, knew that deceased was dead and he wished, in the interests of his own safety, to forestall any suspicions that might arise that deceased might be dead.

"Thus the consideration of this letter suggests to us, first, that the writer knew that deceased was dead, and second that he had reasons for desiring that the fact of the death should not become known or suspected. But the fact of the death could have been known only to the person who killed deceased; and his anxiety to conceal the fact suggests strongly that he had no reasonable defence if he should be charged with the murder of deceased.

"That, I think, is all that I need say. Deceased was evidently killed by some unknown person; and it is for you to decide whether the circumstances, so far as they are known to us, suggest excusable homicide, accidental homicide, manslaughter or wilful murder."

On the conclusion of the summing up, the jury consulted together for a few minutes. Then the foreman announced that they had agreed on their finding.

"And what decision have you arrived at?" the coroner asked.

"We find that the deceased was murdered by some person unknown."

"Yes," said the coroner, "I think that it is the only reasonable conclusion at which you could have arrived. I will record a verdict of wilful murder by some person unknown, and we may hope that the police will presently be able to discover who that unknown person is and bring him to justice."

He entered the verdict in the depositions and this brought the proceedings to an end.

Chapter Seventeen

Thorndyke Retraces the Trail

As the court rose and we all stood up, Miller turned on me fiercely.

"You never told me about that letter," he exclaimed; "and there was not a word about it in the synopsis that the doctor gave me."

"As to me," said I, "there is no question of reservations. I did not refer to it because I had not regarded it as having any particular bearing on the case."

"No bearing!" exclaimed Miller. "Why, it hits you in the face. But if you think it has no bearing, I'll warrant that is not the doctor's view!"

"Naturally," I replied, "I don't know what his views are, but he is here and can answer for himself."

"Well," said Miller, "what about it, Doctor? You knew about that letter and you must know quite well who wrote it and why he wrote it."

"Now, Miller," said Thorndyke, "don't let us misuse words. We don't know who wrote that letter. We may have our opinions, and they may be right – or wrong. But in any case they will be pretty difficult to turn into evidence."

"I suspect you have done that already," grumbled Miller, "and you are keeping that evidence to yourself."

"You are quite wrong," Thorndyke replied. "I have no evidence beyond the facts which are known to you. Actually, I have given very little attention to the letter. It threw no light on the problem which I was trying to solve; whether Penrose was alive or dead, and, if he was dead, where we might look for his body."

"I should have thought it was highly relevant," Miller objected. "If it was good enough for some one to forge a letter to prove that Penrose was alive, when nobody supposed otherwise, that would suggest pretty strongly that the forger knew he was dead."

"So it would," Thorndyke agreed, "but that was of no use to me. I was not out for opinions or beliefs but for demonstrable facts."

"Well," said Miller, "you have produced your demonstrable facts all right, and you have solved your problem. And now, I suppose, you are going on to the next problem: Who murdered Daniel Penrose? And the solution of that problem is to be found in that letter; and as we are both working to the same end, I think you ought to put me in possession of any facts that are known to you."

"But, my dear Miller," Thorndyke protested, "I have no facts respecting this letter that are not known to you. I will hand you the photograph, and you can have an enlargement if you want to employ handwriting experts, or you can have the original. That is all I can do for you."

He produced his letter-case, and, taking the photograph of the forged letter from it, handed it to Miller; who slipped it into his wallet and buried the latter in the depths of an internal pocket. As he did so, he looked round sharply and exclaimed:

"What is the matter, Mr Horridge? Are you not feeling well sir?"

I looked at our friend, who seemed to be groping his way towards the door, and certainly the inquiry was justified. His aspect was ghastly. His face was blanched to a tallowy white, his hands trembled visibly, and he had the dazed, bewildered appearance suggestive of a severe mental shock.

"No," he replied unsteadily. "I am not feeling at all well. This awful affair has been too much for me. It was all so horrible and so unexpected."

"Yes," Miller agreed sympathetically. "I expect it has given you a bad shake-up. Better come along with me to the bar and have a good stiff whisky. Don't you think so, Doctor?"

"I think," replied Thorndyke, "that a hot meal and a glass of wine would be better, if Mr Horridge is returning to town this evening."

"I am," said Horridge, "but I couldn't look at food just now. Besides, my train is due in less than half an hour."

"Well, then," urged Miller, "come along to the bar and have a good, stiff drink. That will pick you up and fit you for the journey home. I happen to be going by that train, myself, so I can see you safely to Charing Cross, and into a cab if necessary."

I think Horridge would sooner have been without the proffered escort, but Miller left him no choice, and he accordingly allowed himself passively to be led away in the direction of the bar.

Thorndyke watched the two men disapprovingly as they passed out, and when they had disappeared, he remarked:

"I am afraid Miller is going to be a nuisance to us. His activity is premature."

"Yes," I agreed, "he is in full cry after Horridge and he thinks that he is on a hot trail. Obviously, he is convinced that Horridge wrote that letter, and I think he is right."

"I have no doubt that he is," said Thorndyke. "The obvious purpose of that letter was to create evidence that Penrose was alive after Oliver's death, and so would inherit his property. But it would be impossible to prove that Horridge wrote it."

"So it may be," said I. "But Miller has got him at a disadvantage, and he is going to push his opportunity for all that it is worth. If he lets on that he is a police officer, Horridge will probably collapse altogether. He is in a fearful state of panic."

"And well he may be," Thorndyke rejoined, "if he wrote that letter. For, quite apart from the suggestion of guilty knowledge that it offers, the mere writing and uttering of that letter is a serious crime. It is a forgery in the fullest sense. It was done with intent to deceive, and the purpose of the deception was grossly fraudulent.

If Miller can frighten him into an admission of having written the letter, he will be absolutely certain of securing a conviction."

"On the charge of forgery," said I. "But that is not Miller's objective. You heard what he said. He is all out on the capital charge."

"Yes, I realise that," said Thorndyke. "Which is why I say that he is going to be a nuisance to us. Because he won't be able to prove his case and he will have set up a disturbance just at the moment when what is needed is a little masterly inactivity combined with careful observation. It is a pity that Miller will not trust us more. He will butt in when the case is not ready for police methods. However, I am glad he is not travelling up with us. His eagerness to acquire knowledge becomes rather fatiguing."

"We are not going up by that train, then?"

"No. We may as well have a little early dinner and take the motor omnibus to Canterbury."

We adopted this plan, and, after a comfortable and restful meal, caught the omnibus and were duly deposited in the main street of Canterbury, not far from the cathedral. As we proceeded thence towards the station, we noticed an "antique" shop, the fascia of which bore the single word "Todd."

"This," I remarked, halting to glance at the antiquities – mostly of the prehistoric type – which were displayed in the window, "seems to be the shop that Horridge referred to as a favourite resort of poor Penrose. Probably some of the things that we saw in the collection came from here."

"One of them almost certainly did," said Thorndyke. "Don't you remember that Saxon brooch? The entry in the catalogue noted its origin as 'Sweeney's Resurrection.' "

"I remember the entry, now you mention it. Lockhart suggested that 'Sweeney' probably meant Todd, and apparently he was right."

We went on our way, discussing the late Daniel Penrose and his harmless oddities, of which I had been so intolerant, and eventually reached the station in time to select our compartment at our leisure. There were few passengers besides ourselves, so that we were able to secure a first-class smoking-compartment of which we were the sole occupants, a matter to which I attended with some anxiety. For the train ran through to Charing Cross without a stop, and the long, uninterrupted journey would afford an opportunity for certain explanations which I felt were now overdue. With this view Thorndyke apparently agreed, for when I presently opened my examination with a tentative question, he replied quite freely, without a sign of his customary reticence and evasiveness.

"Of course," I began, "when Penrose's body was found, I realised at once, in general terms, how I had managed to miss the essential points of the case. The possibility that Penrose might be dead never occurred to me; and it ought. It looks obvious enough now. But still I don't quite see how you contrived to establish the fact of his death – which you evidently did – and locate the place of his burial."

"It was all very hypothetical," he replied, "even up to the last stage. Until Elmhurst reported the discovery I was not certain that my theory of the course of events might not contain some fallacy that I had overlooked. Hence my rather elaborate provisions to cover up a possible failure. But to come back to your own case; the initial mistake that you made was in disregarding the good old Spencerian principle that when certain facts are presented as proving a particular thesis, we should consider, not only that which is presented, but that, also, which is not presented. In other words, we should at once separate fact from inference.

"Now, when Brodribb gave us his narrative of the disappearance of Penrose, he honestly believed that his story was a recital of facts; whereas it was really a mixture of fact and inference. It had not occurred to him that the hospital patient might be some person other than Penrose, and he accordingly presented that patient as Penrose. And you accepted that presentation as a statement of fact, whereas it was only an inference. Hence you made a false start and got on the wrong track from the beginning.

"I was fortunate enough to avoid this pitfall; for even while Brodribb was telling us his story, I made a mental note that the identity of the patient had been taken for granted, and that it would have to be considered, before any action could be taken. But as soon as I began to consider the question, it became clear to me that the balance of probability was against the patient's being Penrose."

"Did it really?" I exclaimed. "Now, I should have said that all the known facts pointed to his being Penrose. And so it seems to me still."

"Then," said Thorndyke, "let us argue the question. We will take two hypotheses: A, that the patient was Penrose; and B, that he was some other person and examine the evidence in support of each.

"Let us begin with hypothesis A. What evidence was there that the patient was Daniel Penrose?

"There were five principal items of evidence. 1. The car was certainly Penrose's car. 2. The patient had been in possession of that car. 3. The coat, which was undeniably the patient's coat, had Penrose's driving licence in its pocket. 4. The initials on the patient's collar were Penrose's initials. 5. A fragment of an ancient object was found in the pocket of the patient's coat. But Penrose was a collector of antiquities and there was reason to believe that he had gone out that day for the purpose of acquiring some such objects.

"Now, you will notice that the first three items are what we may call extrinsic. They afford no evidence of personal identity. They merely prove that the patient was in possession of Penrose's property, and they are thus of very little weight. The other two items we may call intrinsic. They are connected with the actual personality of the patient.

"Of these, the initials on the collar furnished by far the more weighty evidence of identity."

"I should have assumed them to be quite conclusive," said I.

"Then you would have been wrong," he replied, "for you would have been assuming that Penrose was the only man in the world whose initials were DP. Still, the fact that the patient's initials were DP established a very high probability that he was Daniel Penrose."

"I should have put it higher than that," said I. "It would have seemed to me as nearly as possible a certainty. For if he were not Penrose the coincidence would be, as it was, such an amazing one."

"I think you exaggerate the abnormality," he rejoined, "it was a very remarkable coincidence; but there are two things that we should bear in mind. First, the adverse chances were not so enormous as you seem to imply. There are great numbers of men whose initials are DP and, secondly, that the laws of probability relate to large numbers. They must be applied with great caution to particular cases. The tendency to assume that because a thing is improbable it will not happen is a mistake. Improbabilities and coincidences are constantly occurring, and we have to allow for that fact.

"Nevertheless, it had to be admitted that those initials made it, in a very high degree, probable that the patient was Daniel Penrose. But now let us take the alternative hypothesis and see what the probabilities were on the other side. And first, consider the conduct of the patient. Owing to his black eyes and contused face, he was completely unrecognisable. Nobody could form any idea what he was like. But when his injuries cleared up he would have been recognisable; and the extraordinary and determined way in which he absconded from the hospital at a carefully chosen time, is very suggestive. Evidently, during his simulated unconsciousness, he had been watching for an opportunity to get away at night when his odd appearance would be less observed. His behaviour was like that of a man who sought to escape before recognition should be possible.

"Then, there was the man's previous behaviour. Apparently he had abandoned his car. But a car which is abandoned is usually a stolen car. Again, the car which killed the old woman was being driven wildly and furiously. We knew then of no reason why Penrose should have been driving in that manner. But a stranger in unlawful possession of a car would probably have sufficient reasons; and in fact, persons who steal cars usually do drive furiously. Then, if Penrose had knocked down the old woman he would probably have stopped and reported the accident. He was a responsible, decent gentleman and there was no reason why he should not have stopped. But a stranger, in possession of a stolen car – in effect, a fugitive – could not afford to stop and be interviewed.

"Furthermore, if this man had been in unlawful possession of a car, something must have happened to the owner of that car at some place. The stranger would have good reasons for getting away from that neighbourhood as quickly as possible. Thus, the furious driving before and after the accident would be sufficiently explained.

"So, looking at the case as whole, you will see that, on the assumption that the patient was Penrose, his conduct was utterly unreasonable and inexplicable; on the assumption that he was not Penrose, his behaviour was in every respect exactly what we should have expected it to be. For if he was not Penrose, he was under strong suspicion of having made away with Penrose, for the reasons: 1. That Penrose had unaccountably disappeared, and 2. That the stranger was in possession of Penrose's car and his driving licence. Taking all the facts together, I came to the conclusion that, in spite of the initials, the balance of probability was against his being Penrose.

"Nevertheless, those initials presented a formidable objection to the view that I was disposed to adopt, and I decided that the question whether they were Penrose's initials or those of some other person must be settled before any further investigation would be worth while. It was not a difficult question to dispose of, and it turned out to be easier than I had expected. You remember how we obtained the answer?"

"Indeed, I don't," I replied. "I never knew that the question had been raised."

"You never followed this case very closely for some reason," said Thorndyke, "but if you will recall our visit to the garage, you will remember that I was able, quite easily, to extract a statement from Kickweed which settled the question definitely. We learned from him that Penrose was in the habit of marking all his portable property, including his collars and handkerchiefs, with his name, D Penrose, by means of a rubber stamp."

I grinned rather sheepishly. "I remember quite well now you mention it, but I am afraid that, at the time, I merely wondered, like a fool, why you were going into such trivialities at such length."

"Well," said Thorndyke, "you will now see that our conversation with Kickweed cleared up all our difficulties. Penrose's collars were marked 'D Penrose' with a rubber stamp; the patient's collar was marked 'DP' with a marking-ink pencil. Therefore, the evidence of the collar supported all the other evidence; it went to prove that the patient was not Penrose.

"Then, at once, arose two other questions: If he was not Penrose, who was he? And what had become of Penrose? The first question had to be left until we had answered the second. Penrose had disappeared. What had happened to him? Was he alive or dead?

"Now, having regard to the strange and sinister circumstances: the disappearance of one man, the appearance of another man in possession of his property and the anxiety of that other man to escape without being identified, meant that there was only one reasonable conclusion that we could come to. The overwhelming probability was that Penrose was dead and that his body had been concealed by burial or otherwise.

"Adopting this view, as I did, the next questions were: Where did Penrose meet his death? And where was his body concealed? The latter question was the more important, but the answer to both was probably the same. And both questions were contained in the further question: From what place did the car start on that wild journey home?

"Now, in regard to this problem – the starting-point of the car's journey – we had two clues and they were both very imperfect. The place where the woman was killed was in the Canterbury district and the car was travelling via Maidstone towards Gravesend. But the speed at which it was travelling made it difficult to judge how far it might have come, especially as we had no exact information as to the time at which it started. All that we knew was that the car advanced towards the Canterbury – Ashford road from some place to the south and east.

"The other clue was the very distinctive pottery fragment. But this also was a very ambiguous clue. The pocket in which we found it was not Penrose's pocket; and we did not know how long it had been in that pocket. However, when we came to examine these difficulties, they did not appear insuperable. Thus, notwithstanding that the fragment was in another man's possession, I was disposed to associate it with Penrose for two reasons; first, that Penrose was a collector of antiquities, and, second, that, when he started from home he took with him – as we learned from Kickweed – two digging tools and was, apparently, intending to do some sort of excavation. As to the second difficulty, the earth in which the fragment was embedded was of the same kind as that which we scraped from the coat and that which we found later on the car. So it appeared practically certain that the fragment was the product of that day's digging.

"The next question was: Whence had the fragment come? That was a vitally important question; for there could be little doubt that the place where the fragment was dug up was the place where Penrose had met his death and where his body was concealed. But how was that question to be answered? It seemed that the only possible method was that which I had adopted in regard to the other questions; to form a working hypothesis and see whither it led. Now, the broken edges of the fragment showed fresh fractures. It had been broken off the pot at the time of the excavation; and as the digging had probably been done after dark by a very imperfect light, the fragment had apparently been overlooked, the new fracture of the pot being mistaken for an ancient one. It followed that, somewhere, there was a broken pot with a space in it corresponding to this fragment, by which it could infallibly be recognised. If we could find that pot it would probably be possible to ascertain where it had been dug up.

"But where were we to look for that pot? The only possible place known to us was Penrose's collection; and circumstances created an initial probability that it was there. But, further, I had a theory, as I mentioned to you, that the expedition on which Penrose had embarked that day possibly had the express purpose of recovering this fragment to make the imperfect pot complete. Accordingly, I took an opportunity of inspecting the collection, and I took with me my invaluable box of moulding wax.

"You know the result. The pot was there, easily recognisable at sight and conclusively identified by the wax squeeze. There was also a catalogue entry, presumably describing the piece and recording the source whence it had been obtained. But the wording of the entry was so obscure as to present a fresh puzzle. Nevertheless, it was a great advance; for the information was there, if we could only extract the meaning of the words.

"Those words were, you will remember: "Moulin à vent: Julie: Polly." Now, the first term was obvious enough; the piece was a 'Windmill Hill' pot. By the study of other entries in the catalogue, I reached the conclusion that 'Julie' probably represented the locality, and 'Polly' the person from whom the pot was obtained. Accordingly, the first thing to be done was to ascertain, if possible, the meaning of the word 'Julie.'

"To this end, I procured and read various works dealing with Neolithic pottery; and, since our pot had almost certainly been dug out of a long barrow, I gave attention to those also. But the result, for a long time, was very disappointing. I read through quite a large number of books and papers on barrows and pottery without meeting with any name resembling 'Julie'. At last, I struck the clue in Jessup's *Archaeology of Kent*. There, in the chapter dealing with Neolithic remains, I found a reference to a long barrow know as Julliberrie's Grave, in the neighbourhood of Chilham. Looking it up on the ordnance map, I saw at once that its situation fitted the circumstances exactly, for it was quite close to the known track of the car. Thereupon I decided that Julliberrie's Grave was almost certainly the place for which I had been searching; the starting-point of the car's wild career and the place in which the body of Daniel Penrose was probably reposing.

"The question then arose; What was to be done? I had not a particle of definite evidence to support my belief. My whole case was just a train of hypothetical reasoning – guesswork, if you will; and guesswork was not good enough either for the Home Office or the Office of Works. Besides, as you acutely observed, I didn't want to let the cat out of the bag prematurely. Yet it was impossible to get any further in the investigation until the barrow had been explored.

"There was only one thing to do – to organise a scientific excavation of the barrow by skilled and trained archaeologists. That would ensure an absolutely exhaustive exploration without injury to the barrow and without any disclosure of my suspicions if they should prove to be unfounded. Accordingly, I looked up our invaluable friend, Elmhurst, and, to my great satisfaction, found that he had both the means and the will to carry out the excavation if I were prepared to finance the work.

"You know the rest. Everything went according to plan and the first stage of our investigation was brought to a triumphant conclusion. I only hope that the second stage will go as well. It ought to ; for we have now a solid foundation of established fact to build on."

"Yes," I agreed. "We know that Penrose is dead and that somebody killed him. But I don't see much of a lead towards the conclusion as to who that somebody may have been. But I expect that you do. Perhaps the word 'Polly', in that ridiculous catalogue entry, suggests something to you. Apparently, it refers to a person, though it is hardly safe to say even that. The only thing that is certain is that it doesn't mean Polly."

"The meaning of that word," he replied, "really belongs to the second stage of our inquiry, on which we are now embarking; the identification of the person whom we may call 'the murderer' –

though the fact of murder is not established. Penrose was killed with his own weapon, which, as the coroner justly observed, suggests a struggle or conflict. But as to the identity of that person, I have not yet formed a definite opinion. There is one essential question that has to be settled before we begin to theorise. We have got to know whether the alleged burglary at Queen Square was an actual burglary and whether the cupboard in the small room was actually opened."

"You mean," said I, "that, if the cupboard was opened, it must have been opened with Penrose's keys, as you have always maintained, and that, therefore, the person who opened it must have been the murderer."

"I would hardly go as far as that," he replied. "If some person did actually enter that room and open the cupboard he must have opened it with Penrose's keys or with duplicates made from them. That would suggest that he was either the murderer or in league with the murderer. But even if he opened the cupboard, that would not be conclusive evidence that he stole the jewels. He might have found the cupboard empty. That is not probable, but it has to be borne in mind. And then we have to remember that the only evidence of the room's having been entered is the unsupported statement of one person."

"Yes," said I, "and not an entirely unsuspected person. Our friend, Horridge, seems to have had considerable misgivings as to the discreet and melancholy Kickweed; but I didn't think that you had any suspicions in that direction."

"I don't say that I have," replied Thorndyke, "or that I entertain seriously the various possibilities that I have mentioned. I am merely pointing out that we have got a good many eggs in our basket. A sensible man keeps in his mind all the possibilities, no matter how remote; but he also gives his special attention, in the first place, to those that are least remote. And, meanwhile, we have got to begin our quest by settling definitely whether that cupboard has or has not been opened. We have very little doubt as to what was in it when Penrose was alive, and Lockhart will now have to make an explicit statement. If the things are not there, we shall have a definite fact and can consider what follows from it; and if we find the collection intact — well, I shall be very much surprised."

CHAPTER EIGHTEEN

The Opening of the Safe

On suitable occasions, Thorndyke could lie remarkably low and exhibit a most masterly inactivity. But also, on suitable occasions he could act with surprising promptitude. And the matter of the alleged burglary at Queen Square presented such an occasion. Armed with an authority from Mr Brodribb, as joint executor, he proceeded to call on Chubb's and make all the necessary arrangements for the opening of the safe in the small room; and then, as I gathered, he had an interview with Lockhart. What passed at the interview I did not learn, but I suspect that there was some rather plain speaking. Not that it should have been necessary, for Lockhart was a lawyer and knew in what a very questionable position he stood.

But whatever passed on that occasion, he was quite amenable. He frankly admitted that he had seen in the small room a collection of jewels which were almost certainly the Billington jewels, and he gave Thorndyke a written statement to that effect. Further, he wrote a letter to Miller, in somewhat ambiguous terms, referring him to Thorndyke for fuller particulars, and agreed to be present when the safe was opened.

Naturally, this letter brought Miller, hotfoot, to our chambers, and a preliminary discussion was unavoidable in spite of Thorndyke's efforts to stave it off.

"Now, Doctor," the superintendent began, a little truculently, "this is the sort of thing that I was complaining of. You knew those jewels were there, but you didn't let on the faintest hint to me."

"I did not know," Thorndyke protested. "I only suspected; and I don't profess to communicate mere suspicions."

"Well," rejoined Miller, "there they were, at any rate, and we can take it as a certainty that they are not there now."

"I expect you are right," said Thorndyke, "but why not leave the discussion until we know?"

"For all practical purposes, we do know," replied Miller. "We can take it that there was either a real or a pretended burglary, and in either case the stuff is pretty certainly gone; and the question is, who lifted it?"

"You remember," said Thorndyke, "that the keys were stolen from Penrose's body. Presumably they were taken for the purpose of being used; and they could have been used only by entering the premises. Moreover, if the cupboard was opened, it could have been opened only with Penrose's keys."

"Yes, that's a fact," Miller agreed. "but suppose the murderer did enter the premises, how do we know that he found the stuff there? Or, for that matter, how do we know that the place was ever entered? We have got only one man's word for it. And, to an experienced eye, it looks a bit like an indoor job."

"I don't quite see what is in your mind," said Thorndyke. "You are not letting your thoughts run on Horridge?"

Miller grinned sourly. "No," he replied, "though I must admit that I did suspect him very considerably in connection with the murder. But I have squeezed him pretty dry and I can tell you he didn't like being squeezed. But in the end, he was able to produce an undeniable alibi – a club dinner that he attended on the seventeenth of October at which all the members signed their names. So Horridge is now out of the picture."

"He was never in," said Thorndyke. "The proceedings at the inquest made that perfectly clear."

"What proceedings do you mean?" Miller demanded.

"I am referring to Kickweed's evidence," Thorndyke replied. "If you had not been so preoccupied with the forged letter, you would have seen that it excluded Horridge from any possible suspicion in regard to the murder. Kickweed deposed that on the twentieth of October, three days after the murder, and the very day after the flight of the presumed murderer from Gravesend Hospital, Horridge called at Queen Square to see Penrose; and the two of them, Horridge and Kickweed, interviewed a police officer who had come to bring the coat that was assumed to belong to Penrose. Now, if Horridge had been the murderer, he must also have been the hospital patient. But the patient had two very bad black eyes and a severe wound across his right eyebrow. Obviously, he would have been in no condition for paying calls; and you will remember that the police officer was looking for a man with two black eyes and a cut across his right eyebrow."

"Yes," Miller admitted, "I had overlooked that. But it did look as if Horridge had written that letter. Have you any idea who did write it? We have got to find that out."

"My dear Miller," Thorndyke said, a little impatiently, "you had better forget that letter. It is a criminal matter, but it has no bearing on the crime which we are investigating. But if you have dropped Horridge, what do you mean by suggesting that this burglary may have been an indoor job?"

"Well, you know," replied Miller, "this burglary rests on the story told by Mr Kickweed; and Mr Kickweed strikes me as a decidedly downy bird."

"He couldn't have been the murderer, you know," said Thorndyke. "But it was presumably the murderer who had the keys."

"I know," rejoined Miller. "But he was in the house; and there is such a thing as wax."

"You can take it," said Thorndyke, "that Penrose was not in the habit of leaving his keys about."

"No, probably not," Miller agreed, "but I suppose he had a bath sometimes, and I don't suppose he took his clothes in the bathroom with him."

Thorndyke smiled indulgently at the superintendent and admonished him in mock solemn tones:

"Now, my dear Miller, let me urge you to beware of obsessions. At the inquest you allowed yourself to become letter-minded and so you missed a vitally important item of evidence. And now you seem inclined to let yourself become Kickweed-minded. Why not leave Kickweed alone and address yourself to the more obvious lines of inquiry?"

"Still, you know, Doctor," Miller persisted, "somebody must have known that those jewels were there."

"There is not a particle of evidence that Kickweed did. You must remember that Penrose kept their existence absolutely secret from everybody excepting Lockhart; and he swore him to secrecy before he showed them. So far as we know, their existence was known only to two persons; Lockhart, and the man, whoever he was, who supplied them."

"Yes," said Miller, "the chappie who supplied them to Penrose certainly knew that they were there. It would be interesting, quite apart from the murder business, to know who he was. I wonder if it could have been Crabbe, after all."

"You needn't wonder, Miller," said Thorndyke. "It was Crabbe. I think there can be no doubt about that."

Miller sat up in his chair and turned a rather startled face to my colleague.

"Hallo, Doctor!" he exclaimed. "You seem to know a mighty lot about it. And how did you manage to dig up Mr Crabbe? I've been wondering about that ever since that evening when you asked me about him."

"There was a document," replied Thorndyke; "a scrap of paper, apparently a descriptive label, which was found in that small room, on the morning after the alleged burglary. That was what enabled me to connect Crabbe with Penrose's collection."

"Then," Miller exclaimed excitedly, "we have got actual, tangible evidence against Crabbe. Who has got that scrap of paper?"

"Brodribb has the original, but I kept a copy. You shall see it"; and, with this, he rose and went to the cabinet in which Penrose's dossier was kept. Taking out from the collection of notes and papers the copy of Mr Penrose's cryptogram, he brought it over and gravely handed it to Miller, who stared at it aghast while I watched him with unholy glee.

"I can't make anything of this," the superintendent grumbled. " 'Lobster: *hortus petasatus.*' It doesn't make sense. Besides, a lobster isn't a crab; and what in creation is a *hortus petasatus?*"

Thorndyke expounded the meaning of the inscription, explaining the late Mr Penrose's peculiarities of speech, and Miller listened with incredulous astonishment.

"Well, Doctor," he commented. "I take off my hat to you. That thing would have conveyed nothing to me. It's like some damn' silly puzzle game. And you might have passed it all round the CID and no one would have been an atom the wiser. But I am afraid it wouldn't do as evidence in a court of law."

"Possibly not," Thorndyke admitted; "but I am not concerned with the robbery charge against Crabbe. I am investigating the murder of Daniel Penrose; and I am assuming that there was a burglary, that the burglar was in possession of Penrose's keys and that he knew what the cupboard in the small room contained. Of course, if we find the jewels still in the cupboard, we shall know that those assumptions were wrong."

"Yes," Miller agreed. "but we shan't. Burglary or no burglary, those jewels have been pinched. I'd lay my bottom dollar to that. But you realise, Doctor, that, even if there was a burglary, the burglar couldn't have been Crabbe. He was in chokey at the time when it was supposed to have occurred."

"Yes," said Thorndyke, "I had noted that fact; so we shall have to look round for some other person who knew that the jewels were there. And no such person is actually known to us, if we except Lockhart, and I suppose we can hardly suspect him."

Miller grinned faintly at the suggestion and then became thoughtful. After a few minutes of profound reflection he remarked:

"Those locksmiths will make hay with poor old Penrose's safe. Are you going to be present to see how the job is done?"

I was instantly struck by this abrupt change of subject and I could see that it was also noticed by Thorndyke, who, however followed the superintendent's lead.

"No," he replied. "I shall not turn up until they have had time to get the job finished. But Polton will be there to watch the proceedings and pick up a few tips on the correct method of opening a safe."

"Ah!" said Miller, "I shall have to keep an eye on Mr Polton if he is going to qualify as an expert safe-breaker. He is mighty handy already in the matter of locks and skeleton keys and house-breaker's tools."

He pursued this facetious and quite irrelevant topic at considerable length and with no tendency whatever to revert to the subject of the Queen Square burglary. And then he pulled out his watch and, having bestowed on it a single startled glance, sprang up, declaring that, if he didn't look sharp, he would be late for an important appointment. And with this he took his departure hurriedly and with a distinctly purposive air.

"Miller has got a bright idea of some kind," I remarked when he had gone.

"Yes," Thorndyke agreed, "and he thinks he has got it all to himself. You noticed his sudden anxiety to switch the conversation off the subject of Mr Crabbe. Well, it is all to the good if he doesn't get busy prematurely. I suppose you are coming to swell the multitude at Queen Square tomorrow?"

"If there is room," I replied, "I should like to see the fateful question decided. But it will be a bit of an anti-climax if the stuff is there, after all, though I don't suppose Horridge will complain."

"He will have a bad disappointment," said Thorndyke, "if we find the jewels there and he is then told that they are stolen property. However, there is no use in speculating. Tomorrow we shall know whether they were or were not stolen, and until we know that, neither Miller nor I can decide on the next move."

When, on the following morning, we arrived at the house in Queen Square and were admitted by Kickweed, we learned from him that the locksmiths had started their work on the safe about an hour previously and that the operations were still in progress. Our friend shook his head despondently as he showed us into the morning-room and remarked that it was a dreadful business and very disturbing.

"Would you like to wait here until they are ready," he asked, "or will you join the – er – assembly in the great gallery?"

We elected to join the assembly, whereupon he ushered us into the gallery, announcing us with due solemnity as he threw open the door. The word "assembly" appeared to represent Mr Kickweed's state of mind rather than the actual facts, for there were only three persons present: Lockhart, Miller and Horridge, the latter very subdued, care-worn and decidedly gloomy. The cause of his depressed state was made evident presently when he took us apart, leaving Lockhart and Miller amicably discussing the legal position of an accessory after the fact.

"This is a nice state of affairs," Horridge complained. "Do you know that this detective fellow actually accused me, in so many words, of having murdered poor old Pen? Me, his old and trusted friend and an executor of his will! And, if I hadn't had a conclusive alibi, I believe he would have run me in. And now he tells me that even if we find the jewels intact, it will be of no advantage to me because they are all stolen property; which I don't believe. I ask you, is it likely that a man of Pen's character would have been guilty of trafficking in stolen goods?"

"I should say, certainly not," replied Thorndyke, "if he knew that the goods were stolen. But the point is hardly worth discussing if the goods in question have disappeared."

Here our conversation was interrupted by Polton who entered to announce that the work on the lock was completed and that the safe door was free and ready to be opened. Thereupon we followed him into the small room where we found two very superior artificers standing on guard over the remains of a large iron safe, the massive door of which was disclosed by the opening of the wooden case. Miller's prognostications had certainly not over-stated the results of the locksmiths' activities. To say nothing of the wooden door with its shattered detector lock, those artificers had undoubtedly "made hay with" the safe, itself.

"Now, Mr Horridge," said Miller, "you, as executor, are the proper person to open the safe."

Horridge, however, deputed his functions to one of the workmen who accordingly took hold of the battered door and swung it wide open, disclosing a range of shallow drawers like those of an entomological cabinet.

"Are those drawers in the condition in which you saw them when Mr Penrose showed you his collection?" Thorndyke asked.

"Yes, so far as I can see," Lockhart replied. "He took them out, one by one in their proper order from above downwards and carried each over to that table by the window so that we could see the contents better."

"Then," said Thorndyke, "we had better do the same."

But it was not necessary; for when the top drawer was pulled out it was seen to be undeniably empty. Horridge exhibited its vacant interior to the assembled company, turned it upside down and shook it, and glumly returned it to its place. The case was the same with the second drawer and also with the third, excepting that when it was inverted some small object was heard to fall out on to the floor. Miller picked it up and exhibited it in the palm of his hand, when it was seen to be a small opal and was dropped back into the drawer. But that little opal was the solitary occupant of the cabinet. Apart from it and a plentiful covering of dust, the whole range of drawers from top to bottom was empty.

"That burglar," Lockhart commented as the last of the drawers was slid back into its place, "was pretty thorough in his methods. He made a clean sweep of the whole collection; not only the gems but the coins as well. And he must have been fairly heavily laden when he went away for most of the coins were gold and I should say there were some hundreds of them."

"I don't fancy those coins were gold," said Miller. "I think I know where they came from and, if I am right, they were electros – copper, gilt. Still, even copper electros weigh something. But it's surprising what a lot of coins and jewellery you can stow away about your person if you have the right sort of pockets. And it's pretty certain that he had an overcoat as well."

"Do you remember, Lockhart," Thorndyke asked, "whether, when you saw the jewels, there were any labels attached to them?"

"Not attached," Lockhart replied. "There were no fixed labels; only slips of paper like those on the shelves of the gallery."

"Did you notice what was written on those slips of paper? Were they descriptive labels?"

Lockhart grinned. "You know what Penrose's descriptions were like," he replied, "and you have seen the catalogue. So far as I could make out, the descriptions on the labels were similar to those in the catalogue; apparently, unintelligible nonsense."

"You can't recall any of them?" Thorndyke asked.

"I remember one, because I tried to puzzle out what it could mean, and failed utterly. It was Decapod; *jardin à chapeau*. Does that convey anything to you?"

"It does to me, thanks to the doctor's explanations," said Miller, who had been listening eagerly to the questions and answers. "I don't know what a decapod is but I've got enough French to infer that *jardin à chapeau* is much the same as *hortus petasatus*. And the doctor can tell you what that means."

"What does it mean?" Lockhart demanded; and Thorndyke – not very willingly, I thought – gave the required explanation.

"Yes," Lockhart chuckled, I see now, though I hadn't your ingenuity. Poor old Penrose! What nonsense he did write and speak! But I think I also see the point of your questions."

"And an uncommonly good point it is," said Miller. "That chappie was careful to take away the labels as well as the goods, and if he hadn't dropped one of them we should know a good deal less than we do. It's a very significant point indeed."

"And now," said Thorndyke, "as we have done what we came to do, perhaps we had better leave Mr Horridge to discuss the question of repairs. Are you walking in our direction, Miller?"

The superintendent was not. He was proposing, he said, to make a slight survey of the premises to elucidate the circumstances of the burglary, but I suspected that he was unwilling to run the risk of an interrogation by Thorndyke. So we left him to his survey and, having once more condoled with Horridge, we set forth in company with Lockhart, leaving Polton to spy on the superintendent and worm out any trifles in the way of technical tips and trade secrets that he could from the locksmiths.

CHAPTER NINETEEN

Thorndyke's Dilemma

I have referred more than once to Thorndyke's habitual unwillingness to discuss uncompleted cases, excepting in relation to questions of fact, or to disclose any opinions or theories that he had built on the facts which were known to us both. I had come to accept this reticence as a condition of our friendship and usually refrained from any attempts to discover what lines his thoughts were pursuing or what inferences he had drawn. But when me met at our chambers in the evening after our visit to Queen Square, I found him in a mood of unwonted expansiveness, apparently ready to discuss our present case without any reservations.

The discussion opened with a question that I put tentatively, half expecting the usual invitation to exercise my own admirable faculty of deduction.

"I noticed that you and Miller seemed to attach great importance to the circumstance that the burglar had carefully removed all the labels from the drawers. I don't quite see why. Would not a burglar ordinarily take away any labels that might furnish a clue to what had been stolen?"

"I don't see why he should," Thorndyke replied. "An ordinary burglar would assume that the contents of the drawers were known, so that the labels would give no additional information. But these were not ordinary descriptive labels. They gave very definite information as to the person who had supplied the jewels;

and as those jewels were the proceeds of a robbery which was known to the police, the information would be very dangerous to the person named. But that would not concern an ordinary burglar. The labels would furnish no clue to his identity. Of course, we know that he was not an ordinary, casual burglar, since he had Penrose's keys. But the point is that, whoever he was, he seemed to consider it a matter of importance that the identity of the person who sold the jewels to Penrose should not become known."

"But the jewels were sold to Penrose by Crabbe."

"Yes."

"But Crabbe could not have been the burglar. He was in prison at the time."

"Exactly," Thorndyke rejoined. "That is the importance of the discovery. The labels implicated Crabbe. But Crabbe could not have been the burglar. It seems to follow that they implicated some one besides Crabbe; and as the burglar was in possession of Penrose's keys and would thus appear to have been either the murderer or an accessory to the murder, it would be very interesting to know whom those labels could have implicated. I fancy that Miller has a very definite opinion on the subject; and I am disposed to think that he is right."

"The deuce you are!" I exclaimed. "Then it seems to me that you have got the investigation much farther advanced than I had imagined. I had supposed that the search for the murderer had still to be begun. But it seems that there is already a definite suspect. Is that so?"

He reflected for a few moments and then replied: "The word 'suspect' is perhaps a little too strong. My conclusions as to the possible identity of the murderer are at present on an entirely hypothetical plane. I have considered the whole complex of circumstances connected with the murder and have noted the persons who seem to have made any sort of contact with those circumstances; and I have considered each of those persons in relation to the question whether he could possibly be the murderer and whether his known characteristics agree with those of the murderer."

"But," I demanded, "what do we know of the characteristics of the murderer?"

"Very little," he replied, "but still enough to enable us to apply at least a negative test in conjunction with the other considerations. Thus we can exclude Kickweed and Horridge because, although they make certain contacts, neither could have been present at the place and time of the murder. But let us take a glance at the positive aspects.

"We begin with the justifiable assumption that the hospital patient was the murderer. Now, what do we know about him? Of his personal characteristics we have no description whatever. All that we know is that his collar bore the letters, DP, which were presumably the initial letters of his name, and that he had a deep wound crossing his right eyebrow which must have left a rather conspicuous permanent scar. So you see that, little as we know, we have the means of excluding or accepting any given individual. If his characteristics agree with those of the patient, he is a possible suspect; if they do not agree, he is not possible."

"And do you know of any person whose characteristics do agree with those of the patient?"

"Up to a certain point," he replied. "The ascertainment of the scar would involve a personal examination. That will have to come later as a final test. For the present, we must be content with agreement so far as is known."

"But you have some such person in view?"

Again he reflected for a few moments. At length, he replied:

"I am in a rather odd dilemma. I have two theoretically possible suspects and I can make no sort of choice between them."

"And do the names of both of them begin with DP?" I asked, imagining that I was putting a poser.

"But," he exclaimed, "that is the extraordinary thing. They do. There is a coincidence for you if you like. It was a striking coincidence that the murderer should have the same initials as the victim. But this is more than striking. It is almost incredible."

"I suppose we name no names," I suggested humbly.

"I don't know why not," he replied. "We keep our own counsel until we can turn hypothesis into proof. Well, my two possible suspects are Deodatus Pettigrew and David Parrott."

"Parrott!" I exclaimed in astonishment. "I don't see where he comes into it; or Pettigrew either for that matter."

"It is just a question of the contacts that they make with the circumstances of the murder," he replied "Let us take them separately and see what those contacts are. The odd and confusing thing is that their contacts are entirely separate and from different sides."

"Is it possible that they were both concerned in the murder?" I suggested; that they may have been confederates?"

"I have considered that," he answered. "It is possible, but, I think, unlikely. The crime has all the appearances of a one-man job. Moreover, I can find no evidence of any contact between these two men. So far as I know, they were strangers to each other and they persistently remain completely separate. So we will consider them separately.

"Now, as to Parrott. The hospital patient had in his pocket a fragment of pottery which almost certainly came from Julliberrie's Grave. That fragment had been broken off a pot which was in Penrose's museum and which had come from Julliberrie's Grave. The entry in the catalogue relating to that pot consisted of the usual three terms; the description of the piece – 'Moulin à vent' – the place whence it came – 'Julie' – and a third term – 'Polly' – which presumably indicated the person who supplied it."

"Yes," I agreed, "that seems to have been Penrose's custom. So now the question is: Who is Polly? What is she? Have you found an answer to it?"

"I infer, having regard to Penrose's cryptic terminology that 'Polly' indicates Mr Parrott."

"Of course," I exclaimed. "I ought to have spotted that. Poll parrot. Pretty Polly. But still, you know, Thorndyke, it is only a guess, after all."

"It is a little more than that," he objected. "Parrott is referred to frequently in the catalogue, and always by some allusive name, such as Perroquet, Psittacus, or Popinjay. Penrose may well have tried to find a new variant. But I admit your objection. This is not proof; it is only hypothesis. That is all I claim. At present we are only looking for someone whom it would be possible to suspect, as a guide to further investigation. Parrott is such a person, and so is Pettigrew, whose case is equally hypothetical. But you will note that Parrott agrees with the hospital patient in the initial of his name and that we have reason to believe that he knew Julliberrie's Grave and had actually dug into it.

"Now let us consider Pettigrew. He does not appear to be in any way connected with Julliberrie's Grave, or, so far as I know, with Penrose. But there are reasons for connecting him with the burglary. The burglar knew of the existence of the Billington jewels and apparently knew where they were kept. Moreover, he was at pains to take away the labels which contained evidence that the jewels had been supplied by Crabbe. Apparently, he was anxious that Crabbe's guilt should not be revealed. But why? He certainly was not Crabbe himself. What was his interest in the matter?

"You remember that Miller strongly suspected Crabbe of the Billington robbery. And it was not mere suspicion. He had enough evidence to make him consider seriously the possibility of a prosecution, though he decided that the evidence was not sufficient. The difficulty was that the jewels had disappeared and could not be traced. But now they have been traced and are known to have been sold to Penrose by Crabbe. So there is probably a complete case against the latter. But you will also remember that Miller's case against Crabbe included Pettigrew, for the reason – and no other – that Pettigrew was associated with Crabbe at the time of the robbery.

"Now , that robbery was committed by Crabbe, or by his agents – but almost certainly by Crabbe himself. Whether Pettigrew did or did not take part in the robbery, we don't know. But we do know that he was associated with Crabbe at the time, that that association put him under suspicion, and that if Crabbe should be proved guilty, he, Crabbe's associate, would certainly be implicated. You see, therefore, that Pettigrew agrees completely with the special characteristics that we have assigned to the burglar, and we know of no one else who does.

"But that burglar was in possession of Penrose's keys and was, therefore, either the murderer himself or a confederate of the murderer."

"Yes," I agreed, "it is a very complete case so far as it goes. But it is only a string of hypotheses, after all."

"Not entirely," he replied. "The association of Crabbe and Pettigrew is a fact, if we accept Miller's statement. There is really a definite case of suspicion against Pettigrew, at least that is my opinion; and it is certainly Miller's. If I am not greatly mistaken, the superintendent is in full cry after Deodatus. But you see the curious dilemma that we are in. Here are two men each of whom agrees in certain aspects with the characteristics of the murderer. But the characteristics with which they agree are not the same. Parrott is connected with Julliberrie's Grave but seems to have no connection with the burglary. Pettigrew is connected with the burglary but seems to have no connection with Julliberrie's Grave. But the murderer must have been connected with both."

"It almost seems," said I, "that you will have to accept – at least provisionally – the idea of confederacy. The assumption that both men were concerned in the murder would release you from your dilemma."

"That is quite true," he replied. "But it would be a gratuitous assumption. There is nothing to support it. The two men are separate and there is no apparent connection between them; nothing to suggest that they were even acquainted. And again I must say that I have the strongest feeling that the murder was the work of one man absolutely alone."

"It certainly has that appearance," I admitted, "but still – "

I paused as the sound of footsteps on our landing caught my ear. A moment later, an old-fashioned flourish on the little brass knocker of our inner door at once announced the arrival of a visitor and declared his identity. I rose, and, crossing the room, threw open the door; whereupon Mr Brodribb bounced in, looking, with his glossy silk hat and his faultless morning dress, as if he had just bounced out of a band-box.

"Now," said he, holding up his hand, "don't let me create any disturbance. I am only a bird of passage. Off again in two or three minutes."

"But why?" said Thorndyke. "Polton will be bringing in our dinner by that time. Why not stay and season the feast with your illustrious presence?"

"Very good of you," replied Brodribb, "and very nicely put. I should love to. But I have got a confounded engagement. However, I will sit down for a minute or two and say what I have to say. It isn't very important."

He placed his hat tenderly on the table and then continued:

"My principal object in calling, I don't mind admitting, is to bespeak the good offices of the incomparable Polton. I've got a fine old bracket clock – belonged to my grandfather; made for him by Earnshaw, and I set considerable store by it. Now, something has gone wrong with its strike and I don't like to trust it to a common clock-jobber. So I thought I would ask Polton to have a look at it. Probably he can do all that is necessary, and, if he can't he will be able to give me the name of one of his Clerkenwell friends who is equal to dealing with a fine bracket clock."

"Very well," said Thorndyke, "I will undertake the commission on his behalf. He will be delighted, I am sure, to do what he can for pure love of a good clock, to say nothing of his love of the owner."

"Does he love me?" asked Brodribb. "Well, I hope he does, for I have the greatest admiration and regard for him. Then that is settled. And now to the other matter. I thought you would be interested to know that I have got the intestacy proceedings *in re* Penrose well under way."

"You haven't lost much time," I remarked in some surprise.

"Oh, I don't mean that I have got it settled," said he, "that will be a work of months, at least. But I have got the essentials in train. As soon as I got your note informing me that Daniel Penrose was dead and that he died on the seventeenth of October, I set the machine going. Seemed a bit callous, with the body still above ground, but I don't believe in wasting time. None of the law's delay for me if I can help it. So I put out the necessary advertisements at once. You see, it was pretty plain sailing as I had a copy of the Penrose pedigree. That told me at once who the principal next of kin were, though, of course, I didn't know where to find them. But I was able to give names and particulars which were likely to catch the attention of interested parties. And they did. As a matter of fact, there are only two persons who matter and I have got into touch with them both. They are descendants of a certain Elizabeth Penrose, an aunt of Oliver's who married a man named John Pettigrew. What their exact relationship is to each other, I have forgotten, but they are both named Pettigrew. One of them is a young lady named Joan; a nice girl, poor as a church mouse but very independent and industrious. Works for her living and supports her mother – secretary to some professor fellow. And the mother is quite a nice lady. She had a job as manageress of some sort of antique shop, but the proprietor went bust and she lost the billet. It is pleasant to think of these two worthy ladies coming in for a bit of luck."

"You have seen them, apparently," said Thorndyke.

"Yes, they turned up two days after the advertisement appeared, and I liked the look of both of them. The girl, Joan, is very much on the spot and very modern – short skirts, head like a mop, you know the sort of thing. But I like her. She's a good girl and she has evidently been a good daughter."

"And the other person?" Thorndyke asked.

"The other is a man, Deodatus Pettigrew. Quaint name, isn't it? I hope he will justify it, but I have my doubts. Joan and her mother knew him, but they were mighty reticent about him. Rather evasive, in fact. Made me suspect that he might be a sheep of the brunette type. But we shall see. In any case, his personal character is no concern of mine."

"You haven't met him yet?" Thorndyke suggested.

"No. He didn't seem keen on an interview. Joan and her mother turned up in person, but he just wrote and seemed to want to do the whole business by correspondence. Of course, I couldn't have that in the case of a big estate like this. Must know the people I am dealing with."

"What do you reckon these two persons are likely to receive?" Thorndyke asked.

"The whole estate is about a hundred and fifty thousand pounds and, as there are practically no other claimants, they can hardly get less than fifty thousand apiece."

"Fifty thousand pounds," I remarked, "ought to be worth the trouble of an interview."

"So I told him," said Brodribb, "and, in effect, he agreed. So he is coming up to see me tomorrow."

"At what time?" Thorndyke asked.

"The appointment is for twelve o'clock, noon, sharp. But why do you ask that?"

"Because I rather want to see Mr Pettigrew."

"Ho, ha!" said Brodribb. "So you know something about him."

"Not very much," replied Thorndyke. "I am interested. I should like to have a look at him in a good light to see if he agrees with a description that I had of a person of that name. Can you manage that?"

"I can and I will. Would you like an introduction?"

"No," replied Thorndyke. "I don't want to know him and I don't wish him to know who I am. I just want to have a good look at his face."

"Ha!" exclaimed Brodribb. "I scent a mystery. But I ask no questions. You will bear me out in that, Jervis. I ask no questions though I am bursting with curiosity. I just do what I am asked to do. I shall arrange for you to be shown in to the waiting-room — where, by the way, the clock is. Pettigrew will come to the clerk's office, but when he goes away I shall let him out through the waiting-room. So, if you sit or stand close to the outer door, which is by the window, you will have a good view of him in an excellent light. I wonder why the devil you want to see him. But I don't ask. No, not at all. I know my place."

Here Brodribb consulted a fat gold watch. Then, as he sprang up and seized his hat, he concluded:

"Now I must really be off. Tomorrow at noon; and don't forget to tell Polton about the clock."

When he had gone, I reopened our previous discussion with the inevitable comment.

"This communication of Brodribb's throws a fresh and lurid light on the case and lets you out of your dilemma. It looks as if Parrott might be dismissed from the role of suspect."

"It does," Thorndyke agreed. "But we mustn't exaggerate the significance of these new facts. Because a man stands to benefit by another man's death, it doesn't follow that he is prepared to murder that other man."

"True," I replied. "But that is not quite the position. It is not merely a case of a man standing to benefit by the death of another. The benefit was actually created by the murder. If Penrose had not been murdered, he would have taken practically the whole estate and the others would have received nothing. There is no blinking the fact that the murder of Daniel Penrose was worth fifty thousand pounds to Pettigrew, and that without the murder he would have got nothing. I should say that you might pretty safely forget Parrott."

"You may be right, Jervis," he rejoined. "You are, certainly, in regard to the reality of the motive. But that motive is no answer to the positive evidence that seems to implicate Parrott."

Here Polton stole silently into the room (having let himself in with his key), bearing the advance guard of the materials for dinner, and the discussion was necessarily suspended. Thorndyke lapsed into silence, and, as his invaluable henchman laid the table in his quietly efficient fashion, he watched him thoughtfully as if noting his noiseless, unhurried dexterity. As Polton retired to fetch a fresh consignment, he rose, and, stepping over to the cabinet, pulled out a drawer and took from it the cardboard box in which the pottery fragment and its mould and the other objects from the pocket of the hospital patient had been deposited. From the box he picked out the cigarette-tube – the existence of which I had forgotten – turned it over in his fingers, looking at it curiously, and replaced the box in the drawer. Then he walked over to the table, and, having laid the tube on the white cloth, went back to his chair.

I watched the proceeding with a good deal of curiosity but I made no comment. For the immediate purpose was plain enough and it remained only to await the further developments. And I had not long to wait. Presently Polton returned with the remainder of the materials for our meal on a tray.

The latter he set down on the table and was about to begin unloading it when the cigarette-tube caught his eye. He looked at it very hard and with evident surprise for a few moments and then picked it up and turned it over as Thorndyke had done, examining every part of it with the minutest scrutiny.

"Well, Polton," said Thorndyke, "what do you think of it?"

Polton looked at him with a cunning and crinkly smile and replied comprehensively in a single word: "Tims."

"Tims," I repeated. "What on earth are Tims?"

"Mr Tims, sir," he explained, "now deceased. Mr Parrott's cabinet-maker."

"You think it once belonged to Mr Tims?" Thorndyke suggested.

"I don't think," Polton replied. "I know. I saw him make it. The way it came about was this; there was a little cabinet of African ebony sent to the workshop for some repairs, and the owner of it sent with it a piece of the same wood that he had managed to get hold of – queer-looking stuff of a sort of brownish-black, rather like a lump of pitch, with a streak of grey sap-wood running through it.

"Well, Tims did the repairs and he was mighty economical with the wood because there was none too much of it. However, when the job was finished, there was a small bit left over, mostly sap-wood. But Tims cut most of that away and then put the piece in the lathe and turned up this tube, finishing the mouthpiece with a paring chisel; and he made these white dots by drilling holes and driving little holly-wood dowels into them before he finished the turning. He was quite pleased with it when it was done."

"Did he keep it for his own use?" Thorndyke asked, "or did he sell it?"

"That I can't say, sir. But he would hardly have kept it, because he didn't smoke cigarettes. I supposed at the time that he had made it to give to Mr Parrott, who smoked cigarettes a lot and always used a tube; and the one that he had was burned to a stump. Still, Tims may have given it or sold it to someone else. Might I ask, sir, how it came into your hands?"

"We found it," Thorndyke replied, "in the pocket of a raincoat that was left by the unknown man who was in possession of Mr Penrose's car."

"Oh, dear!" said Polton. "Then I am afraid it has been in bad company."

He laid it down on the table and resumed the business of unloading the tray. Then, having removed the covers, he made a little bow to intimate that dinner was served, and retired, apparently wrapped in profound thought.

"There, Jervis," said Thorndyke, picking up the tube and restoring it to its abiding-place, "you see how the evidence oscillates back and forth and still keeps a rough balance. Here we are, back in the old dilemma. First comes Brodribb and weights the balance heavily against Pettigrew; so heavily that you are disposed to drop Parrott overboard. But then comes Polton and weights the balance heavily against Parrott – and, by the way, I think he has his own suspicions of the Popinjay. He looked mighty thoughtful after I had answered his question."

"Yes," said I, "it seemed to me that your answer had given him something to think about. But with regard to this tube. There is not a particle of evidence that it was ever in Parrott's possession."

"Not of direct evidence," he admitted. "But just look at the prima facie appearances as a whole. Here was a man who was evidently intimately acquainted with Penrose, for they had been digging together in the barrow. He had in his pocket an object which had been dug up in that barrow and which was part of another object, dug up from the same barrow, and almost certainly dug up by Parrott and sold by him to Penrose. That, at least, suggests the possibility – even a probability – that the man was Parrott. Now we find in that same man's pocket an object that was certainly made in Parrott's workshop. That is a very striking fact. It makes, at least, another connection between Parrott and the hospital patient. And then there is the very strong probability that Tims made the thing as a gift to his employer; that it was actually Parrott's property. By the ordinary rules of circumstantial evidence, all these agreements create a very definite probability that the man was Parrott."

I had to admit the truth of this. "But," I objected, "this suspicion of Parrott is no answer to the positive evidence against Pettigrew. If you refuse to entertain the idea of a joint crime by two confederates – which still seems to me the only way out – you are left in a hopeless dilemma. You have got evidence suggesting that Tweedledum is the guilty party and evidence that Tweedledee committed the crime; and yet – on your one-man theory – they can't both be guilty. I don't quite see how you are going to resolve the puzzle."

"Don't forget, Jervis," said he, "that there are certain final tests which, if we can only apply them, will carry us out of the region of inference into that of demonstrable fact. If our inferences are correct, one of these men is pretty certainly in possession of the Billington jewels. And there are other confirmatory tests equally conclusive. The purpose of our hypothetical reasoning is to discover the persons to whom the tests may be applied."

CHAPTER TWENTY

The Dilemma Resolved

It wanted some minutes to the appointed time when Thorndyke and I, accompanied by Polton and a burglarious-looking handbag, arrived at Mr Brodribb's premises in New Square, Lincoln's Inn. The visitor, we learned from the chief clerk, had not yet made his appearance, and we were shown at once into the private office, where we found Brodribb seated at his writing-table sorting out a heap of letters and documents. He rose as we were announced, and, taking off his spectacles, proceeded to the business on which we had come.

"You had better come out into the ante-room at once," said he, "as Pettigrew will come in through the clerks' office. I don't think you will have so very long to wait. The interview needn't be a very protracted affair as there isn't much to discuss. It is really only a matter of my making his acquaintance."

He opened a small, light door and ushered us through into the ante-room, a rather long, narrow chamber, lighted by a large window at one end which was close to the door of exit. A large office table occupied a good deal of the floor space and extended to the neighbourhood of the window, leaving a space just sufficient for a couple of chairs.

"There," said Brodribb, indicating the latter, "if you take those chairs you will be close to the window and the door. He will have to pass quite near to you and you will be able to inspect him in an

excellent light. And I think this table will do for you, Polton. There
is your patient on the mantelpiece. He is ticking away all right but,
when he tries to strike, he makes a most ungodly noise."

Polton walked round to the mantelpiece and surveyed the clock
with a friendly and appreciative crinkle.

"It's a noble old timepiece," said he. "They don't make clocks
like that nowadays. Don't want 'em, I suppose, now that you can
get the time by counting the hiccups from a loud-speaker."

He listened for a few moments with his ear close to the dial,
and then lifted the clock, cautiously and with loving care, on to the
table. The keys were in the front and back doors, and, when he had
unlocked and opened them, he placed his bag on the table and
began to discharge its cargo of tools and appliances. First, he took
out a roll of clean, white paper, which he spread on the table,
weighting it with one or two tools and a couple of lignum-vitae
bowls. Then he started the strike, which was accompanied by the
most horrid asthmatical wheezing, and having listened critically to
these abnormal sounds, he took off the pendulum and fell to work
with a screwdriver to such effect that, in a jiffy, the clock was out
of its case and lying on its back on the sheet of paper.

At this point a clerk appeared at the door of the private office
and announced that Mr Pettigrew had arrived; whereupon Mr
Brodribb directed him to show the visitor in, and, after a last,
anxious glance at the clock, went back into his office and shut the
communicating door.

But the latter, as I have said, was by no means a massive
structure, and, in fact, hardly seemed to meet the requirements of
a lawyer's office in the matter of privacy. Brodribb's voice, indeed,
was hardly audible, but I heard quite distinctly the visitor's reply:
"Yes, sir. I am Mr Pettigrew."

But I was not the only person who heard that reply. As
Pettigrew spoke, I noticed that Polton seemed to pause for an
instant in his operations and listened with a rather odd expression
of interest and attention. And so, as the interview proceeded, each
time that Pettigrew spoke, Polton's movements were arrested and

227

he sat with his mouth slightly open, listening, without any disguise, to the voice that penetrated the door.

It was a rather peculiar voice, resonant, penetrating and clear; and its quality was reinforced by the deliberate manner and distinct enunciation. The disjointed sentences that came through the door might have been spoken by an actor or by a man making a set speech. But I think that Brodribb must have done most of the talking, for the sounds that came through took the form, generally, of an indistinct rumble which certainly did not proceed from Pettigrew.

The interview was not a long one, but to me the inaction, coupled with an ill-defined expectancy, made the time pass slowly and tediously. Thorndyke relieved the tedium of waiting by following Polton's operations and discussing – almost in a whisper – the construction of the striking mechanism and the symptoms of its disorder. The latter did not appear to be very serious, for, presently, Polton began to reassemble the dismembered parts of the movements, applying here and there, with a pointed style, a delicate touch of oil."

He had got the greater part of the striking movement together when the sound, from the private office, of a chair being drawn back seemed to herald the termination of the interview. Thereupon Thorndyke went back to his chair and Polton, softly laying down a pair of flat-nosed pliers, suddenly became immobile and watchful. Then the door opened an inch or two and Brodribb's voice became audible.

"Very well, Mr Pettigrew," he said, "you shall not be troubled with unnecessary journeys. I shall let you know, from time to time, how matters are progressing and not ask for your personal attendance unless it is absolutely necessary."

With this he threw open the door and ushered his client into the ante-room, filling up the doorway with his own rather bulky person as if to prevent any retreat. I glanced with natural curiosity at Pettigrew and saw a rather large man, dark-complexioned and wearing a full beard and moustache, the latter turned up fiercely at the ends in a fashion slightly suggestive of wax. Apparently, he had supposed the room to be empty for he looked round with quick, uneasy surprise. And then his glance fell on Polton; and I could see at once that he recognised him and was rather disconcerted by the recognition. But he made no sign after the first startled glance, walking straight up the room in the narrow space between the table and the fireplace, looking neither to the right nor left. But just as he had advanced midway, Polton rose suddenly and exclaimed:

"Why, it's Mr Parrott! Bless me, sir, I hardly knew you with that beard."

Pettigrew cast a malignant glance at the speaker and replied, gruffly:

"My name is Pettigrew."

"Ah!" said Polton, "I suppose Parrott was the business-name."

Pettigrew made no reply, but stalked up the room until he passed between our chairs and the table to reach the door. And then he suddenly clapped on his hat. But not soon enough. For I had already noted – and so certainly had Thorndyke – an irregular, rather recent, scar crossing his right eyebrow. And when I saw that, I realised what Thorndyke had meant by "the final tests."

As Pettigrew grasped the handle of the door, he cast a swift, apprehensive glance at my colleague. Then he opened the door quickly, and, when he had passed out, shut it after him. Instantly, Thorndyke rose and followed him, and, of course, I followed Thorndyke; and so we came out in a sort of procession into the Square.

As we emerged from the house, I became aware of a man loitering on the pavement at its northern end. He was a stranger to me, but I diagnosed him at once as a plainclothes police officer. So, perhaps, had Pettigrew, for he turned in the other direction, towards the Searle Street gate. But that path also was guarded, and by no less a person that Superintendent Miller. When I first saw him, he was standing in the middle of the pavement, apparently studying a document. But as we turned in his direction,

Thorndyke took off his hat; whereupon Miller hastily pocketed the paper and awaited the approach of his quarry.

It was evident that Pettigrew viewed the superintendent with suspicion for he turned and crossed the road to the railings of the garden; and when the superintendent also crossed the road, with the evident purpose of intercepting him, the position was unmistakable. Pettigrew paused for a moment irresolutely, thrusting his hand into his pocket. Then, as Miller rushed towards him, he drew out a revolver and fired at him nearly point blank. The superintendent staggered back a couple of paces but did not fall; and when Pettigrew, having fired his shot, dodged across to the pavement and broke into a run, he clapped his hand to his thigh and followed as well as he could.

The swift succession of events has left an indelible impression on my memory. Even now I can see vividly with my mind's eye that strange picture of hurry and confusion that disturbed the peace and repose of New Square; the terrified fugitive, racing furiously down the pavement with Thorndyke and me in hot pursuit; the plainclothes man clattering noisily behind; and the superintendent hobbling after us with a blood-stained hand grasping his thigh.

But it was a short chase. For hardly had Pettigrew – running like a hare and gaining on us all – covered half the distance to the gate when suddenly he halted, flung away his revolver and sank to the ground, rolling over on to his back and then lying motionless. When we reached him and looked down at the prostrate figure, his aspect – wretched as he was – could not but evoke some feelings of pity and compunction. The ghastly face, the staring, terrified eyes, the retracted lips, and the hands, clutching at the breast, presented the typical picture of *angina pectoris*.

But this, too, was but a passing phase. Before any measures of relief could be thought of, it was over. The staring eyes relaxed, the mouth fell open, and the hands slipped from the breast and dropped limply to the ground.

The superintendent, hobbling up, still grasping his wounded thigh, looked down gloomily at his prisoner.

"Well," he commented, "he made a game try, and he has given us the slip, sure enough. It's a pity, but it's no one's fault. We couldn't have got him any sooner. Hadn't we better move him indoors before a crowd collects?"

It did seem desirable; for the pistol shot and the sounds of hurrying feet had brought startled faces to office windows and now began to bring curious spectators from office doorways.

"Do you mind if we carry him into your ante-room?" Thorndyke asked, turning to Brodribb, who had just come up with Polton.

"No, no," Brodribb replied. "Take the poor creature in, of course. Is he badly hurt?"

"He is dead," Thorndyke announced as I hastened with the assistance of the plainclothes officer to lift the body.

"Dead!" exclaimed Brodribb, turning as pale as his complexion would permit. "Good God! What a shocking thing! Just as he was coming into a fortune too. How perfectly appalling!"

He followed the gruesome procession as the officer and I, now aided by Thorndyke, bore the corpse back along the pavement to the doorway from which we had emerged but a minute or two previously and finally laid it down on the ante-room floor; and he stole softly into the room and shrank away with a horrified glance at the ghastly figure. And his agitation was natural enough. There was something very dreadful in the suddenness of the catastrophe. I was sensible of it myself as I rose from laying down the corpse and my glance lighted on the clock and the litter of tools on the table, lying just as the dead man had seem them when he passed to the door.

"I think," said Thorndyke, "that we had better telephone for an ambulance to take away the body and convey the superintendent to the hospital. Where is he?" he added anxiously.

"The question was answered by Miller in person, who limped into the room, his gory hand still grasping his wound and a trickle of blood running across his boot.

"My God, Miller!" exclaimed Brodribb, gazing at him in consternation, "you too! But aren't you going to do something for him, Thorndyke?"

"We had better see what the damage is," said I, "and at least control the bleeding."

"I don't think it is anything that matters," said Miller, "excepting to Mr Brodribb's carpet. However, you may as well have a look at it."

I made a rapid examination of the wound and was relieved to find that his estimate was correct. The bullet had passed through the outer side of the thigh leaving an almost impercetible entrance wound but a rather ragged wound of exit which was bleeding somewhat freely.

"You haven't any bandages or dressing material, I suppose?" said I.

"I have not," replied Brodribb, "but I can produce some clean handkerchiefs, if they will do. But bring him into my private office. I can't bear the sight of that poor creature lying on the floor."

We accordingly moved off to the private office where, with Brodribb's handkerchiefs, I contrived a temporary dressing which restrained the bleeding.

"There," said I, "that will serve until the ambulance comes. Someone has telephoned, I suppose?"

"Yes," replied Brodribb, "the police officer sent a message. And now tell me what it is all about. I heard a pistol shot. Who was it that fired?"

"Pettigrew," Thorndyke answered. "The position is this: the superintendent came here on my information to arrest Pettigrew and charge him with the murder of Daniel Penrose and Pettigrew fired at Miller in the hope of getting away."

Brodribb was horrified. "You astound me, Thorndyke!" he exclaimed. "I have actually been conferring with poor Penrose's murderer. And not only that. I have been aiding and abetting him in getting possession of the plunder. But I don't understand how he comes to be dead. What killed him?"

"It was a heart attack," Thorndyke replied. "Angina, brought about by the excitement and the intense physical effort. But I think I hear the ambulance men in the ante-room. That sounded like a stretcher being put down."

He opened the door and we looked out. At the table Polton was seated, apparently engrossed in his work upon the clock and watched with grim amusement by the plainclothes officer, while the ambulance men, having lifted the body on to the stretcher, were preparing to carry it away. I was about to help Miller to rise from his chair when Thorndyke interposed.

"Before you go, Miller," said he, "there is one little matter to be attended to. You had better get Pettigrew's address from Mr Brodribb; and you had better lose no time in sending some capable officer there with a search warrant. You understand what I mean?"

"Perfectly," replied Miller. "But there isn't going to be any sending. I shall make that search myself, if I have to go down in an ambulance."

"Very well, Miller," Thorndyke rejoined. "But remember that you have got only two legs and that you can't afford to part with either of them."

"With this warning he assisted the superintendent to rise and when the latter had received and carefully pocketed the slip of paper on which Brodribb had written Pettigrew's address, we escorted him out to the ambulance and saw him duly dispatched *en route* for Charing Cross Hospital.

As we turned to re-enter the house, our ears were saluted by the cheerful striking of a clock; and passing into the ante-room, we found Polton, still seated at the table, surveying with an admiring and crinkly smile the venerable timepiece, now completely reconstructed and restored to its case.

"He's all right now, sir," he announced triumphantly. "Just listen to his strike."

He moved the minute hand round, and, having paused a moment for the "warning," set it at the hour and listened ecstatically as the hammer struck out six silvery notes.

"Clear as the day he was born." He remarked complacently; and forthwith moved the hand round to the next hour.

"You must stop that noise," exclaimed Brodribb. "I can't bear it. Have you no sense of decency, to be making that uproar in the house of death, you – you callous, indifferent little villain?"

Polton regarded him with a surprised and apologetic crinkle (and moved the hand round to the next hour).

"But, sir," he protested, "you can't set a striking clock to time any other way, unless you take the gong off. Shall I do that?"

"No, no," replied Brodribb. "I'll go outside until you've finished. And I apologise for calling you a villain. My nerves are rather upset."

We accompanied him out into the Square and walked up and down the pavement for a few minutes giving him some further explanations of the recent events. Presently Polton made his appearance, carrying his bag, and announced that the clock was now set to time and established in its place on the mantelpiece. Brodribb thanked him profusely and apologised still more profusely for his outburst.

"You must forgive me, Polton," he said. "My nerves are not equal to this sort of thing. You understand, don't you?"

"I understand , sir," replied Polton, "and I suppose I *was* callous. But he was a bad man, not worth troubling about, and the world is the better without him. I never liked him and I always suspected him of fleecing poor Mr Penrose."

"Probably you were right," rejoined Brodribb, "but we must talk about that when I am more myself. And now I will get back to my business and try to forget these horrors."

He shook hands with us and retired into his entry while we turned away and set a course for the Temple.

"I suppose, Thorndyke," I said presently, "you were not surprised by our friend's recognition of Parrott. I am judging by the fact that you took the opportunity of having Polton with us."

"No," he replied, "I was not. The assumption that Parrott and Pettigrew were one and the same person seemed to offer the only way out of my dilemma if I rejected – as I certainly did – the idea of confederacy. There were the two men, making separate appearances. Each of them seemed, by the evidence, to be the murderer. But there was only one murderer. The only solution of the problem was the assumption that they were the same man. There was a perfectly reasonable assumption and there was nothing against it."

"Nothing at all," I admitted. "In fact, it is rather obvious – when once it is suggested. But I have found this case rather confusing from the first; it has seemed to me a bewildering mass of disjointed facts."

"That is a mistake, Jervis," said he. "The facts form a perfectly coherent sequence. Some time, we will go over the ground again, and then I think you will see that your confusion was principally due to your having made a false start."

CHAPTER TWENTY-ONE

Afterthoughts

"It seems to me," Lockhart suggested, "that this case is, to a certain extent, left in the air. The essential facts, in a legal sense, are perfectly clear. But there is a lot that we don't know, and, I suppose, never shall know."

The remark – which fairly expressed my own view – was made on the occasion of a little dinner-party at our chambers, arranged partly to celebrate the completion of the case, and partly to enable Lockhart – who had developed unexpected archaeological sympathies – to make the acquaintance of Elmhurst. The dinner was supplied by the staff of a neighbouring tavern, an arrangement which not only relieved Polton of culinary labours but included him in the festivities; for he was enabled thereby to entertain, in his own apartments adjacent to the laboratory, no less a person than Mr Kickweed.

Both of our guests had been, in a sense, parties to the case; but each had made contact with it at only a single point. It was natural, then, that when the meal had reached its more leisurely and less manducatory stage, the desultory conversation should have subsided into a more definite discussion, with a demand from both for a complete exposition of the investigation. And it was then, when Thorndyke readily complied with the demand, that I was able, for the first time, to realise how clearly he had grasped the essentials of the problem from the very beginning and how steadily and directly he had proceeded, point by point, to unravel the tangle of false appearances.

I need not report his exposition. It contained nothing but what is recorded in the foregoing narrative of the events. It consisted, in fact, of a condensed summary of that narrative with the events presented in their actual sequence with a running accompaniment of argument demonstrating their logical connections. When he had come to the end of the story with an account of its tragic climax, he paused to push round the decanters and then proceeded reflectively to fill his pipe; and it was then that Lockhart made the observation which I have recorded above.

"That is quite true," Thorndyke agreed. "For legal purposes – for the purpose of framing an indictment and securing a conviction – the case was as complete as it could well be. But the death of Pettigrew has left us in the dark on a number points on which we should probably have been enlightened if he had been brought to trial and had made a statement in his defence. At present, the circumstances surrounding the murder – if it was a murder – and the motive – if there was a clear-cut motive – are more or less wrapped in mystery."

"Are they?" Elmhurst exclaimed in evident surprise. "To me it looks like a simple murder, deliberately planned in cold blood, for the plain purpose of getting possession of a very large sum of money. Fifty thousand pounds would seem to furnish a very sufficient motive to a man of Pettigrew's type. But you don't take that view?"

"No," replied Thorndyke, "I do not. I am even inclined to doubt whether the money was a factor in the case at all. We must not lose sight of the conditions prevailing at the time. When Penrose left home, that is to say on the day of his death, his father was alive and well and the question of the disposition of his property had not arisen. At that time, the only persons who knew that state of affairs were Penrose, Horridge and Brodribb; and even they knew it very imperfectly. Brodribb, himself, was not certain whether there was or was not a will. As to Pettigrew, there is no evidence, or any reason for believing, that he had any knowledge, or even suspicion, that Oliver's estate was not duly disposed of by a will."

"Penrose knew, more or less, how matters stood," said Lockhart, "and he may have 'let on' to Pettigrew."

"That is possible," Thorndyke admitted, "though it would be rather unlike the secretive Penrose to babble about his private affairs to a comparative stranger. For it seems pretty certain that he had no idea as to who Parrott was. Mrs Pettigrew almost certainly knew who he was, but she must have been sworn to secrecy, and she kept the secret loyally. Still, we must admit the possibility of Penrose having made some unguarded statements to Parrott, unlikely as it seems."

"Then," said Lockhart, "if you reject the money as the impelling motive, what is there left? What other motive do you suggest?"

"I am not in a position to make any definite suggestion," replied Thorndyke, "but I have a vague feeling that there may have been a motive of another kind; a motive that would fit in better with the circumstances of the murder – or homicide – in so far as they are known to us."

"I am not sure that I quite follow you," said Lockhart.

"I mean," Thorndyke explained, "that the money theory of motive would imply a deliberate, planned, unconditional murder with carefully prepared means of execution, and the method would involve the necessary detail of taking the victim unaware and forestalling any possibility of resistance. But that is not what happened. The weapon with which Penrose was killed was not brought there by his assailant. It was his own weapon. So that the method of homicide actually used must have been improvised. And Penrose must have been either on the defensive or offensive. There was an encounter. But it was a deadly encounter, as we can judge by the formidable weapon used, not a mere chance 'scrap'. And the deadliness of that encounter implies something more than a sudden disagreement. There is a suggestion of something involving a fierce and bitter enmity. Perhaps it is possible to imagine some cause of deadly strife between these two men. But I knew very little of either of them; and before I offer even a tentative suggestion, I would ask you , Lockhart, who at least knew them better than I did, if anything occurs to you."

"They were both practically strangers to me," said Lockhart. "I knew nothing of their relations except as buyer and seller. But could you put your question a little more definitely?"

"I will put it quite definitely," Thorndyke replied. "Looking back on your relations with these two men, and considering them by the light of what we now know, does it appear to you that there was anything that might have been the occasion of enmity between them or that might have caused one of them to go in fear of the other?"

Lockhart looked at Thorndyke in evident surprise, but he did not reply immediately. He appeared to be turning the question over in his mind and considering its bearing. And then a little frown appeared on his brow as if some new and rather surprising idea had occurred to him.

"I think I see what is in your mind, Thorndyke," he replied at length; "and I am not sure that you aren't right. The idea had never occurred to me before; but now, looking back as you say, by the light of what we know, I am disposed to think that there may have been some occasion of enmity, and especially of fear. But you don't want my opinions. I had better relate the actual experiences that I am thinking of.

"I have told you about my visit to Penrose when he showed me his collection of jewels, which we now know to have been the stolen Billington collection."

"Do you think," Thorndyke asked, "that Penrose knew they were stolen property?"

"I can hardly think that," Lockhart replied, "or he would surely never have let me see them. But I do think that he had some uneasy suspicions that there may have been something a little fishy about them. I have told you how startled he seemed when I jocosely suggested that the Jacobite Jewel was a rather incriminating possession. My impression is that he may have got

239

the collection comparatively cheap, on the condition that no questions were to be asked."

"Which," I remarked, "usually means that the goods are stolen property."

"Yes," Lockhart admitted, "that is so. But I am afraid that your really acquisitive collector is not always extremely scrupulous. However there the things were, obviously property of considerable value, and I naturally raised the question of insurance. Penrose was quite alive to the desirability of insuring the jewels. But he was in a difficulty. Before they could be insured, they would have to be valued; and he had an apparently unaccountable objection to their being seen by a valuer. I put this down to his inveterate habit of secrecy. Now, of course, we know that he was doubtful of the safety of letting a stranger – and an expert stranger, too – see what they were. But he agreed in principle and promised to think over the problem of the valuer.

"Now, on the only occasion when I met Parrott in the flesh, it happened that Penrose was present. The meeting occurred in Parrott's workshop when I was waiting for a table that poor Tims had been repairing and Penrose was waiting for Mr Polton. By way of making conversation, I rather foolishly asked Penrose what he was doing about the valuer. I saw instantly that I had made a *faux pas* in referring to the matter before Parrott, for Penrose – usually a most suave and amiable man – snapped out a very short answer and was obviously extremely annoyed.

"At the moment, Parrott made no comment and seemed not to have noticed what had passed. But as soon as Penrose had gone, he opened the subject of the insurance and the valuer; and as I, having been sworn to secrecy, was necessarily evasive in my answers, he pressed the matter more closely and went on to question me in the most searching and persistent fashion as to what I had seen and whether Penrose had shown me anything more than the contents of the large gallery. It was very awkward as I could not give him a straight answer, and eventually I had to cut the interrogation short by making a hasty retreat.

"Looking back on this interview, I now see a new significance in it. Parrott was undoubtedly angry. He was quiet and restrained, but I detected an undercurrent of deep resentment, the occasion of which I entirely misunderstood, putting it down to mere pique on his part that Penrose should have contemplated employing a strange valuer when he, Parrott, could have managed the business quite competently. And I also misunderstood the drift of his questions, for I assumed that he knew nothing of the jewels and was merely curious as to whether Penrose had any things of value which had been obtained through some other dealer. Now I see that he suspected Penrose of having shown me the jewels and was trying to find out definitely whether he had or had not. And I think that my evasive answers must have convinced him that I had seen the jewels."

"Yes," said Thorndyke, "I think you are right. And what do you infer from that?"

"Well," replied Lockhart, "by the light of what we now know, certain conclusions seem to emerge. The jewels were sold to Penrose by Crabbe, but I think we are agreed that Parrott – I will still call him Parrott as that is the name by which I knew him – was the go-between who actually negotiated the deal. Now, as these jewels were a complete collection, instantly identifiable by anyone who had seen them, and of which the police had a full description, I think it follows that they must have been sold to Penrose with the condition that he should maintain inviolable secrecy as to their being in his possession and that he should neither show them nor disclose their existence to anybody. Do you agree?"

"I do, certainly," Thorndyke replied. "It seems impossible that they could have been sold on any other conditions."

"Moreover," Lockhart continued, "there is nothing improbable in such a condition. Penrose wanted the things, not for display, but for the purpose of gloating over in secret. In consideration of a low price, he would be quite willing to accept the condition of secrecy. Very well, then; we are agreed that Penrose must have been bound by a promise of secrecy to Parrott, on the faithful performance of which Parrott's safety depended. Consequently, when it appeared to Parrott that Penrose had broken his promise by showing me the jewels and that he was actually contemplating their disclosure to a valuer (who would almost certainly recognise them), he would suddenly see himself placed in a position of great and imminent danger. Penrose's indiscretion threatened to send him to penal servitude. In your own phrase, Parrott must thenceforth have gone in fear of Penrose. But when a man of a criminal type like Parrott goes in fear of another, there has arisen a fairly adequate motive for the murder of that other. I think that answers your question."

"It does, very completely," said Thorndyke. "It brings into view exactly the kind of motive for which I have been looking. The money motive, even if Pettigrew had known about the intestacy, would have seemed hardly sufficient. Deliberate, planned murder for the purpose of pecuniary profit is rare. But murder planned and committed for the purpose of removing some person whose existence is a menace to the safety of the murderer, is relatively common. The motive of fear is understandable, and, in a sense, reasonable. It may even be, in certain circumstances, justifiable. But in any case, it is a strong and urgent motive, impelling to immediate action and making it worth while to take risks. You don't remember the date of your interview with Parrott, I suppose?"

"I don't," replied Lockhart, "but it must have been quite a short time before Penrose's disappearance, for, when I came back to London, he had been absent for a month or two. It looks as if the murder had followed pretty closely on that interview."

"And now, Thorndyke," said I, "that you have heard Lockhart's story, what is your final conclusion? Apparently you exclude the money motive altogether."

"I would hardly say that," he replied, "because, after all we have no certain knowledge. But I see no reason to suppose that Pettigrew knew anything about his position as next of kin until he saw Brodribb's advertisement. On the other hand, from the moment when he became a party to the sale of the jewels, he was at Penrose's mercy; and as soon as he formed the definite suspicion that Penrose was not keeping faith with him, he had a perfectly understandable motive for making away with Penrose."

"Then," said I, "you think it was deliberate, premeditated murder?"

"I think that is the conclusion that we are driven to," he replied. "At any rate, we must conclude that Pettigrew lured Penrose to that place with the idea of murder in his mind. The intention may have been conditional on what happened there; or whether, for instance, Penrose could or would clear himself of the charge of bad faith. But the remarkable suitability of the time and place, both for the murder, itself, and for the secure disposal of the body, seems to imply a careful selection and a considered intention."

"What makes you suggest that the intention may have been conditional?" Lockhart asked.

"There are two facts," Thorndyke replied. "which seem to offer that suggestion. The piece of pottery that we found in Pettigrew's pocket shows clearly that an excavation was actually carried out by the two men. There would certainly have been no collecting of pottery after the murder. Then the fact that Penrose was killed with his own weapon suggests a quarrel, and a pretty violent one, for Penrose must, himself, have produced his weapon. But when Pettigrew had got possession of that weapon, his behaviour was unmistakable. He struck to kill. It was no mere tap on the head. It was a murderous blow into which the assailant put his whole strength.

"So, taking all the facts into account, I think our verdict must be wilful murder, not only in the legal sense – which it obviously was – but in the sense in which ordinary men use the words. But it is an impressive and disturbing thought that only by a hair's-breadth did he miss escaping completely. He had abandoned and hidden the car and was sneaking off in the darkness to disappear for ever, unknown and unsuspected. But for the incalculable chance of his being knocked down by that unknown car or lorry, he would have got away without leaving a trace, and we should still be looking for the missing Penrose."

There was a short interval of silence when Thorndyke had concluded. Then Elmhurst remarked: "It is rather a gruesome thought, that of the two men digging away amicably into the barrow when one of them must have known that the other was almost certainly digging his own grave."

"It is," I agreed. "But Thorndyke's interpretation of the facts suggests some other strange and gruesome pictures; that, for instance, of the murderer reading Brodribb's advertisement and realising that his murderous blow had been worth fifty thousand pounds; and his visit to New Square to collect his earnings."

"Yes, indeed," moralised Elmhurst, "and he collected them truly enough. It is a satisfaction to think of that moment of disillusionment when he saw his ill-gotten fortune turn to dust and ashes and realised that, for him as for others, the wages of sin was death."

R Austin Freeman

The D'Arblay Mystery
A Dr Thorndyke Mystery

When a man is found floating beneath the skin of a green-skimmed pond one morning, Dr Thorndyke becomes embroiled in an astonishing case. This wickedly entertaining detective fiction reveals that the victim was murdered through a lethal injection and someone out there is trying a cover-up.

Dr Thorndyke Intervenes
A Dr Thorndyke Mystery

What would you do if you opened a package to find a man's head? What would you do if the headless corpse had been swapped for a case of bullion? What would you do if you knew a brutal murderer was out there, somewhere, and waiting for you? Some people would run. Dr Thorndyke intervenes.

R Austin Freeman

Felo De Se
A Dr Thorndyke Mystery

John Gillam was a gambler. John Gillam faced financial ruin and was the victim of a sinister blackmail attempt. John Gillam is now dead. In this exceptional mystery, Dr Thorndyke is brought in to untangle the secrecy surrounding the death of John Gillam, a man not known for insanity and thoughts of suicide.

Flighty Phyllis

Chronicling the adventures and misadventures of Phyllis Dudley, Richard Austin Freeman brings to life a charming character always getting into scrapes. From impersonating a man to discovering mysterious trapdoors, *Flighty Phyllis* is an entertaining glimpse at the times and trials of a wayward woman.

R Austin Freeman

Helen Vardon's Confession
A Dr Thorndyke Mystery

Through the open door of a library, Helen Vardon hears an argument that changes her life forever. Helen's father and a man called Otway argue over missing funds in a trust one night. Otway proposes a marriage between him and Helen in exchange for his co-operation and silence. What transpires is a captivating tale of blackmail, fraud and death. Dr Thorndyke is left to piece together the clues in this enticing mystery.

Mr Pottermack's Oversight

Mr Pottermack is a law-abiding, settled homebody who has nothing to hide until the appearance of the shadowy Lewison, a gambler and blackmailer with an incredible story. It appears that Pottermack is in fact a runaway prisoner, convicted of fraud, and Lewison is about to spill the beans unless he receives a large bribe in return for his silence. But Pottermack protests his innocence, and resolves to shut Lewison up once and for all. Will he do it? And if he does, will he get away with it?

Printed in Great Britain
by Amazon.co.uk, Ltd.,
Marston Gate.